REBEL MAGIC

THE WITCHES OF HOLLOW COVE
BOOK NINE

KIM RICHARDSON

FABLEPRINT

FablePrint

Rebel Magic, The Witches of Hollow Cove,
Book Nine
Copyright © 2022 by Kim Richardson
All rights reserved, including the right of
reproduction
in whole or in any form.
Cover by Kim Richardson
Printed in the United States of America

ISBN-13: 9798430907822
[1. Supernatural—Fiction. 2. Demonology—Fiction.
3. Magic—Fiction].

BOOKS BY KIM RICHARDSON

THE WITCHES OF HOLLOW COVE
Shadow Witch
Midnight Spells
Charmed Nights
Magical Mojo
Practical Hexes
Wicked Ways
Witching Whispers
Mystic Madness

THE DARK FILES
Spells & Ashes
Charms & Demons
Hexes & Flames
Curses & Blood

SHADOW AND LIGHT
Dark Hunt
Dark Bound
Dark Rise
Dark Gift
Dark Curse
Dark Angel
Dark Strike

REBEL MAGIC

THE WITCHES OF HOLLOW COVE
BOOK NINE

KIM RICHARDSON

CHAPTER

1

What do Davenport witches do when one of them announces they're getting married? They throw a party, of course.

Following the Hollow Cove Pie Festival, we threw a combination party for Ruth and Beverly—Ruth for winning first place in the best pie competition and Beverly for her engagement to Derrick, the dirtbag who'd made her feel she needed a boob-booster spell.

The party lasted until the early morning hours, though I left around midnight, scrambling up the stairs to fall asleep in my clothes like a seasoned drunk. Much of how I got there was a blur. However, I do remember floating at one point. Either the vodka I'd drunk had superpowers, or House had helped me up.

My pounding headache was a testament to the four huge glasses of wine I had plus the vodka shots Beverly *made* me take. Marcus left around ten, around the time the vodka shots appeared on a tray held by my beautiful Aunt Beverly. Thank the cauldron he'd left when he did and didn't witness my slurred speech or when I joined Dolores on the coffee table for a rendition of "The Hills Are Alive" from *The Sound of Music*. Julie Andrews would have shot us both.

All the contestants from the festival, plus the usual invites, such as Martha and a few shop owners, had come to celebrate Ruth's victory.

All but one. Our town mayor.

Gilbert was a no-show. Though I was surprised Ruth had even invited him, the little shifter owl had chosen not to come. He was still struggling with the fact that Ruth had bested him in the pie competition. Fine by me. He was irritating as hell.

Now that the party was out of the way, it was time to get to work.

And the toaster hadn't stopped toasting—or whatever it's called.

I sat at the kitchen table, eyeing the toaster and waiting for any signs of rattling. Turns out, most of our Davenport relatives and relations didn't believe in modern technology, which was basically the old landline phone or even email. No. They believed in magic, which was why I was on message card duty this morning.

The toaster shook, followed by a rattling sound from the inside. Then, with a pop, a white card shot out of one of the toasting slots like a Pop-Tart, and I caught it in midair. I flipped the card between my fingers and glanced at it:

THIS WITCH IS GETTING HITCHED!
RSVP
Kindly respond by Tuesday, April 28th by phone or by any magical means of communication of your choosing.
Ms. Teresa Toots accepts with pleasure
Seats at the cauldron: 2
Magic: White magic

"Why is it necessary to specify the type of magic?" I'd asked Dolores after glancing at my first message card. "Isn't that a little discriminatory?"

"Just a formality," she'd answered, like that was supposed to explain it all before she'd left. I seriously doubted that. I suspected it was more of a precaution to separate the White witches from the Dark witches if a fight broke out. However, I didn't really see the reason. Iris was a Dark witch, and we all loved her like she was part of the family. And as a Shadow witch myself, I could harness both White and Dark magic, plus my newest demon mojo, so I didn't see what the big deal was. Still, I was curious to see how it would all turn out. I wanted to find out if they'd get along or if they'd start a magical fight. I was hoping for a fight. Maybe then Beverly would call off this ridiculous sham of a wedding.

I placed the card on the "Accepts" pile, which was now as high as my coffee mug and the only pile. No one had declined the invitation. Well, not yet.

The wedding was to take place on Wednesday, April 29—which was an insanely short amount of time to plan a wedding, especially when the accepted guests totaled 106 so far. Besides, who got married on a Wednesday? Aren't weddings supposed to be on weekends?

Beverly had decided to get married here in Davenport House, on the grounds, rather. It was going to be a garden wedding, which I thought were the most beautiful, to be honest, especially at this time of the year. The fruit trees were in blossom, and the air was sweet with the scent of honey and the spicy scent of lilacs. I had no doubt it would be quite the event. I just didn't know how they were going to pull off a massive wedding in four days.

Magic was the answer. It couldn't happen without it. If anyone could pull off a big wedding in four days, my aunts could.

After I gulped down another sip of delicious coffee, I grabbed my pen and went back to work. I stared at what I'd written so far, wondering what else to add to my list.

"Whatcha doing?"

A black cat leaped up on the table and padded over to me. His silky fur caught the sunlight through the window, making it sparkle like a precious stone.

I rapped the notepad with my pen. "This, my dear four-legged fellow, is my 'How to get back at Allison' list."

The cat's yellow eyes rounded. "Oooh, sounds like fun. Can I help?"

I grinned. "You may."

"Excellent." The black cat lay down on the table, his eyes half closed in that lazy-cat way, with the tip of his tail twitching. "What do you have so far?"

"Ah… I have a permanent-butt-rash hex— courtesy of Iris. I've got an extra-long-chin-hairs curse, the kind that even when you pluck, they just keep growing back. I've got a permanent-baldness curse, and then my favorite… chlamydia."

Hildo laughed. "You're evil. You're like one of Disney's top ten villains. I like it." The cat crossed his front paws. "You know, I just so happen to have in my possession a curse that makes it so she can no longer remember any of her passwords."

"Ha!" I laughed, excitement rushing through me. "That's a really good one. Thanks. I'll take it."

I hadn't forgotten or forgiven Allison for what she'd done. By disobeying Marcus and bringing me to the mourning werewolves' parents with basically a sign on my forehead that said "Witch... I killed your sons," she'd wanted me hurt or worse; she'd hoped the werewolves might have taken me out of the picture so she could finally have Marcus all to herself. I wasn't a vindictive person, but this time Gorilla Barbie had gone too far.

It was game on as far as I was concerned. And I *was* going to win.

The toaster rattled and bounced. A message card came soaring in the air, and I snatched it up again.

I smiled. "I'm getting really good at this."

"How many have acceptive so far?" asked the cat familiar, his gaze shifting to the pile of message cards.

I glanced down at the card and then at the cat. "One hundred and seven now."

A sound came from the cat, which I suspected was his attempt at a whistle, but it came out like a long, weird hiss. "How many invitations were sent?"

"No idea. Ruth was in charge of sending those."

"It's going to be a *big* wedding," remarked the cat between bouts of licking his front paw in a rather stately fashion.

"A big, fat, witchy wedding." I hadn't been to many weddings in my life, never a witch wedding or any type of paranormal one. I was probably just as excited to be there as Beverly was. Well, maybe not *as* much but a close second.

Speaking of Beverly.

"Did you get some more scoop on this Derrick character?" I asked the cat, my mouth curled in displeasure at the name.

The cat lowered his ears. "Nothing new since last night. Though I did hear he was coming over for dinner tonight to meet the sisters and the family."

My eyebrows shot to my hairline. "That is *excellent* news, my furry friend. Just excellent."

Hildo flashed me his pointed teeth. "I aim to please, my dear witch."

I'd asked Hildo to help me get some intel on Derrick since none of my aunts knew anything about him apart from Beverly. I'd even asked Marcus to look into him, but so far, the guy was as squeaky clean as a hand sanitizer. I didn't like it.

I'd never met this Derrick character, and I'd already formulated an opinion of him. Said opinion—he was a bastard. Okay, not exactly mature of me. But after what I'd seen Beverly do to herself just to please a man, well, it made me do my "crazy eyes" a lot more often. I didn't know if he was a witch, a vampire, a werewolf, or even a human. But something wasn't right about this guy, and I was determined to find out.

Starting tonight.

What would I do with this information after? I wasn't sure yet. I just wanted to make sure my aunt was marrying someone decent and not a douche.

"Have you heard from the queen of all that is evil?" asked the cat in the sudden silence.

I flinched, my blood pressure rising at the thought of the queen of hell and the pact we made.

It wasn't a pact, per se. It was more of an obligation—a favor that wasn't really a favor—since if I refused, well, Lilith would kill me.

Two days ago, the queen of darkness had basically ordered me to help her kill her husband, aka Lucifer, the king of hell—a deity rumored to be the most powerful, if not the most evil. And little witch me was going to help her. Yeah, it sounded insane.

Then she did something totally out of character and restored Davenport House to its former glory.

Lilith was a complicated goddess, if not a tad insane. I got that now. I really didn't want to get involved in her crazy, but she'd made it so.

"Not yet," I finally answered the cat, my heart pumping faster. "But I'm sure I'll see the red-eyed goddess soon, unfortunately."

"You know what she's planning?" meowed the cat.

I shrugged. "She says she wants me to help her kill Lucifer. So, I'm guessing it's going to suck in celestial proportions."

"It is," agreed the cat.

"Tell me something I don't know."

Worse was how livid Marcus was. He was still on the mend after the attack he'd suffered from the Dark wizards. But it seemed the better he got, the angrier he became about the deal I'd made with the goddess.

It's not like I had a choice in the matter either. It seemed when I thought my life was finally heading in the right direction, I was suddenly going up shit creek without a paddle again.

Yet, an angry Marcus sent delicious little thrills all over my body. Was it wrong that his overprotective ways turned me on? Maybe. But they still did. That fierce, alpha-male protectiveness was really, really hot. What warm-blooded female wouldn't want a strong, gorgeous, clever, and affectionate man protecting her? This one did.

"You can stop glowering at me, Dolores," came my Aunt Beverly's voice as she came through the kitchen's back door. "And you really need to rethink those eyebrows."

I glanced up to find Beverly walking into the kitchen, her hips swaying and looking as glamorous as always in her black capri pants and light-blue blouse, which accentuated her tan skin and shoulder-length blonde hair. Her kitten heels clicked on the floor as she dropped a shopping bag and sizeable white box with a metallic sheen onto the kitchen island.

"I'm just saying you'd be a damn fool to think you can wear white at your wedding," commented my Aunt Dolores as she pushed through the kitchen back door, her long, gray braid swaying down her back. At five-ten, she was tall for a woman and broad-shouldered, with a sharp tongue and a knife-edge wit. Her dark brown eyes were bright and clever as she stood with the stance of a professor, provoking a floundering student.

"No one is going to believe you're a *virgin*," pressed Dolores with a knowing smile. "And *this* isn't the first time you're getting married. Or have you forgotten?"

I eyed the great big box on the kitchen island, knowing that Beverly's wedding dress was probably in there. I knew they'd gone out shopping. I just didn't realize it was for *the* dress. I grabbed my coffee mug and took a sip, wishing Iris were here to enjoy the show with me. 'Cause, the gloves were coming off, and the wands were coming out.

"But it *feels* like the first time. Shouldn't that be reason enough?" answered Beverly, tracing her hand lovingly over the box. "Why shouldn't I wear white? It's *my* wedding, and I'm going to wear what *I* want. I don't care what anyone else says."

Dolores clamped her jaw. "You're going to be the laughingstock at your own wedding. Is that what you want?"

"She has a point," said Ruth as she pushed in behind her sister. Nearly a head shorter and bursting with youthful energy, her white hair was stacked into a bun and held in place with two chopsticks. She smiled innocently and said, "Everyone knows you're a slut."

Coffee flew out of my mouth, spraying Hildo in the face. The cat hissed and leaped off the table. Whoops. There went my partnership.

Ignoring her sisters, Beverly walked over to the table, grabbed the pile of accepted RSVP cards, and shuffled through them. She paused at one, her green eyes narrowing, and then tossed it.

"You can burn that one," she said, shuffling through the others.

I wiped my mouth with my hand and stared at the card on the kitchen floor. "What? Why?"

My aunt gave me a one-shoulder shrug. "Violet Ricci has a better ass than me. I don't want anyone at my wedding who looks better than me. I'm going to be the most dazzling, gorgeous bride there ever was."

"*Was* being the crucial word here," mumbled Dolores.

Beverly's gaze swung back to me. "How many have accepted so far?"

I shifted in my seat. "There are a hundred and seven—*six* acceptances. It's going to be a large wedding."

"Good," said Beverly, tossing another card. "Go big or go home. Right?" She smiled and added in a sultry voice, "That's what I told Derrick last night."

Ew.

"It's going to be a *big* catastrophe. That's what," expressed Dolores as she moved to the kitchen table and grabbed her newspaper. "Where are we going to put them all? We don't have a hotel in Hollow Cove. We have no choice but to book all the hotels in Cape Elizabeth. Which is really *not* ideal."

I looked at Dolores. "Why not? It's not that far from here. I don't think they'll mind driving a few extra minutes."

Dolores shook her head and splayed her hands on the table. "That's not it. Some of our guests have never been around the nonmagical."

I snorted. "You're kidding."

"Dolores never does," said Ruth, moving her eyebrows suggestively. "Have you ever heard Dolores tell a joke?"

She had a point. "Where have they been all this time? In a cave? I find that hard to believe." The idea of some paranormal folk never mixing with humans in this day and age sounded absurd.

Ruth's eyes widened to match her enormous smile. "Cousin Johnny and his wife, Patty, live in a cave. They've got Wi-Fi and everything."

Okay. Weird.

"So, how are you with the seating arrangements? Where are we getting the chairs?" I asked.

Beverly set the RSVPs back on the table, seemingly having approved the rest of the guests. "Gilbert is helping us with that. He's placing orders through his shop."

"Gilbert? That ought to be interesting. Make sure he doesn't charge you extra." That little shifter was a sneaky one, and I wouldn't put it past him to overcharge my aunts.

"Why isn't Derrick helping out with the bill?" It came flying out of my mouth before I could stop myself.

I felt Dolores's glare before I saw it. She'd told me to let it go yesterday when I'd asked the same question. It was apparently a taboo subject around Beverly.

Color rushed to Beverly's face as she turned around and joined the white box on the kitchen island.

Crap. I regretted upsetting my aunt, but I was more ticked off and curious as to why the Davenport witches were paying for the wedding. I mean, what kind of man lets his future wife, sisters, and niece pay for everything? The wrong kind. And seeing how things were going, this wedding was costing us a small fortune.

"What are your plans if it rains?" I asked to change the subject. The last thing I wanted was to embarrass my Aunt Beverly further. But I *was* going to find the dirt on this Derrick character.

Ruth waved a hand at me. "I'm working on an overlay spell. It's like a huge blanket in the sky that'll cover the entire backyard and house from any rain," she said, spreading out her arms over her head and grinning. "Boy, it's going to be great fun."

She was so cute. I smiled at her. "Impressive." Not that I wanted it to rain on Beverly's big day, but it would be cool to see that.

Ruth's face went bright red as she hurried over to the kitchen. She was so easy. It made it fun to compliment her just to see how many different shades of red would flush on her face.

"Are you hungry, Tessa?" asked Ruth as she washed her hands in the sink. "It's nearly lunchtime. I can whip up something for you. Veggie burritos? An omelet?"

I thought about it for two seconds. "Come to think of it, I am hungry. A veggie burrito sounds divine."

Beaming, Ruth grabbed a fresh apron and went to work, humming some tune. With a flash of black, Hildo appeared next to the stove. He lowered his eyes when he caught me staring. Guess the kitty was still angry about the coffee incident.

Dolores leaned over my shoulder. "What's that you're writing?"

Crap. I snatched my list and folded it in half. "Nothing."

Dolores bore her dark eyes into mine, a suspicious frown forming on her forehead. "Hmm. What kind of nothing?"

"The kind you wouldn't even want to know. Trust me."

Dolores wasn't about to back down, not when she had her teeth sunk into the meat. "Leave it be, Tessa. I'm warning you. Don't start trouble."

"Me? Never. I stay away from trouble." I knew she thought this was about Derrick. Something was off with this guy, and I couldn't, in good conscience, let Beverly marry him. Not until I figured out what he was about.

"Oh! Is that the time?" Beverly stared at the digital clock on the stove. "Oh shoot. I'm going to be late for my appointment with Dr. Howard."

"Dr. Howard? I didn't know you were seeing a new doctor," questioned Dolores, her brows knit into a frown.

"I am." Beverly smiled, her eyes glittering. "A vagina therapist."

Okaaayyy.

Dolores was watching Beverly like she'd grown a third eye on her forehead. "Ah… a what kind of therapist?"

Beverly placed her hands on the kitchen island's counter. "A vagina therapist. You know. To teach your vagina how to be young again. Isn't it wonderful?"

I blinked. "I want to die."

Ruth laughed as she dropped some chopped onions in a simmering pan. "A vagina therapist? Sounds like fun."

I gave my head a little shake. "I think this is the strangest conversation I've ever had. No—I *know* this is the strangest conversation I've ever had."

"Tessa darling," said Beverly. "I need you to do me a favor." She reached inside the bag and handed me a small red box.

I took the box. Written in elegant gold letters was the name Pot of Gold. "What's this?" I opened it. A large ruby pendant fitted with a gold chain rested on a tiny cushion. It was exquisite, and I didn't even know anything about precious stones.

"It's for Lilith," she answered.

"What?" I stared at her, openmouthed. "Why would you want to give her this?"

"We wanted to thank her for giving us back our home," answered Beverly. "She's a goddess, we know, and we know she can have anything she wants with a snap of her gorgeous, manicured fingers."

"But it's the thought that counts," interjected a smiling Ruth.

Beverly gave me a dazzling smile. "And it matches her eyes. She's going to *love* it. I'm sure of it. So, can you give it to her?"

I hated how they thought she was like my new best friend. Guilt hit. I still hadn't told them about my little pact with Her Ladyship of Night. I was pretty sure they wouldn't be spending good money on jewelry for her if they knew.

"Tessa?" prompted Beverly.

"Hmmm?"

A frown formed on Beverly's perfect features. "Are you going to give it to her?"

"Sure." What the hell was I supposed to say? One thing was for sure. I was going to have to tell them about Lilith eventually before they started offering her more gifts, or worse, they started praying to her and offering naked male virgins.

17

The doorbell rang, echoing through the house.

"I got it." I stuffed the box in my jeans pocket just as another RSVP card sputtered out of the toaster. I spun around. My bare feet slapped against the wood floors as I hurried down the hallway, wondering who it could be.

Maybe it was Marcus. He'd been badgering me for two days to tell my aunts about Lilith, hoping they'd either change my mind — which they couldn't — or help me with the whole *let's kill Lucifer* thing. Perhaps he was coming to invite me to lunch? Which would translate to a *very* naked lunch between two *very* naked people. My kind of lunch.

I grabbed the doorknob and pulled open the front door.

My horny, fantasy-filled smile vanished.

I felt like I was having a twilight zone moment because what stood before me was just too incredible to be real.

Three witches — and I say witches by the strong scent of pine leaves, earth, wildflower meadows, and witchy vibes I was getting from them — loomed in the doorway.

But that wasn't the reason my facial muscles went slack. Hollow Cove was filled with witches and other paranormal folk. It was our normal.

However, the striking resemblance to my aunts had me do a double take. No, wait—a triple take.

I was staring at my aunts' doppelgängers.

CHAPTER

2

The tallest of the three could send grown men scrambling away with that deep scowl. She had a look like she was disappointed with just about everything life had to offer. Her hair was bundled on the top of her head with a sheen of black and blue highlights from a box die, which were a hard contrast to her pale skin. She was Dolores's match in every sense of the word, in terms of height and looks, complete with Dolores's million-dollar frown.

Next to her was a brunette witch in her mid-fifties that put twenty-year-olds to shame. Fit, with a voluptuous figure, she had a sexy, exotic flair and could easily pass as Monica Bellucci's sister. She oozed sensuality with a kind of beauty that would have anyone turn their head at any age.

The last witch was even shorter than Ruth. But, unlike the other two, her hair was white. It hung just above her shoulders in spiraling curls, which gave her a few inches in height. Her right eye wandered slightly outward, giving the impression she was trying to see into the back of her head. Her plain face was in a constant state of movement as though she wasn't sure if she should be smiling, frowning, or crying.

"Well, don't just stand there like a coatrack," said the tall witch, sounding annoyed and disturbingly like Dolores. "Are you going to let us in, or do we have to remove you from our path?"

"You even sound like her," I said, amazed and trying really hard not to laugh. It was so surreal. I had to be dreaming, but even dreams couldn't come up with this stuff.

"Like who?" Dolores's twin gave me the once-over, her left eye twitching.

"Ah-ha! I thought I recognized that annoying nasally voice." Dolores appeared next to me at the entrance. "Didn't think you'd show up," continued my aunt, her hands on her hips, giving the tall witch a disdainful glance. "Not after the last time."

"Why not?" Dolores's twin moved forward until she was nose to nose with my aunt and pressed her hands on her hips as well, mirroring her posture. "This is *our* house."

I frowned. This was news to me. "Your house? What is she talking about?" This visit turned out to be *very* interesting. Now I just wished I had a glass of red wine, a comfortable chair, and some cheese and crackers. I'd be all set.

Dolores let out a short laugh and rolled her eyes. "Not this again. You just can't let it go. Can you, *Davina*?"

The witch called Davina sneered. "Why should I? This is our house just as much as it is yours, *Dolores*. Or have you forgotten who built it?"

"It's true," agreed the small witch, who reminded me of Ruth, her voice as mousy and small to match her frame. "It's our house too."

Dolores scoffed, color showing on her cheeks. "Like hell it is. This is *Davenport House*. Always has been. Always will be." She glowered at Davina, her eyes glinting. "A wise witch accepts defeat and knows when she's down."

I felt eyes on me, and I turned to find the pretty witch eyeing me with a tiny, knowing smile on her face, which made me feel slightly uncomfortable. Did she know who I was?

Davina's posture turned stiff. "Our grandfather built this house alongside yours. Our family magic, our magical roots are here, same as yours."

Huh? Very *interesting.* I felt a smile creep over my face. This was soooo good. *Where the hell is my wine?*

"More. I can feel it," added Ruth's doppelgänger. "A lot more of *our* magic is here than yours." She raised her hands as though she were sensing residual magic from her family, her right eye swirling in its socket and making me feel ill.

Dolores grimaced as though they'd just told her that her spell work was substandard. "If that were true, which is it *not*, it would be your house. Wouldn't it? But it's not. Nothing but lies. It's never been yours. Look around you. This is Davenport House."

"It was never yours to claim," accused Davina, her dark eyes hard and full of contempt. "Your grandfather cheated ours. Our family. He took what didn't belong to him. This is *our* house."

"It should have been our house from the very beginning," commented the sexy witch, speaking for the first time. Her sultry voice matched her body.

Clearly, I was missing out on some serious family history, or rather, family drama. And I *loved* drama. When it wasn't mine, of course.

I looked from the strangers to my aunt. "Who are these witches?" I didn't know what, but my witchy instincts were telling me there was more to these strangers than Dolores was letting on.

Some serious history was here, radiating from them in nearly palpable waves.

A sneer appeared on Dolores's face. "These unfortunate, magical drones are our first cousins. The Wanderbush witches."

I choked on my air and then nearly fell forward with the strength of Dolores's hand as she smacked my back. Beverly was right. Those were some serious man hands.

I straightened, face reddening from the choking and the physical attack, but mainly from the collective glares from the Wanderbushes.

It was a good thing Ronin wasn't here. He'd have a field day with that surname. He'd never let it go. The said surname wasn't familiar, and I was pretty sure I'd never seen any pictures. Yet the family resemblance was uncanny. Trippy, really.

Davina's eyes, framed by crow's feet, were bright and sharp. "That's right. Cousins. And we have every right to claim this house as our own."

It was Dolores's turn to stiffen. "It'll never be your house, you old hag."

Yikes.

Davina smiled. "Old? At your age, when you fart, it turns to dust!"

I snorted and was rewarded by Dolores's scowl that felt like a slap in the face.

My tall aunt glowered at the cousins. "Well, you can't come in. The wedding's in four days, and the house is not open to guests. Best be on your way."

"We'll just see about that." Davina made to move forward, but Dolores blocked her way.

"Where do you think you're going?" Dolores's eyes darkened with cold anger.

Davina lifted her chin, and her eyes sparkled with something equally challenging. "To *our* rooms."

"Ha!" Dolores threw back her head and laughed, making me wince. "I just told you we're not accepting any guests. You're not staying here, if that's what you think."

Davina splayed her hands at her sides, like she was about to spell my aunt. "Oh, yes we are."

"Over my dead body," spat Dolores.

Davina smiled. "If you insist." Purple energy danced about her fingers, coiling around her wrists like moving jewelry.

Instincts kicking in, I pulled on the elements around me, drawing even from the ley line that was so conveniently placed under my toesies. A burst of sudden energy hit me, and I inhaled deeply, feeling a tremor on the floor and all around me.

I was going to blow them to pieces if they tried anything. I didn't care if we were related.

Was I an evil witch? Possibly. I guess we were about to find out.

The three witches' attention homed in on me, their expressions changing from surprise to wonder and even traces of fear.

Yup. They could feel the magical juices.

It wasn't the best way to greet guests, but they started it. If Dolores didn't want them here, that was good enough for me.

"It wasn't my idea to invite you to the wedding, but you weren't invited to stay here," said Dolores, though the witches were still staring at me. I wasn't one to shy away from a few stares, so I stared right back.

"Dolores?" came Beverly's voice from somewhere down the hallway behind us, the clicking of her heels on the hardwood loud in the sudden silence. "Who are you being so unforgivably rude to? Oh. You're early."

The scent of a flowery perfume filled my nose as my Aunt Beverly squeezed in beside Dolores and me and positioned herself right in front of the *other* sexy witch who reminded me so much of her.

"Beverly," said the pretty witch by way of greeting, "I see you've aged since the last time I saw you. You need to stay out of the sun if you don't want to add more wrinkles to your already weathered face. One more wrinkle, and everyone will start calling you grandma."

A smile came over Beverly's face. "Belinda. I love what you've done with your hair. How do you get it to come out of your nostrils like that?"

Ouch. The control on my magic slipped as a burst of giggles bubbled up before I could suppress it.

Belinda's face went white and drawn. Her expression twisted into something ugly as red sparks shot out of her fingers like she was short-circuiting.

Ruth's familiar laugh reached me. "Who's got hair up their noses? Oh. It's you." I turned my head to see her smiling face morph into the most profound scowl I'd ever seen on her, giving her a bulldog appearance. I never imagined her face could do that, but she was still cute.

Ruth stood face-to-face with her apparent nemesis. "You stole my truth potion, *Reece*." She added the name with such anger and intensity that I wasn't sure I was still staring at my angel of an Aunt Ruth.

Reece's right eye swirled as she tried to focus both eyes on Ruth but failed. "I don't know what you're talking about."

Pink stained Ruth's cheeks. "You were the only one there with me. The only one who knew *where* I put it."

Reece scoffed. "It's not my fault you lost your potion. Though I'm not surprised. You're a hoarder. There's no order in the way you catalog your potions. It's disgraceful—a disgrace to the art of potion making. It's a miracle you find anything in that pigsty of a house."

Ruth fisted her hands. "Take that back."

"I will not," commented Reece.

Ruth narrowed her blue eyes. "Give it back," she said tightly. "It took me three years to get it just right. I know you stole it."

"Just like every other Davenport witch," cackled Reece with a laugh that sounded like a crow's call. "Always blaming others. Always pretending to be perfect."

I felt like I was watching a fight about who was allowed on the swings in a school playground. It was clear the two witch clans despised each other.

"Give it," demanded Ruth.

Reece smiled. "Or what?" she challenged.

"Or you'll regret it," threatened Ruth, her tone taking on a dangerous edge.

The air shifted as Davina pulled on her magic again. Belinda and Reece did the same.

Of course, I answered with a tug of my own. And when I say *tug*, it was more of a forceful push. Oops.

"Inflitus," I muttered as a kinetic force ripped out of my splayed hand and hit the three Wanderbush witches, pushing them back a few steps. It was barely anything, and I wanted them to know this was just an inch of what I could do to them if they didn't leave and kept threatening my aunts with magic.

Shock and outrage were the winning emotions on the sisters' faces as they steadied themselves. I could be wrong, but I was pretty sure I'd just assaulted them, and I was certain I'd just broken some witch law. My bad.

From their shared rage and displeasure, I was also confident I'd just made new enemies. What else was new?

Davina straightened and glowered at me, all tall, sour, and severe. Her eyes met mine. "Who's this?" she demanded.

"I'm Tessa Davenport," I answered before any of my aunts could.

Recognition flashed across the tall witch's face as she stared at me for a beat too long. Her eyes focused on me like she was trying to peel away my forehead to see what was inside. "You're Amelia's child," she said with such disdain, I nearly hit her again with my magic. "I thought she was a dud like her mother. Seems we were... *misinformed*."

My lips parted, and I cocked my head. "Did you just call me a dud?" I laughed. I really shouldn't have, but I couldn't help it.

Davina ignored me and looked at Dolores with a knowing smile that had the hairs stand up on the base of my neck. "Looks like you've been keeping secrets from the White witch court. Though, that's no surprise, coming from you."

"I have nothing more to say to you. I think it's time you leave," ordered Dolores, her hands still at her sides, fingers twitching and ready in case she needed to cast a spell.

"Yes. I think we have more now than we came for." Davina never stopped smiling. Her eyes flicked to me one last time, and then slowly, very slowly, she turned on her heel. "Come along, sisters."

Belinda raised her eyebrows suggestively at Beverly before turning around and joining her sister down the front porch.

Reece's face pulled and stretched, never settling on one expression as her right eye spun in her apparent stress. I thought I was going to puke. But then she, too, turned and left to join her sisters down on the walkway.

And then the front door slammed shut, making me jerk. My view of the three sisters was cut short.

"That was… interesting." I let go of the hold I had on my magic, my skin tingling as I felt it leave. "Strangely, I enjoyed it."

"Horrible witches," muttered Ruth, a cute frown on her face. "I really don't like them. I can't believe we're related." Her blue eyes darted past me and focused on something down the hall. "I think I'll check my potions room just in case." And with that, my small aunt ran down the hall, her bare feet slapping the hardwood loudly until she disappeared through the room to the right, just off the kitchen.

Beverly smiled and placed a hand on her cocked hip. "Belinda put on weight. Ten fabulous pounds or more. She looks like a well-fed cow," she added happily as though this was the best news of the day. "I think I'll have a glass of wine to celebrate." She spun around and headed for the kitchen.

I thought Belinda looked amazing. Hell, I'd love to have a body like that, but I kept that to myself, not wanting to upset the bride-to-be.

Dolores turned and marched back toward the kitchen behind her sister. I ran up to her.

"Is there any truth to what they said?" I asked, watching her face closely. "About House being theirs too?"

Dolores never stopped walking. "Absolutely not. If there were, this house would be theirs. Wouldn't it?"

"She did say that your grandfather cheated theirs. What was that about?"

Dolores halted. "People will say anything when they want something, even when it doesn't belong to them. Desperate people are capable of horrible things."

"If you despise them so much, why did Beverly invite them?"

Dolores shrugged. "They're our first cousins," she answered as though that was answer enough. "Of course we have to invite them."

Right.

She stared at me a moment. "Tessa. Whatever you do, do not let on about who your father is. The Wanderbushes must never know. Do you understand me?"

I searched my aunt's face, sensing a tad bit of urgency in her tone. "Does this have to do with what Davina said about the White witch court?"

Dolores grabbed me by the shoulders, her face wrinkled in concern. "Do you understand? Promise me. Promise me you will never tell them."

"Yes," I answered, shocked at the sudden panic in her voice. "I promise."

Dolores sighed. "Good. Well, it appears I also need a drink to calm my nerves."

Okay, what the hell was that about?

I followed my tall aunt, my mind whirling with questions as to why I should never let on to the cousins who my father was. I had the strangest feeling it had everything to do with the White witch court.

I watched as Dolores and Beverly toasted two very large glasses of red wine with strange little victory smiles on their faces. Yeah, there was definitely more to the Wanderbush witches' claim to the house than they were letting on.

And I was going to do some digging of my own. I was going to find out what really happened between the cousins.

"Tessa," called Hildo from the kitchen table. The black cat eyed the toaster and gestured with his front paw. "You're back on the job."

Right on cue, the toaster rattled, and another card flew out from the toasting slot. I had no idea how the cat knew there'd be another card. Maybe familiars had some psychic abilities. I rushed forward and caught it in midair.

"I should get paid for this," I muttered, wondering how long I had to work the RSVP station.

I pulled the card closer and examined it. My brows wrinkled in confusion, and a nervous trepidation rose in my gut. I turned it over, expecting there to be more, but there wasn't.

Only two words were written on the card in big, bold letters.

HELP ME

CHAPTER

3

"And it said *help me*?" asked Iris, sitting on my bed.

"Here. Read it." I came out of my walk-in closet, grabbed the card from the top of my desk next to the red box that contained Lilith's gift, and handed it to the Dark witch.

She looked up at me. Her black hair was pulled back into a low ponytail, which accentuated her pixie-like features. "You look great," she told me. "Dresses really suit you. I don't know why you don't wear them more often. You've got the body for it."

"I've got *a* body," I pointed out, making Iris laugh. "Without it the dress would have nothing to hold on to." I stared down at the black wrap dress I'd gotten at Banana Republic on the sales rack and ran my hand over the smooth, silky fabric. My hand moved to my stomach, and I patted my small wine gut that didn't seem to want to go away no matter how many sit-ups I did. "Have you met my newest addition?"

Iris let out a howl of laughter. "You're crazy."

"I know. Well… it's not what I would have chosen. I'd be a hell of a lot more comfortable in jeans, but Beverly insisted I wear a dress for dinner tonight. I didn't want to argue with her. She's all spazzy and neurotic."

Iris smiled and crossed her legs, looking beautiful and elegant in a white-and-navy-striped dress. "She wants to impress Derrick. I think it's sweet. Have you met him yet?"

"No. I'm not even sure Dolores and Ruth have met him either." Which was very unlike my Aunt Beverly. She usually loved to parade her lovers in front of her sisters. It was by far one of her favorite pastimes.

Iris shrugged. "It sounds like Beverly wanted to keep him to herself."

I thought about it. "More like she wanted to keep him secret." Which was something entirely different. It didn't settle well with me. And after Beverly felt the need to mutilate her body for this guy, it made things worse.

But after tonight, I'd know a lot more about this mysterious Derrick.

"Too bad Marcus couldn't make it," said the Dark witch. "With his detective skills and wereape instincts, he'd size him up in no time. I haven't seen him since the pie festival. How are you guys doing? It's getting really serious. Isn't it?"

"I'm good. We're good. He's… *very* good."

A giggle escaped from Iris. She was so easy.

The Dark witch fanned herself. "I'm not surprised. Something about that male just says he's got some serious skill in the bedroom."

"He does. He's ruined my vajayjay with his weapon of mass destruction."

Iris let out a peal of laughter and had to catch herself before she fell off my bed.

My heart sped up a little faster at the thought of mesmerizing gray eyes framed with thick black lashes. "I'm meeting him later after dinner. He's still interviewing for Jeff's replacement. He must have interviewed at least ten possible candidates so far, but he hasn't picked one. Maybe he just can't." The memory of the pain I'd seen on the chief's face when Jeff had been killed tore a tiny hole in my heart.

"Poor Marcus," said Iris, her eyes sad. "Must be really hard for him."

"It is. He lost a colleague and a friend. I tried to get that big beast to open up, but he doesn't want to talk about it. So I'm just letting him deal with it on his own. He knows I'm here when he's ready."

He'd been quiet after Jeff's funeral, but I could see the turmoil in his eyes, the anger, the pain, the frustration. He was stiff with emotions, and it pained me to see him this way. I'd wanted to wrap my body around his, to absorb some of the pain, to release some of what he'd bottled up. But he'd pushed me away, his body tight like it was about to fall apart.

"Well, I hope you help soothe his worries properly," teased the Dark witch, raising a brow suggestively.

I grinned and hooked thumbs at myself. "Why do you think I'm wearing this dress? Because it comes off *really* easily."

The sex was still mindboggling with earth-shattering orgasms. I got to thinking that Marcus really did have a magic wand.

It seemed to be the only thing that released some of the chief's tension, as he visibly relaxed after every session until he was *up* and ready again. Hey? Who was I to say no to multiple historical vagigasms?

Iris snickered and reached out to check her phone. "Ronin's really excited to be invited. He couldn't shut up about it before I left his place to get changed." She let out a tiny giggle. "I'm surprised he's not here yet."

"Probably still standing in front of the mirror debating what to wear." If I knew the half-vampire well enough, he was either still undecided about his attire, or he was still fussing around with his hair.

The Dark witch set her phone down and grabbed the card. "Could this be Lilith? She seems like the type to play games."

"Lilith?" I shook my head. "I doubt it. I've made the mistake once thinking she'd waste her time torturing paranormals. I think Lilith is only interested in Lilith." And of course, killing her husband, aka Lucifer.

"It's magical," continued Iris. She closed her eyes and pressed the card between both of her hands. A tiny frown appeared on her forehead. "I can feel residual magic on it," she said after a moment before opening her eyes. "The person who sent it has magical knowledge."

"I felt it too." I sat on the edge of the bed next to her. "Not much. Just an echo, but it's there."

Iris traced a finger over the words. "What do your aunts make of it?"

"They think it's a prank," I answered, shaking my head and remembering their dismissal a few hours ago when I showed them the card. "Orchestrated by their cousins."

"The Wanderbush witches," agreed Iris, a smile curling her lips at the mention of that stellar surname.

I'd told her about the weird encounter with the three doppelgängers earlier while I was getting dressed, and I enjoyed watching and hearing her laugh. I did tell good stories.

Iris looked at me. "And by that short tone in your voice, I'm guessing you don't agree."

I shook my head again. "No. I don't know… this feels different. Not a prank but real. I can't really explain it. It's a feeling. Like someone out there is in need of our help." My witchy instincts were all over this. I couldn't just dismiss it as a prank. Even if my aunts did, I still felt obligated to see it through. Besides, my gut told me this wasn't a joke. Somewhere out there, someone, a witch maybe, needed my help. They sought us out, the Merlins, because they expected help. And I was going to help them.

The Dark witch let out a little sigh and shook her head. "Any ideas who would send this?" She held up the card, inspecting it and turning it around, just as I had done.

"Someone who can do magic and needs our help?" It sounded lame, but it was all I had. I stared at the card in her hands. "I was hoping you might be able to help me with it. Like maybe try a locator spell or something? Possibly tell us where it came from. If I knew that, I might be able to do something about it. I don't have much more to go on. The only lead I've got is that this person is most probably a witch."

Iris stared down at the card for a moment. "Hmm. I don't know. The fact that it was sent by magic might have erased any residual traces of where it originated and the lasting energies of the person who sent it. But I'll try."

39

"Thanks. It's all I ask. I'd asked Ruth to help me at first, but she got all weird and angry, muttering something about cursed cards and that I should burn it. She's been reclusive and jumpy since the cousins showed up."

Iris shook her head. "Those Wanderbush witches really did a number on your aunts." She set the card down on her lap. "And if it doesn't work? What then?"

"Then"—I sighed, thinking I didn't have much to go on—"hopefully, they'll send another card." It was a long shot, but I might get lucky.

"Girls! Get down here!"

I jerked as Beverly's voice boomed from downstairs, which was surprisingly loud even with the door closed, sounding like she was in the room with us. She'd obviously used some sort of amplifying voice spell.

"Derrick will be here any minute!" Beverly shouted.

I laughed. "I don't think I've ever seen her this nervous. That can't be good."

Smiling, Iris pushed herself up from my bed. "We better go before Beverly has a heart attack," she said, handing me back the card. "She must really love him."

I cringed. I hadn't even met the guy, and he had already set my teeth on edge.

"He doesn't deserve her," I told Iris as I walked over to my desk and slipped the card in the top drawer before sliding it shut. "She could have any man, *any* man, and she picked him. Why? I have no freaking clue. But I'm going to find out."

Because after tonight, I'd have a much better idea of who the hell he was.

I stood and moved toward the bedroom door, but I halted as the unmistakable deep rumble of a masculine voice wafted up from downstairs.

"And this is my sister Dolores," I heard Beverly say, her voice unnaturally high and angsty, sounding like a nervous teenager bringing her boyfriend to meet her parents for the first time.

My mood brightened, and I smiled, my pulse quickening with anticipation.

Derrick was here.

CHAPTER

4

Ladies are taught *not* to run down stairs. Good thing I wasn't a lady.

I ran down the staircase two at a time, my bare feet gripping on the hardwood steps and keeping me from slipping and breaking my neck. I liked my neck. I liked it even better when Marcus placed tiny little kisses all over it. Yeah, we were keeping the neck.

I realized only once I neared the bottom that I was going too fast and couldn't stop my forward momentum without seriously injuring myself.

I was going for a crash landing.

Holding my breath, I landed with a thundering boom at the bottom. I smiled, thrilled that I managed to stay upright.

"Must have been a gymnast in another life." My smile vanished at the mortification on Beverly's face at the sight of me, and when her eyes moved to my feet, her face twisted in frustration.

I stared down at my toes. Okay. So I'd forgotten to wear shoes *and* failed to do a pedicure. My toes looked like I'd trekked through the Peruvian jungle. Too late to do anything about that now. They'd all seen the travesty of my phalanges.

I straightened and flicked my gaze away from Beverly to the tall man standing next to her.

He was lean with handsome enough features to make him stand out in a crowd. He was about Marcus's height, but where the chief was thick with hard muscle, this guy was slim and had more of an athletic physique, like a tennis player. A dark jacket hung from his broad shoulders over a black shirt and a pair of dark jeans. His brown hair was cut short on the sides and swept back on top in a modern style, with hints of gray gracing it. He looked younger than my aunt, mid-forties, if I had to guess. His skin had the smooth dark tan of someone who spent lots of time in the sun.

I got why Beverly was attracted to him. He was certainly handsome. But what were looks if the person inside was an asshole?

"Derrick, I'd like you to meet my niece, Tessa," said Beverly. Her voice had that high edge to it again. And when I looked back at her, her face was flushed, traces of sweat already forming on her pretty forehead. I felt a pang in my heart at her nervousness.

Derrick stuck out his hand. His smile was whiter than white. I practically needed sunglasses from the glare. "It's nice to finally meet you, Tessa." His voice was calm and confident, like that of a businessman accustomed to getting what he wanted. "Your aunt tells me you're an artist."

I stared at his hand. His manicure was the best I'd ever seen. Even with Martha's magic, you couldn't get a manicure *that* good. I debated whether I should shake it or not. I didn't want to embarrass my aunt any further, but his teeth were creeping me out.

"I am," I answered as I took his hand and shook it. Trying to keep my face straight, I cringed again inwardly at the hot, clammy touch of his skin on mine and the soft handshake. This was not a man who worked with his hands. He had the smooth hands of a banker or a guy who spent most of his time on the phone.

The strong scent of musky cologne assaulted my nostrils, making my eyes water and my head spin. But then I noticed an underlying acrid scent of something else, something burned, like the smell of burnt hair.

And then something weird happened.

I sent out my witchy senses and felt winding veins of some kind of cold energy pulsing beneath his skin, writhing strings of power that were hidden from the surface.

I yanked my hand away, glad not to be touching his anymore. He was a paranormal. And I was also certain that what I felt was a magical concealment, like a glamour but different. Stronger, more permanent. He was definitely trying really, really hard to hide something.

I smiled. "It's nice to meet you, Derrick. I'm glad you're here. We've got so much to talk about." This was going to be a lot more fun than I first thought.

"We do?" Derrick watched me, and I saw a crack in his casual, poised features.

The staircase behind me squeaked as Iris came to join me.

"This is my friend Iris." I watched as the two of them shook hands. I stared at Iris to see her reaction to his touch, but the Dark witch didn't even flinch. Either she was good at hiding her emotions, or she hadn't felt what I'd felt.

Beverly hooked her arm around Derrick's. "Come on, darling. Let me get you a drink before dinner," she said and steered him away toward the living room.

"Did you feel that?" I asked Iris, my voice low. I kept my eyes on Derrick as he sat on the sofa.

"What are you talking about?" The Dark witch leaned closer, her eyebrows knitting together.

"That concealment charm or whatever. He's hiding something."

"What?" asked Iris, her eyes wide just as the doorbell rang.

"Never mind."

I yanked the front door open, grabbed a stunned-looking half-vampire, and hauled him inside.

Ronin eyed me as I let him go, raising his hands. "I'm getting mixed signals here."

I rolled my eyes. "Come on. I don't want to miss anything."

Ronin cocked a brow. "Clearly *I'm* the one who's missing something."

I hurried into the dining room to the buffet table where a tray of wine bottles and glasses sat. Then I poured three glasses.

"Cheers," I said, handing Ronin and Iris both a glass.

"Excellent. And… what are we toasting?" asked the half-vampire as he took his glass.

"To secrets and how I will uncover them," I said loudly enough for Derrick to hear. I wanted him to know that I was onto him.

My gaze slid over to him, only to find his dark eyes on me. I flashed him my teeth and gave him a thumbs-up.

Iris smacked her forehead. "You're insane. It's going to be a disaster. I can feel it. Beverly's going to have a fit." She took a rather large gulp of wine.

"I don't know what the hell you're talking about, but I'm in," said Ronin, swirling his wine, his gaze directed at Derrick. "So, this is the guy?"

"If you mean the asshat who's been manipulating my aunt somehow, yes," I answered, keeping my voice low so that only Ronin and Iris could hear.

"What do we know about him?"

"Nothing. That's why tonight is so perfect." My pulse thrummed with excitement. "Prepare yourselves. It's going to get ugly."

The sounds of conversations drifted around me, and the chime of Beverly's loud laughter made me sick to my stomach. She was trying too hard. Way too hard. That was really concerning coming from a woman who never had to try hard for anything, especially for the attentions of a man.

I felt nauseated as I eavesdropped on Beverly and Derrick's discussions, which were basically all about him, how successful his business was, how he was about to purchase a house in Southampton, and how good he looked. After only a few sips of my red wine (I had to keep my wits about me), we all assembled at the dining room table.

Of course, Dolores was the first to sit at the head of the table. Following her example, Beverly sat on her right with Derrick beside her. He leaned over and muttered something in her ear, making her turn almost purple. She looked like she'd just stepped out of a sauna fully clothed. The constant blushing and the sweating was getting worse, and I felt my anger stir.

I quickly took the seat facing Derrick. I didn't want to miss anything. I wanted him in my zone so I could catch him weave his web of lies. This guy was hiding something. It was crazy obvious, so why couldn't Beverly see it?

Iris took the seat at my left, while Ronin pulled out the chair at the end of the table, watching Derrick, with a strange smile on his face.

I pulled my attention away from Derrick for a moment to admire the table. Ruth had once again outdone herself.

The table was stunning. Above a flower-patterned green, red, and blue tablecloth sat a spectacular centerpiece. It was two feet high and just as wide. It looked like a miniature boza tree, except it was pink, glittering, and had tiny fairies flying around it, leaving sparkling fairy dust in their wake. Utensils, napkins, water, and wineglasses rested perfectly in front of each assigned spot. The dinner plates were again mysteriously absent.

Ruth came rushing from the kitchen, her eyes round and cheeks pink. "Dinner is on its way," she announced as she watched the happy faces, her blue eyes shining with excitement.

"Are we ordering in?" asked the half-vampire, leaning forward. "Whatever you do, *don't* order from Igor's Steakhouse. I found one of Igor's toenails in my fries."

Before I could comment, Ruth snapped her fingers, and I felt a tingle of warm energy over my skin. I stared at the spot where I'd expected my dinner plate to magically materialize as it had done before, but nothing was happening.

At the sound of happy exclamations, I glanced up.

"No way."

Plates piled with roasted Chile renello, black beans, and a baked sweet potato next to a serving of Mediterranean salad soared from the kitchen and headed to the dining table in a straight line, like a floating food locomotive.

The plates hovered a moment above the table and then dropped into place without spilling a single bean.

Iris clapped enthusiastically, and then I joined her. I couldn't help it. My Aunt Ruthy was awesome.

Ronin raised his glass. "Ruth… if I were into threesomes, it would be on, baby."

Iris tossed her napkin at him, but Ruth laughed, looking rather pleased with the compliment.

"Show off," muttered Dolores, though smiling.

Ruth took the last empty seat at the table, looking exhausted but with a broad, very pleased grin on her face.

"I hope you like it, Derrick," commented Dolores as she placed her napkin on her lap. "Ruth slaved all day in the kitchen, making sure everything was perfect for you since you are our special guest."

Derrick gave her a pleasant smile and dipped his head. "I'm sure I will. I'm more of a meat lover myself, but I've heard all about Ruth's culinary talents. I'm sure I'll love it. It smells delicious." His gaze flicked to mine again before glancing over at Beverly. My creep-meter just went up a few notches.

I waited for everyone to have had a good fill before putting my plan in motion, which was right about now.

I cleared my throat because that's what you did when you were about to drill someone with questions. "Tell me, Derrick, are you a witch?" I knew he had some sort of magical know-how. I just didn't know if he was a witch or some sort of regular paranormal. He could be just a guy with lots of money to buy the right potions from an experienced witch.

"Tessa, don't be rude," warned my Aunt Beverly. She then flashed me a false smile with too much bottom teeth and narrowed eyes that reminded me of Jemma, the Stepford witch.

"I'm not being rude. I just want to know more about the man, witch, or whatever he is, who's going to be my uncle."

Derrick choked on his wine, and my smile grew as I heard Ronin's laughter.

"Good one." Ronin smiled.

"You're obviously not human," I went on, not caring that he hadn't stopped choking. "I can feel the energy about you," I said, wiggling my fingers at him to add more of an effect. "All that paranormal mojo. But it's weird because I just can't put my finger on it, you know? I just can't tell if you're a vampire? Or a werecat? A shifter, or even a fae? Weird, huh? It's almost like, well, it's going to sound silly, but, it's almost like you don't want us to know?"

Derrick watched me, his expression empty, his eyes inhumanly blank.

"So… which one is it?" I asked, seeing Iris lean forward in her chair from the corner of my eye.

"Well, if you must know," said Beverly as she rubbed Derrick's back gently. "Derrick comes from a line of very famous and powerful werewolves—an ancient family. The Baudelaires," she added with a note of importance like that was supposed to mean something to me.

I raised my brows. "Never heard of them." And I really doubted Derrick was a werewolf. I didn't get the werewolf vibe from him or the scent of wet dog that was always associated with a werewolf. In fact, I didn't get any of the energies that most weres or shifters emitted. This guy was something else. And the fact that he was lying about it only cemented my opinion that he was hiding something and that he was false.

Derrick cleared his throat, his gaze flicking from Ruth to Dolores. "I'm the youngest of four brothers and the last to get married. Suffice it to say, my mother is very excited about the wedding."

Suffice it to say? Nobody talked like that. I leaned forward in my chair, watching him. "She's coming? Your mother is coming? Wonderful. I can't wait to meet her. She must have some great stories about you." I didn't believe for a second that his mother, or rather, his make-believe mother would come. If I was right about him, there's no way she would.

Derrick cast his gaze my way, and a muscle in his jaw twitched. "Unfortunately, her health won't permit her to travel. She lives in Spain, and her doctors won't allow her to make the trip. It's too dangerous."

"Right. Sure." I hated being right. "What about your brothers? Are any of your family members going to attend the wedding? Or maybe they're sick too?" I wasn't giving up that easily.

Beverly flushed with embarrassment and cast me an ugly scowl, but I ignored her.

Derrick leaned back in his chair. He breathed through his nose, visibly trying to control the temper I knew was brewing behind those cold, dark, lying eyes. "We're a very busy family in real estate. We buy and sell properties and land all over the world. My brothers are working on a major deal at this moment, worth *billions*. Unfortunately, they can't make it." He grabbed his wineglass and took a sip, staring at me.

I pursed my lips. "How convenient." *I got you*, I told him with my eyes.

Something vicious in Derrick's eyes flashed with a cold fury, and his grip on his glass tightened.

"I think that's enough of that," snapped Beverly, looking angrier than I'd ever seen her. "Forgive my niece, darling. She's lost her head tonight."

"I'm not the one who's lost her head," I mumbled.

Beverly flicked her gaze in my direction. Her green eyes flared, and if I wasn't mistaken, I'd say she was ready to murder me. But I also saw a hint of insecurity on her face, a vulnerability I'd never seen before. It was as though she felt like she didn't deserve him. It made my chest tighten. I hated to see her like this. I hated that a man could make her feel this way. Not my Aunt Beverly.

I wasn't going to give up, but for my aunt's sake, I would let it go for now. Besides, I had a pretty good idea that this guy, this Derrick, if that was even his real name, was up to no good. He was hiding his true identity. Only people with something to hide did this. He was a paranormal in disguise and lying to everyone.

But the question remained, why did he want to marry my aunt?

I turned my attention to Dolores and Ruth. "Have you thought about the card we got today?" I thought it best to change the subject before Beverly's head exploded.

"Not this again," exclaimed Dolores, her scowl returning to her face. "I told you, this is the work of the Wanderbush witches."

"I'm sorry." Ronin interlaced his fingers on the table, a strange smile twitching his lips. "Did you just say… *Wanderbush*?"

Dolores ignored him. "This is exactly the thing they would do. They manipulate and spread lies. The only thing they can master is the twisting of the truth. Odious witches."

I shook my head. "I don't think so. I mean... I don't know them, but what would they gain by pretending someone needs our help? It doesn't make sense."

Dolores shrugged. "You can't cure stupid, but you can numb it with a two-by-four."

Okay. "I still don't think it's them. Just think about it for a second."

Dolores blinked. "There. I have. It's not them. Are you satisfied?"

I cocked a brow. "Very mature."

"Wait." Ronin waved his hands around. "Can we go back to the Wanderbush witches?"

"What are we talking about?" asked Derrick, his eyes on me, and I didn't miss the slight anger that still shone there. Oh yeah, he was pissed at me.

Dolores sighed and took a sip of wine before answering. "We received a card this morning that had the words *help me* written on it. And Tessa seems to think this is a real case, when I'm telling her it's not. Our unfortunate cousins are the culprits here. Nothing else."

I stared at her, my frustration creeping up. "How can you be so sure?"

"And how can you be so sure it's not?" countered my tall aunt. "Don't you think it's convenient that we get this card *the morning* the Wanderbush witches show up at the house? Claiming it's theirs? I thought you were smarter than this, Tessa," she added with a tight smile.

I scowled at her. I knew she was just trying to piss me off by insulting my intelligence, her way of making me let it go. It was not going to work.

"Wanderbush," repeated Ronin, his expression sly and suggestive. "It has a nice ring to it. Doesn't it? Like it's telling you to go wandering into *that* bush."

I caught sight of Beverly going to remove what I suspected was lint from Derrick's jacket, and he smacked her hand away, looking annoyed and not at all like a happy groom-to-be.

Yeah, I really hated this guy.

"I think it would be irresponsible *not* to look into it," I told them. "As Merlins, we have a responsibility to everyone here in town and to any others who might need our help. I think this person could be in real trouble."

"She has a point," said Ruth. "Maybe we should examine the card more closely. Just to make sure. We could do a few spells to see who sent it—"

"And *I'm* telling you it's a waste of time," growled Dolores. "With the wedding on the way, we don't have time to play along in this game with them."

Ruth leaned back, looking worried. "That's true. I don't know if I'll have time with all the food and preparations for the wedding. I'm swamped."

"I can help," announced Iris. "I was going to try a locator spell, but if you have any suggestions to peel away at the layers of residual magic and get to the source, I'm willing to help."

Ruth's eyes lit up, and she clasped her hands together. "We can start after dinner."

"Good." Dolores smacked the table with the flat of her palm. "Then it's settled. I don't want to hear any more about that card until we've finished our dinner."

A buzzing came from Derrick's jacket, and he retrieved his phone. "Excuse me." The tall man moved from the table and disappeared somewhere into the hallway out of sight, but not before I noticed the dark scowl on his face.

"Tell me more about this card," prompted the half-vampire, giving Dolores a shrug. "Can I see it?"

"Sure. I'll get it." If Ruth and Iris were going to work on it later, I might as well go and fetch it.

I pushed my chair back and made my way to the staircase. I didn't see Derrick in the hallway. I had a feeling he'd stepped out to the front porch to get some privacy with whatever lies he was spewing.

When I reached the landing to the attic, I was out of breath.

"Damn. I really need to work on my cardio," I panted, thinking up any excuse for some sexy time with my wereape. Best cardio that ever was, really.

But when I walked into my room, I halted. Because someone was already in there.

And that someone was Derrick.

CHAPTER

5

"**W**hat the hell are you doing in my room, dick?" No point in pretending anymore. The guy was scum and should be addressed as such.

Derrick stood next to my dresser. He smiled at me, and the white from his teeth could have left scars on my retinas. "I wanted to see the house. It has good bones. I prefer a more modern, luxurious home, but I guess it's charming in a classic, simple sort of way."

Did he just insult Davenport House? I glared at him. "It looks like you were going through my things. Looking for my underwear? Pretty pervy for an uncle."

He laughed at the use of that word. "I'm not your uncle."

"No. You're something else. Aren't you? You're not a werewolf. What are you?"

He watched me a moment, and I felt a shiver roll up my spine at the intensity in his eyes. "I don't get it. Why do you hate me so much? We've never met. And I know I've never done anything to offend you. This makes me think that perhaps… it's jealousy."

I laughed hard. "Jealousy? Wow. Your maker really didn't waste time filling your head with stupid. Why would I be jealous of you?"

Derrick took a slow step in my direction, and all my warning flags sailed high. "Jealous of your Aunt Beverly. Be honest, Tessa. We're closer in age, in personalities, in looks. Appearances are everything. You and I are very attractive people. And you are *very* beautiful."

I held up a finger. "Wait—did you just hit on me?" Next, I held up my entire hand. "Wait—I think I just threw up in my mouth."

"You want me," said Derrick, his voice low. "Admit it so we can be together. We can dine, drink, and feast on all the parts we like. You and me, our warm, naked bodies touching, thrusting. It'll be the most satisfying sex you've ever had."

Yeah, this guy was the king of creeps. Hell, a throne out there somewhere had his name on it.

The air tightened around me. I felt a pulse of energy, wet, like a spray of mist. It glided over me like a cold, greasy oil, something foul and nauseating that made me want to rub it off and jump in the shower.

What the hell was happening? What kind of magic was that? I'd never felt anything like it before, but then again, I wasn't very well-versed in all things magic.

My anger resurfaced. Derrick had just pulled some magic crap on me.

Oh hell, no.

"Admit it," he said again. "I can see it written all over your face and the way your body moves in my presence, your sensuality. You crave it. I saw it the moment we met. Your face was flushed with desire for me."

I raised a finger again. "Okay. Ew. All that was seriously gross and visually disturbing. Of course my face was flushed. I had just run down the stairs, you idiot." I felt a snarl materialize on my face. If he didn't leave my room soon, I was going to kick his ass.

He halted for a second, confusion written on his face. Either he wasn't accustomed to being turned down, or he was astounded that whatever magic he'd tried didn't have the effect on me he was hoping it would.

My tension rose. "There's no way I'm going to let you marry my aunt now, you sick sonofabitch. Not after what you just said."

"Tessa. Tessa. Tessa." He laughed a deep rumble. "Of course I'm still going to marry her. Don't worry. It doesn't mean that we can't be together."

"How can you do this to her," I growled, and I swear I felt steam coming out of my ears. "She doesn't deserve this, you twisted jerk. She deserves a hell of a lot better than you. My aunt deserves the best. And you ain't it, buddy."

"People aren't meant to be with only one partner." He said like it was the most obvious thing in the world, and I was the moron who hadn't gotten the email. "Especially our kind."

"The cheating kind."

He laughed quietly. It sounded evil. "The paranormal kind. We all have lovers. Many lovers. No one stays with just one partner for the rest of their lives. It's absurd and unnatural."

"I do." And I knew in my bones that Marcus was a one-woman man. And I suspected Iris and Ronin were in that group as well.

"I don't know what your deal is, Derrick Baudelaire, if that's even your real name. Nah, I think you pulled it out from the bottom of a Cracker Jack box. I know you're not a werewolf, and I know you're a liar."

"Did any of your lovers tell you how your eyes light up when you're angry?" he said, his voice gaining a soft, velvet quality. "Anger and desire are similar emotions."

Derrick stepped toward me, his stare a relentless gaze of a predator sighting his prey. It awakened my senses, my magic.

"I hate slimy guys like you." Power words hammered from the inside as he neared, threatening to tear out of me and whip this guy's ass.

But I didn't move. I didn't want him to think I was afraid, because I wasn't.

"You know"—Derrick prowled closer—"Marcus and I are very much alike."

"I seriously doubt that. He's awesome. You're a douche."

Derrick laughed softly. "We both fall prey to lust for a beautiful woman. We both guard our pride and suffer from jealousy. We both employ our resources to get what we want. I use my wealth and my power. He uses his strength and position."

"I think you should get your cheating ass out of my room before I kick it," I told him, giving voice to my rage.

A narrow smile curved his lips. "I know you want me," he purred, and bile rose the back of my throat. "I want you too. I'm really turned on right now. Can't you tell?" He looked down at himself, at the tent in his jeans.

That's it. I'd had enough of this shit.

"Get the fuck out of my—"

Derrick's hands were all over my butt and my waist before I had a chance to blink. Damn, he moved fast. And before I could move away or even blink, the bastard kissed me.

His soft, hot lips pressed against mine—stiff, awkward, and vile. I was so shocked that I just stood there like an idiot. But when he stuck his tongue in my mouth, I lost it.

I hit him. Not with my magic. Not with my demon mojo. With something else.

I kneed him in his man-berries as hard as I could.

A cry escaped Derrick as he keeled over, his hands on his man junk. I could see tears leaking out. Huh. Must have hit him harder than I thought. All that going up and down stairs had given me some serious nut-crushing strength.

"Does it hurt? Tell me it hurts. Ah, poor wittle Werrick."

A whimper and a moan came from Derrick. "You bitch. You fucking bitch."

"You should think twice before you force yourself on a woman," I told the still-moaning Derrick.

"Tessa? What's going on here?"

I whirled around as Beverly came inside my room. At the sight of Derrick on the ground, she halted for a half second, her green eyes widening. "Derrick? Oh my cauldron! What happened? Is it a heart attack? Should I get Ruth?" She hurried over to her fallen fiancé.

Derrick pointed a finger up at me. "She attacked me," he said, his voice coarse and full of pain. Yeah, I'd gotten him good.

I smirked. "Nice try."

But Beverly's face turned to worry as she kneeled next to him, her hands on his shoulder and back. "Have you lost your mind! Why would you do this, Tessa? What's the matter with you?"

I raised my brows. "Me? I didn't do anything. Well, okay. Except for kneeing him in the balls. But that was his fault. I found him in my room going through my things."

Beverly's face went still, and I saw an almost panicked look on her face. She stared at Derrick. "Derrick? Is that true?" I heard the distinct hint of worry in her tone, like it was something she feared might happen.

Derrick took hold of Beverly's hand. "I was on the phone. So I went upstairs not to disturb anyone. And the next thing I knew, she was pulling me inside her room. She threw herself at me. She wanted to have sex."

Oh. My. God.

Something inside me snapped, and I pulled on my magic as I leaned over him. "You're a dead man."

"How could you do this, Tessa? How could you do this to me?" accused my aunt, and I felt the hold on my magic waver.

A frown came over me, and I looked at her incredulously. "What? You can't seriously believe him? He came on to *me*. Ask yourself. *Why* was he in my room? He had no business being there."

Conflicting emotions flickered across Beverly's face—confusion, hurt, anger. I was not used to seeing her like this. She looked… devastated.

"She came on to me, and I tried to push her away," continued Derrick. "I told her there was only one woman for me. You, my darling. But she didn't like that. She got angry and jealous. And then she attacked me."

I gritted my teeth, my blood pressure rising. "You lying son of a bitch. That's not what happened. You're the one who threw yourself at me."

Derrick moaned as he strained to get up, and Beverly clasped her arms around his chest to help him up, her arms never letting him go.

"Beverly," I pressed and waited until her green eyes settled on mine. "You believe me. Don't you? I didn't do what he says."

Beverly's mouth opened and closed like she was struggling with what she wanted to say, what she was feeling. She opened her mouth again. "I… I don't—"

"You know how much I love you, darling," said Derrick, and I wanted to kick him in his balls again. Maybe they'd come out through his mouth. He leaned closer. "You're the only woman for me, darling. Just you. I want to be with you for the rest of my life."

At that, my aunt's eyes sparkled, and a smile blossomed on her face. I felt sorry for her. Sorry that she was being led on and lied to by this fool of a man.

And in that moment, I knew that whatever I said would make no difference. It was clear Beverly wouldn't believe me.

"Beverly?" I tried again, hopeful.

My aunt turned her attention to me, her eyes hard. "I never thought you'd be capable of something so vicious as this. To try and steal another woman's man."

"Trust me," I said, my anger bubbling. "I don't want him. But neither should you."

"You're a very sad and desperate woman, Tessa," said Derrick. A sheen of sweat covered his face. "But you should know that Beverly and I are in love. And nothing can break our special bond."

Another kick in the nads would.

Beverly's eyes filled with love and admiration for the lying scumbag. "You glorious man," she purred. "I'm going to make sure little Derrick's taken care of later."

Okay, now that was gross.

I threw up my hands. "I can't believe this. You know me." I pointed at him again. "You're going to believe him over me? Your only niece?"

I'll admit that hurt. But my aunt acted really weird with this guy around her. She wasn't herself.

"Family's overrated," she said.

"You're making a mistake marrying him," I said in a desperate attempt to make her see reason. "He's not who he says he is."

"Really?" Beverly laughed, though her face flushed red with anger. "Then who is he?"

She had me there. "I don't know yet." Derrick laughed, and I was tempted to send his man nuggets on the ley line express without the rest of him.

Beverly swiped a delicate finger over her sweaty brow. "I'm really surprised at you," she said. "What would Marcus think of you if he knew his girlfriend was throwing herself like a whore at unavailable men. At *my* man?"

I felt my expression turn ugly. "Really? Is this what you think of me? That I'm some slut who likes to steal attached men? Come on. You know me."

Beverly raised her hands. "What do you want me to think?"

"How about the truth. Don't you have a brain?" Yeah, maybe I shouldn't have said that, but she was starting to tick me off.

Beverly narrowed her eyes, her face shifting like she'd bitten something sour. "What did you say?"

I gestured to Derrick. "I'll make this easy. This guy is a dick. Don't marry him."

"Darling." Derrick squeezed Beverly closer and kissed her gently on the lips. "After what happened, I really don't think she should be at the wedding."

I had to pick up my jaw from the floor. "Excuuuuse me? You can't *uninvite* me? I'm family." Technically, I knew that was untrue, but my aunt would never go for this. Not in a million witch years.

"She's going to ruin the wedding," he continued, ignoring me. "You wouldn't want that. Would you? You wouldn't want people to talk."

Beverly thought about it a moment. "You're right." Her eyes found mine. She put a hand on her hip and said, "Tessa. You're not invited to my wedding anymore."

Guess I was wrong.

Giving me one last glare, my aunt grabbed her fiancé by the arm and steered him out of my room.

Neither of them looked at me as they disappeared from the landing, their happy chatter drifting as they made their way down the staircase.

I stood there, my fists trembling with white-hot fury and shock. The steady anger in me flared into a full-blown rage. My hair lifted off my shoulders, swaying in my sudden release of magic. I had my crazy eyes, but what did that matter if no one was there to appreciate them.

Okay, so I was uninvited to their wedding. It didn't matter.

Because there wouldn't be a wedding.

Not if I could help it.

CHAPTER

6

"**Y**ou'll never guess what happened to me," I said as I barged into Marcus's apartment without knocking. He had given me a key a few weeks ago, so I figured this was one of those perfect occasions to use it.

I'd been torn about whether I should tell Marcus what that creep Derrick did. Once I told the chief, I knew he would most probably have a talk with the guy. And when I said *talk*, I really meant the sound of Derrick's teeth spitting out of his mouth in time with the pounding of his head on the hard pavement.

I didn't want to upset Beverly more than she already was. But my legs seemed to have driven

71

my body here, and I'd already opened my big mouth.

The chief looked up at me from the dining table. He was eating alone, all proper and refined and sexy as hell. The gray T-shirt he was wearing seemed to be painted on, doing absolutely nothing to hide the ridiculous amount of chest muscles. He might as well just take it off. I wouldn't mind. His black hair was wet, telling me he'd just taken a shower.

His lips curled into an earth-shattering smile. "Did you burn your father's eyebrows off again?"

"No." I kicked off my shoes and made my way to the kitchen in search of some wine. "Do you have any wine? I need a glass to calm my nerves. Make it a bottle." It was to calm my nerves, yes, and tame the waves of anger and disappointment.

The sound of a chair pushing across the hardwood reached me, and then Marcus was in the kitchen with me, a bottle of Pinot Noir in his hand.

I frowned. "How did you do that?"

He grinned, the kind of smile that made my heart skip a few beats and made me want to rip off my clothes before I knew what I was doing. "Magic," he purred, his voice low and rough, which had my blood pounding low in my lady regions.

I swallowed as I watched him grab a glass and fill it with thick burgundy liquid.

"I'm sorry I've interrupted your dinner," I told him. Yeah, not really.

"You haven't told me what happened." The chief poured himself a glass and turned back to me, his gray eyes searching my face before resting on my lips.

I raised a finger and took a gulp of wine. Then another. "The scumbag grabbed me and kissed me."

The glass in Marcus's hand exploded. Then he went deadly still with wine dripping from his hand and fingers like blood.

Uh-oh.

Then the muscles on his neck and shoulders popped, literally popped as they bulged and moved under his skin. It was as though he was controlling his beast and wasn't sure whether to say hello to King Kong or stay in his expensive-looking jeans.

Me? I'd prefer him in nothing at all. But hey, I didn't come here to see him naked.

Yeah. Yeah, I did.

Rage shivered at the edges of his mouth. He stalked back and forth like a caged lion. He was furious. The fury in his eyes simmered, and a growl burst from his throat, making my skin erupt in goose bumps and my heart thrash faster. I froze. I was part terrified, part excited. Let's be honest. I was a little horny too.

Having a sexy, strong man like Marcus show this much affection and protectiveness toward me was all kinds of hot. I didn't care if you were thirty or seventy, it made you want to rip your clothes off and shout hallelujah at the top of your lungs.

He was silent for a long moment, his body shaking with rage as he pushed it away, bringing himself back under control. It was a monumental effort of will, and it was scary as hell.

He took a calming breath and asked, "Which scumbag?" His voice was a deep snarl that shook with suppressed rage.

"Derrick. The guy my Aunt Beverly wants to marry," I said, watching him.

Marcus's gray eyes met mine as he said in a very calm voice, which I was almost certain was scarier than his snarling voice, "He's a dead man."

Shit. Shit. Shit. "Wait. Just hang on a second. I didn't tell you so you could go all ape-shit on him."

"Dead. He's dead," repeated the wereape. "He's going to regret the day he touched you. I'm going to remove his head from his neck."

"Okay there, you overgrown baboon. I can take care of myself, you know." I waved my hands in front of his body to the ridges of hard muscles barely contained by his teeny-weeny T-shirt. "I might not be blessed with Geralt of

Rivia's muscles and good looks like you, but I have magic. I'm more of a Yennefer. Besides, right now, he's nursing some very sore balls."

A smile twitched his lips, and I saw some of the tension loosen around his shoulders. "You hit him in the balls?"

I grinned, proud of myself. "You bet I did. Really, really hard. There was contact. I believe it was along the lines of a vasectomy."

"Good." Marcus grabbed a dishrag and began to mop up the broken glass and wine from the floor. "I'm still going to have words with him. You know that. I can't let that go. He needs to know."

"I know," I said, smiling as I imagined Marcus squeezing Derrick's neck until his head popped off like a dandelion.

"There'll be some yelling."

"I know."

"Possibly a bit of violence."

"You wouldn't be you if there wasn't."

Marcus dumped the contents into the trash. "Did you tell Beverly what he did? Or any of your aunts?"

I sighed, remembering how quickly Beverly took his side. "I told Beverly."

"And?"

"And… she uninvited me to her wedding," I told him, my voice so bitter I could practically taste it.

He stared at me, mute for a moment. "She did? She couldn't have."

Saying it out loud sounded absurd. "Trust me. She did. She didn't believe me. She believed that nasty guy over me." A feeling of frustration and guilt bubbled up inside me at the memory of that conversation with my aunt. "I feel like I've been here before, you know, with the whole Dolores and the Sisters of the Circle thing. If you remember, she didn't believe me either, that the Stepford witches were a bunch of evil-worshiping crazies. And look what happened."

"You saved her, and now she loves you even more," said the wereape, a smile on his handsome face.

"The point is… the guy is a cheating bastard. How do I get my aunt to believe me? She practically caught him in the act, in my room, by the way, and still, the witch thought I had hit on him."

Marcus shook his head. "Beverly is a complicated woman," said the chief.

"You say that like you *know* her, know her," I teased, knowing full well that the chief thought of Beverly as his family, as his aunt too.

"I've known her for a long time," said the wereape, and his voice grew soft. "I care about her, just as I care about all of your aunts. They're part of my family."

My heart swelled at the emotion in his voice. He really did love them. Could he be any more perfect?

"There's no way in hell I'm going to let her marry him," I said. "Not after what he did. Besides, if he did this to me, her own niece in her own home, I'm betting he's done it before. And will keep on doing it." I might be a tad prejudiced when it came to cheaters, having been cheated on myself, but this guy was oily, gross, and I wasn't going to let my beautiful aunt marry that scumbag.

"What do you plan on doing?"

I cocked a brow and threw a smile in his direction. "Sabotage the wedding."

Marcus stared at me for a beat. "You sure that's wise?"

"Hell, yeah."

"Beverly'll never forgive you."

"I know. But better that she hates me than marry that dirty bastard." I hesitated, thinking. "Can you pull up everything you can find on Derrick Baudelaire? I know it's not his real name, but it's the only name I've got."

Marcus leaned against the counter, facing me, and crossed his arms over his enormous chest. His biceps bulged, stretching the sleeves of his T-shirt even more. "Is he a witch?" asked the chief.

I dragged my eyes away, nearly having to literally pull my eyeballs from his ample biceps.

Soooo distracting. "No, but he's something. He's paranormal, but I just haven't figured it out yet. He's pulling some hard magic. I could sense it. And I could also sense that he was using this magic to hide who he is or what he is. He wants us to believe he's a werewolf, but I'll bet my life he's not."

Marcus's gray eyes rolled over my face. "Why do you think he wants to marry Beverly?"

I shook my head. "I don't know. It's not like she's rich, so it can't be that. And he's loaded. Maybe he's got some mommy issues."

The chief laughed, and it sent delicious tremors into my belly. "She owns Davenport House," said the chief. "It's worth a lot in terms of real estate and power."

"Partly owns it," I told him. "She's only a part owner. Dolores and Ruth own the house too. I'm pretty sure Dolores is going to have him sign a prenup that keeps his dirty hands off Davenport House." I thought of the Wanderbush witches and their claim to the house and wondered if they had any part in Derrick's plan. But it didn't make sense.

"I met our cousins today." I relayed the strange encounter with my aunts' doppelgängers, and my heart thumped harder every time he laughed. I would never get used to that laugh. That deep roll, the way his shoulders and biceps popped. It sent warmth pooling in my core.

"There's something else," I said, trying hard to focus as I thought back to the strange card I'd gotten this morning.

"What?" His face went hard again.

"Has anything out of the ordinary been happening in Hollow Cove recently? Or maybe in Cape Elizabeth that you know?"

"Like what?"

"A missing person?"

Marcus thought about it. "No. Not that I can think of, but I can check tomorrow if you want. Why? Who's missing?"

"I got a card this morning while I was on wedding RSVP duty. It said… *help me*. Nothing else was on the card. My aunts said their cousins are taunting them, but I know it's not them. Someone is in trouble out there. I have to find them. I don't want to lose any more people. Not on my watch."

Marcus's face twitched, and I could see the traces of pain there. He was still mourning his friend Jeff and all the others we'd lost recently.

"I'm sorry." I moved forward and rubbed my hands over his arms, letting them slide up and down his biceps and enjoying their hardness, their warmth. "I haven't asked how you're doing. You're a bit tense. You okay? How did the interviews go?"

Marcus's arms closed around me and pulled me to him. "I think I might have found a new deputy," he answered, and I noticed that he didn't answer my other question.

"That's good."

"She starts tomorrow."

"She?" I smiled. "Is she pretty? *Please* tell me she's pretty." Allison was going to *love* this. If the new deputy was good looking, she'd take that as a threat. I couldn't be happier at this very moment. Wait. I'd be happier at this moment if Marcus and I were naked with some whipped cream and strawberries.

The chief laughed. "Not as pretty as you."

I showed him my teeth. "I've trained you well."

"Don't go," he purred, looking at me as if I wore nothing.

Right. Like I was going to go anywhere when such a man was staring at me with my flabby arms and my little potbelly like I was the most precious thing in the world.

We stared at each other for a moment, forgetting our troubles. And in that moment, there was only him and me.

His gray eyes stared into mine. They reflected lust and possessiveness.

Oh yeah. It was happening.

He grinned a crazy feral smile and pulled me closer. I slid my arms around his waist, crushing my body to his. His hot breath brushed against my jaw, and he kissed my neck, sending tickling warmth down to my lady regions.

I was so tired and wired from my encounter with Derrick and Beverly that I felt a sort of desperation to be with Marcus.

I turned my head so he could kiss me on the mouth as I pressed against his body, wanting to melt against him.

"I love you, Tessa," he whispered in my ear, the L-word that terrified me more than Dolores's scowl.

I opened my mouth to answer and stopped. Did I love him? Of course I did. I'd loved him for a long time. I was just too afraid to admit it, fearful of letting go and being hurt again.

My lips parted as I tried to say those three words, but his lips found me again. His tongue found mine, eager and hot. It was a possessive kiss, and my eyes nearly rolled back into my skull.

I gulped to catch my breath. He released me, breathing hard. The lust in his eyes nearly sent me over the edge.

In a flash, the wereape pulled off his T-shirt, jeans, and underwear to stand in his naked glory, his long, perfect manhood pointing in my direction.

I stared at it. "Is it me… or is it *bigger* than the last time?"

Marcus laughed, but it was cut short when a feral growl emitted from his throat. Damn. He was hot and wild. I'd never been this excited to see him naked.

Okay. Let's get this show on the road.

Clever as I was, glad to be wearing my wrap dress, I pulled at the belt. The bow came off quickly. "See? Not bad, huh? Look at me in my rip-your-clothes-off-in-a-second outfit."

I'd barely finished before the wereape leaped at me.

I screamed out in glee as he ripped off my panties, tearing them in one pull. No idea what happened to my bra. Once second it was there holding the girls and gone in the next.

He crushed me against him again, letting me feel the hardness and hotness of his skin on mine. I kissed him, fast and fierce, stealing his breath. I never wanted to let go. His scent and the heat coming off him drove my hormones off the scale.

His rough, calloused hands slid over my back, my shoulders, and my waist, caressing my skin. He cupped my breasts with his hands, his fingers brushing my nipples and sending shivers into my core. Heat rushed through me, making me crazy and impatient.

I jumped on him, I really did, and wrapped my legs around his waist. He growled as he grabbed my ass and hoisted me higher on his hips.

I smiled. We were going for a ride.

Marcus swung me from the kitchen and into his bedroom. Well, what I thought was the bedroom, but I couldn't see anything. I was too occupied with his mouth, his face, and his ears.

He lowered me carefully onto his bed, his big body on top of mine, all the while sending tiny kisses along my jaw, my neck, and my collarbone. The man knew how to turn me on.

Delicious heat pounded through my core, my fingertips, and everywhere. He dragged his mouth from my lips, staring down at me as hunger flashed in his eyes—

I jerked as the cramp of the century exploded in my stomach.

Wow. That hurt.

I pushed Marcus away as another cramp hit.

I bent over, feeling like I was about to be sick. Heat rushed to my face. I was not about to be ill in this hot man's bathroom, not when we were just about to do the horizontal tango.

"What's wrong?" Marcus's worried face was an inch from mine. "Did I hurt you?"

"No." I shook my head, thinking Ruth's cooking wanted an early exit. But then another cramp hit, only this time in my chest and my lungs. I couldn't breathe.

Frightened, I stared at Marcus. "Something's not right," I panted. "Something's wrong." I pressed my hands to my chest as another massive cramp hit, just as darkness blurred my vision.

I couldn't see Marcus anymore. I couldn't see anything but a smothering darkness, like a blanket was thrown over me. My ears were shut off from sound, like I'd stuffed them with cotton balls.

Now I was really panicking.

The cramping stopped. And I could see again. A wave of nausea hit, and I took a gasping breath, then another, shivering and feeling cold as I sat on a hard surface.

Hard surface?

A second later, I became acutely aware of another presence in the room. More than one. I blinked as my eyes adjusted, looking around, and I nearly had a stroke.

Across from me, at the end of a long table, sat a woman with red hair and red eyes, who was no mere woman at all, surrounded by paranormals and demons.

Lilith stared at me, her red eyes filled with mischief. "Oh my. Did I interrupt something?"

CHAPTER

7

Okay, not panicking.

I stared down at my arm and pinched myself, just in case I was having that weird, recurring nightmare where I was naked in a room filled with strangers, all staring at me and laughing at my body.

Pain flared up where I'd pinched my skin. "Guess I'm not dreaming."

Lilith threw back her head and laughed, her long, luscious red locks cascading down her back in rippling crimson waves. "This isn't a dream, my little demon witch. You're really here."

"No shit."

Apart from the fact that I was most certainly buck naked and very much in front of a group of strangers whose eyes were fastened on me like I was the "meat of the day" at some demon buffet, I should have been embarrassed. Hell, I should have run out screaming or attempted to hide my lady bits.

But I didn't move. I was pissed. Too ticked off to think of anything but strangling the queen of hell.

Recognition flashed on Lilith's face. She leaned forward in her chair and rested her elbows on the table as she interlaced her fingers. "Oh, you hate me right now. Don't you? I can see it all over your face." She giggled, making my blood pressure rise. "I understand. You were about to have sex with that gorgeous male. I would be angry, too, if someone had interrupted *that*."

"Your timing sucks," I snapped, anger thrumming through me. I had no idea the queen of hell could magically transport me wherever she wanted. But then again, she was a goddess.

Lilith had the face of a beautiful thirtysomething woman, with long waves of glorious red hair that shimmered like it was on fire. She wore a black leather ensemble with tight leather pants and a bustier top under a short black leather jacket.

She lounged back in her chair and crossed her legs at the knee, bouncing a knee-high boot. I caught the scent of her perfume, something rich and spicy.

Lilith watched me. "You're so tense. Why do you look tense?"

"I've had better nights," I answered. *And that tension was about to be burned off with a hot male until you just interrupted.*

A snicker came from the table, and my eyes found that familiar, blue-skinned female demon I'd met when I went looking for Lilith in New York. She had answered the door... with an attitude. She watched me with her black, smiling eyes, laughing at my expense because I found myself without clothes in front of strangers.

My life couldn't get any weirder.

But I wasn't ashamed of my body. I was cold, yes, but not embarrassed. A year ago, I would have been mortified. But I was a different woman now. I'd grown some serious lady balls along with an "I don't give a crap" attitude. I didn't have the patience for drama anymore. Not even Lilith's.

I flicked my gaze over the others at the table. Excluding the blue-skinned bitch, two others were here, both male. The one sitting next to the blue-skinned demon wore a dark suit of questionable material. His arms were a bit too long and his shoulders a bit too wide, with a smallish head. His mouth was spread in a wide grin, his black eyes unsettling. Demon, if I had to guess. The pressure of his black eyes was like nothing I'd ever felt before—an empty darkness that if you stared too long would suck you right in.

Across from him sat the other male who looked to be in his late fifties.

His features were like bronzed leather, his eyes unconcerned. He wore an old multicolored robe, something out of a medieval movie or a role-playing game. The magic that emanated from him was impressive. He was a witch—a Dark witch.

The blue-skinned demon still watched me with that snide smile, along with the other demon and shady witch, as I stood.

A round of snickers from those at the table echoed through the room, which, when I paid more attention, was clearly a boardroom. City lights flickered through the tall windows, stretching far out into the distance. I heard the pulling of leather as they all turned to have a good look at my birthday suit.

I met Lilith's gaze. Her red eyes shone with admiration and respect as I walked to the table. Ignoring the soft laughter coming from those gathered, I brought my naked self to the empty chair across from Lilith and sat. My butt stuck to the leather, pulling and squeaking as I found a comfortable position.

"Nice rack," said Lilith.

"Thanks." I folded my hands on the table. "Are you going to tell me why I'm here? If you're thinking of an orgy, I'm out."

Lilith laughed, the sound so mundane and natural, it annoyed me. "There's that sense of humor I like. I didn't bring you here for an orgy, but if you want, I can make it happen."

"I think I'll pass, thanks."

Laughter brought my attention to the blue-skinned demon again. "What's your problem?"

The blue-skinned female demon made a face as though I was a simpleton. "You're naked."

I blinked. "You're blue. I win."

She glared at me, and I glared right back.

"Let's fix that, shall we," announced Lilith suddenly. "Your hard nipples are a distraction." She waved her right hand in my direction, and I was hit with the sudden scent of rich spices filling my nose. A faint flicker of energy washed over me. I felt it dance and glide over my skin like a cool wind. The power was different, yet familiar the way witch magic was familiar to me.

The energy left me in a rush, and I felt something rub my skin. I looked down. My black wrap dress covered my body. I even had on my bra, and the underwear Marcus had shredded were whole again.

"Nice touch," I told the goddess, giving her a nod of approval. If I wasn't so mad at her, I might have applauded.

KIM RICHARDSON

She smiled lazily. "I know."

My stomach churned as I thought of Marcus. He was probably going out of his mind with worry. Not exactly the romantic evening we'd planned. I had to get back to him before he ransacked the town in search of me.

I shifted in my seat and crossed my arms over my chest. "Why am I here, Lilith?" I asked again, knowing full well the reason. I was here because of the deal I'd made with her, which only fueled my tension further.

Lilith's red eyes blazed with that ancient, hellish fury. "It's time," she answered. "It's time for my treacherous husband to get what he's owed. Payback, as you call it."

The deal I'd accepted was insane. Yet I was curious and frightened, but more curious as to how she thought she could do this and with *my* help. I was just a mere witch. Yes, I had some awesome demon mojo at my disposal, and the ley lines were badass. But I wasn't a god or a goddess.

I stared at the goddess without blinking. "And how do you plan on doing that?" It seemed I would have to drag it out of her.

"I thought about it a long time," answered the goddess, her red eyes gleaming with some animalistic fury. "A *very* long time. It's all I thought about while in my cage... ways to kill the bastard who did this to me." The air in the room thickened as magic pulsed and thrummed, making my ears pop. I swallowed down my sudden fear. Yet I understood her anger. I'd want to get back at my scumbag husband if he'd locked me up in a cage for over a thousand years.

"It consumed me," she went on. "So many plans, so many different ways I could kill him… but they were all complex and required the help of many. And then I realized I had the perfect plan. Simple, yet effective. The best plans usually are."

"Which is?"

Lilith's smile widened for a second and then faded. "I'm going to do what he did to me. I'm going to trap him, take away his power, and when he's down and at his weakest… I'm going to kill him."

"Sounds great," I told her. "But where do I fit in in all this? I mean, what exactly do you want me to do?"

Lilith's red eyes pinned me for a beat too long. "Do you remember why you were the only one who could set me free?"

Uh-oh.

"Yes," I ventured, my unease growing. This was not going to go over well. I could feel it in my witchy bones.

The goddess rolled her creepy red eyes over me. "It is in you. Your… *uniqueness*, your exclusive brand of witch."

Don't say it. Please don't say it.

A smile played on her full mouth as she cocked a brow. "Because of the demon blood that runs in your veins, my little demon witch."

Shit. Shit. Shit.

My gaze traveled over the table. My secret was out and in front of these shady characters, no less. Now the Netherworld leaders would know I wasn't a dud, that my magic was strong and getting stronger. They'd sent Vorkan, a demon hit man to try and kill me a few times. He'd only let me live because of my demon blood, more specifically, my father's blood, which he'd transferred after I was cut with Vorkan's death blade. The blood transfusion (if you want to call that) had awoken my demon heritage. I knew the demon lords of the Netherworld would be back. I'd just hoped I would have been in my seventies by then.

And let's not forget Lucifer. He would be my number-one problem if word reached him about who I was. My father's warning came back to me. If found out by the king of hell, he would use me for his own purposes and enslave me. If Lucifer knew who I was, there was no telling what he'd do to me.

I also had to worry about the witch councils. He had no ties to my family or me. If he opened his mouth to the Dark or White witch council about me, I'd be done for. And my aunts would lose everything.

My secret was out, and there was no place for me to hide.

I knew she'd called me "demon witch" earlier in front of these strangers, but I was hoping they thought I was a Dark witch, using demons to further my magical power.

"Are you worried about your little secret getting out?" asked the goddess, reading my thoughts. That, or it was written all over my face.

I nodded. "Of course I am. If they open their big mouths, I'm screwed. And if I'm screwed, I can't help you with your plan." I didn't really care about her plan. I cared about my life and my family's.

"Don't worry. I trust them," said the goddess, dismissing my concerns with a wave of her hand, like my life was no big deal. "They won't blab. I promise. Your dirty little secret is safe."

I narrowed my eyes at her use of the word "dirty." "How can you trust them? They look as trustworthy as an addict next to a heroin needle. No offense," I added, but I really didn't care. I felt the blue-skinned demon glare at me, but I ignored her.

Smiling, Lilith shrugged, barely lifting her shoulders. "Simple. If they utter a word of your special blood... they die."

I thought about it. "Okay then. That works for me." Not really, but what else was I supposed to say?

"Marvelous." Lilith gestured to the male witch. "Rada will work on a spell to trap Lucifer. And with *your* blood, my little demon witch, this is where the fun starts. Your blood will act as the final seal to keep him from using his power, his magic." A dark smile shifted on her face. "He'll be powerless. Weak, like the humans he despises. I'm going to take the time and explain to him the errors of his ways." Which translated to torture. "And when he's at his worst, that's when I'm going to kill him."

It all sounded easy enough. If it was just my blood they needed, I didn't mind giving them a gallon of it, but I did spot a few holes in her plan. Said holes were that I doubted Lucifer would be so easily trapped. Lucifer's strengths and powers outweighed even Lilith's considerable gifts.

"The strong dominate, and the weak are dominated," added the goddess, looking pleased with herself.

"Awesome." I felt some tension leave my shoulders. "And all you want from me is my blood? Okay. Do you need it in a blood bag or something?" I was pretty sure I could find the tools to pump out half a liter or so of my blood, in Hollow Cove. I felt ill just thinking about it.

The male witch called Rada snickered. "This is the witch? She's even more simple than most humans."

"It doesn't matter that she's stupid," said the blue-skinned demon. "We don't need her brain. We just need her blood. She can be dead too."

I glared at them both. "Excuse me for not having all the details. I just got here." Clearly, I was missing some vital elements in Lilith's plan.

"The thing is," said Lilith, and I turned my attention back to her, "for the seal to work, you need to be there, my little demon witch."

My heart thrashed in my chest so fast, I felt dizzy. "What do you mean? How exactly do you want me to do this?" Though I had an idea, it was just too crazy. No. I had to be wrong. Right?

"Simple." Lilith leaned forward. She smiled at me with very white, perfect teeth. "I need you to go to the Netherworld."

Great.

I sat there feeling the blood drain from my face and pool somewhere around my middle. This was insane. This was nuts. This was precisely the type of crazy-ass thing the goddess would want from me.

Lilith watched me for a moment. Her smile faded, and her jaw clenched. "Is there a problem?"

Yes. "No problem." I flashed a smile. "It's just… well… this is as crazy as goat yoga."

Lilith threw back her lovely head of red hair and laughed. "There's that sarcasm I love so much. Isn't she funny?"

"Hilarious," mumbled the blue-skinned demon.

"Just one problem," I told Lilith, seeing her eyes harden. "What if I can't cross into the Netherworld? I'm only part demon. What if I don't survive the trip?"

Lilith blinked and leaned back into her chair. "Then you die, my little demon witch."

"Great. Just great." I let out a sigh and rubbed my eyes. I was going to hell, literally. "And when are we going on this delightful trip?" I was going to be sick all over the table. I just knew it.

"Soon." Lilith's lovely and dangerous mouth curled into a smile. "I have a few things to take care of first, and then we'll kill my husband." Her eyes flashed with sudden anger.

I shifted in my seat. "Soon as in tomorrow or soon as in next year?" Please say next year.

The goddess blinked. "Soon," she repeated.

"Can't wait."

The last thing I saw was the flick of Lilith's wrist, and my world faded to black.

Chapter

8

I woke up the following morning to the loud chatter coming from downstairs. Dolores's deep voice rumbled up the stairs with a few high-pitched hysterics that sounded like Beverly's thrown in the mix. My head throbbed from lack of sleep, and from being pulled magically from Marcus's bedroom to Lilith's boardroom.

It was no surprise I hardly slept last night after Lilith told me her plan to trap and kill her husband, with me going to the Netherworld.

I wouldn't lie, I had thought about it, me going to my father's home world. I just never thought I'd be going there for the sole purpose of destroying the god who'd created it.

Granted, Lilith had helped him in the creation, but it was still a crazy-ass plan. Would I survive the trip? That was a question I had to ask my father. It wasn't a conversation I was excited about having since I would have to tell him why I had to go there in the first place, but I wanted to be prepared. If he told me the trip would kill me, I was screwed. It was suicide. I'd have to come up with something to give Lilith instead. I would have to change her mind somehow.

Worse was that, I had no idea when this *let's kill Lucifer* plan was going down. Lilith had said soon, but that could mean anything coming from her. It could mean today or tonight, or even next month.

Still, I needed to speak with my father. Now.

I yanked my sheets off and swung my legs over my bed. My chest tightened as I pressed my bare feet on the soft, plush Persian carpet. I still had to face my Aunt Beverly. Knowing her, she was probably still furious at me, though I was innocent, thank you very much. And the fact that she was angry at me made me infuriated with her. Talk about some healthy dose of family drama right here. I never imagined she'd take the word of a man over mine. Yes, the word came with a handsome face, but inside the man was nothing but rot. He had the face of an angel, but he was foul and wrong somehow.

The longer I stayed sitting on my bed, contemplating, the more I thought about it. I decided that waiting for my aunts to be out of the house might be the way to go before summoning my father. The last thing I wanted was to burden my aunts with Lilith's plans. They had enough on their plates with the coming wedding.

The wedding.

Derrick was *not* going to marry my aunt. I wasn't going to let it happen. And to do this, I needed to show her somehow that he was the cheating, evil sonofabitch that I knew he was.

If he was so determined to come on to me once, I was sure, given the opportunity, he'd do it again. The fact that he'd tried to pull some magic on me cemented my belief. Maybe it was his version of some magical ecstasy, an easy lay charm. It hadn't worked.

Nothing was easy about me, but I could use that. I would use that. I'd make him come on to me again and have my aunt see him in action.

But to make my plan work, I needed that bastard alive, which meant I had to make sure Marcus didn't find him first.

Last night, Lilith had teleported, magicked, whatever me back to my wereape's place only to find it deserted—and destroyed. Marcus always kept his place tidy and clean, like his person, but when I got back, it looked like a hurricane had swept through.

Marcus the hurricane.

The bed was shredded; foam, feathers, and wood splinters littered the floor. The bed frame was upturned. Holes had been punched in the walls like someone had practiced boxing with the drywall. I didn't need to have witnessed the event to know what had happened here.

Marcus, in his fear, had beasted out into his King Kong alter ego and ripped apart his bedroom in search of me, or just because he was angry. Maybe a little bit of both.

When I found the silverback gorilla, he was pacing around Davenport House's front yard like he was debating going in. Or maybe he was trying to control his temper, but remembering the last time he'd lost his temper there, House had thrown him out on his ass. He froze at the sight of me.

And then, with a powerful lunge of his back legs, the next thing I knew, a four-hundred-pound gorilla was rushing my way.

The gorilla scooped me up in his big, furry arms and crushed me against him, which I would have thought romantic if my airways weren't obstructed.

"Can't. Breathe," I managed, feeling like my ribs were about to crack if he didn't let go soon.

"Sssaury," said the gorilla in a deep growl as he gently pulled back and let go.

My eyes rolled over the magnificent gorilla. The muscles on his chest flexed as he stood on all fours, his front hands resting on his knuckles. His face was wrenched tightly with worry, and his gray eyes shone with fear. He looked like he'd been out of his mind with fear—fear for me.

I pressed my hand to my chest, feeling around my ribs to make sure no bones were broken. "That's what I call a lot of gorilla love."

The gorilla smiled impishly and shrugged. Then his gray eyes hardened. "Wat appen? U gonne?"

Here it comes. I exhaled and said, "Lilith happened. She took me from your place to her boardroom."

The gorilla's eyes disappeared under his deep scowl as a roar sounded in his throat. "Urr deeel?" he said, his sharp canines gleaming in the streetlight.

I nodded. "That's right. She wanted to discuss our deal."

The gorilla pounded his fists on the ground. "Usifer," growled the big gorilla, and he flexed his biceps. "No. Deel." He roared, thrashing his head to the side, and I found myself taking a step back at his sudden rage. He raised himself on his two legs and let out a piercing roar, pounding his chest in a show of strength. Not like he needed it. We all knew how strong he was. The silverback gorilla was no joke when it came to his strength and sheer power—an uncrowned king of his kind, a majestic beast. He was a force to be reckoned with. And he was mine.

I shook my head. "It's not like I have a choice. She's going to kill me if I say no."

"Usifer, keel yuu."

"Maybe. Maybe not. I'm really hoping for the latter. Maybe I'll get lucky, and Lilith and Lucifer will end up killing each other."

The gorilla snarled. "Naat fuhnee." His face twisted again, and when I met his eyes, they were flooded with pain. "Naat looze yoo."

Well, my heart just about exploded.

I reached out and buried my face into his chest. "I'm sorry you're worried about me," I said and sighed as he cradled me with his big ol' gorilla arms. His thick, coarse, springy hair rubbed against my face, rough and delicious. I breathed in his scent, strong and musky with a bit of animal scent, which was nice and familiar. Part of me wanted to bury my face in his fur and fall asleep in his arms. Only I knew I couldn't.

We stood there, holding each other for a while with me listening to his heartbeat. I only pulled away once it reached a slower, much more regular beat.

"You need a new bed, you big dope." I laughed, wanting to change the subject.

The gorilla shook with laughter. "I noo."

I watched him. "You can share my bed tonight if you want. But if you steal the covers again, I'm going to beat you. Got it?"

The gorilla showed me his teeth. He shook his head and pointed at the street behind us. "Neeed uh waak."

"Sure," I answered. "A walk will do you some good. You need to calm down. All that testosterone in a knot, you need to walk that off. But don't go looking for Derrick. Okay?"

The gorilla avoided my gaze.

"Marcus? Promise me."

"Rromisss," answered the gorilla.

With my hands, I grabbed his large head and kissed the top of his forehead. The rough skin grazed my lips.

I'd stayed out for a moment longer, watching as the gorilla made his way down the street, his gait commanding but not erratic. And only when he disappeared at the corner of Stardust Drive and Charms Avenue did I pick myself up, walk straight to Davenport House, and clamber straight to bed.

Now, the morning after, even though a shitstorm was brewing between me and my Aunt Beverly, I couldn't hide in my room all day. I had things to do and bastard secrets I needed to uncover.

And there was still the question of that mysterious note I'd gotten yesterday morning. Last night, Ruth was going to help Iris with a locator spell, and I was dying to know if they'd discovered anything.

My curiosity finally convinced me to get my ass out of bed.

I moved over to my desk, where I'd put the card in the small first drawer. I pulled it open, seeing only scattered bills. No card.

"Maybe Iris took it," I thought out loud.

After a quick shower, I got dressed in my usual blue jeans and T-shirt and went in search of Iris. I popped by her room first, but it was empty.

I made my way downstairs, following the commotion to the kitchen. The aroma of fresh coffee wafted up my nose along with something sweet, like apple pie or cranberry muffins. My stomach growled in approval.

I could see Ruth at the stove, smiling as she whisked something in a stainless-steel mixing bowl. Hildo sat next to her, dipping his front paw in the batter of another bowl.

Dolores, Beverly, and Iris were seated at the kitchen table, each with a fork in their hand and each with a slice of a different colored cake placed before them.

At least twenty cakes sat on the table—of varying sizes, colors, and presentations. I saw a butter cake, a pound cake, sponge cake, angel food cake, black forest cake, genoise cake, and many more I didn't recognize. They all looked scrumptious.

Cake for breakfast sounded just about right. Add coffee, and I was in heaven.

The toaster rested on the table in front of Iris, and judging by the pile of message cards next to her, she was on RSVP duty.

Iris looked up as I approached, her features wrinkling in question. "Hey. I thought you were staying at Marcus's last night."

"I did. I was. Long story." When Iris gave me a *what's going on* look, I quickly dismissed it with a shake of my head. "So. Are we tasting cakes for the wedding I've been uninvited to?" A low blow in the early morning, but I couldn't help it.

Dolores's half-chewed cake piece went spewing out of her mouth and hit her coffee mug like a bowling ball hitting a pin. It was a pretty impressive hit.

Iris slowly put her fork down, the whites of her eyes showing as she leaned back stiffly in her chair. Even Ruth had stopped stirring and was still.

Beverly let out a huff and stood. She pushed a strand of her perfectly styled blonde hair back on her shoulder and said, "I think I'll be going now." An emerald dress that matched her eyes wrapped around her shapely body, accentuating all her womanly curves. She looked beautiful. Too bad she was being an irrational, wicked witch.

I raised a brow. "You're leaving because of me? Seriously? Is this what we're doing now?"

Beverly grabbed the compact from her purse and applied red lipstick with an expert hand. "I don't care what *you* do." She smacked her lips together. "But I have a date with *my* fiancé."

I wanted to vomit. "You deserve better."

Beverly's face flushed with sudden anger. Her green eyes flashed with resentment as they pinned me. "A bit rich, coming from the woman who tried to *steal* my fiancé."

"Wow. Who licked the red off your candy?"

Beverly held her lipstick like she was about to gouge my eyes out with it.

I raised my hands in surrender. "I didn't try to steal him. He came on to me. Remember?" This witch was clearly still delusional. But I'd fix that problem. "What you should do is toss him in the basement. Let House deal with him."

Beverly grabbed her purse. "You know nothing. You don't know anything about him or our relationship. He's the best thing that's ever happened to me, and I won't let you ruin it." With a last frustrated glare, she sashayed her way out of the kitchen. A few seconds later, the house shook with the sound of the front door slamming shut.

"Nice touch, Tessa, really delicate." Dolores stood up from her chair. "I'm very surprised at you, especially when you have Marcus. What were you thinking taking Derrick to your room?"

My jaw fell open, and I saw Ruth whip around, giving us her back. Her shoulders hunched, looking like she wanted to be anywhere but in her kitchen at the moment.

I thought about protesting and declaring my innocence, but I could see it wouldn't make a difference. They believed their sister. Of course they would. And I wouldn't bring it up again, not until I had definite proof that Derrick was the scumbag I knew he was.

"You're leaving too?" I asked instead, wondering if I was the reason for it.

Dolores drained her coffee mug. "I have to meet Gilbert." She grabbed a piece of paper from the table that I hadn't noticed. "That scoundrel of a mayor is charging us *double* for the wedding chairs. Says it's a rush fee. I'll show him a rush fee. He won't get away with it."

I shook my head. "Can't say I'm surprised."

"Oh, can you give me a lift?" Ruth set her mixing bowl next to Hildo, who proceeded to taste this new batter. "I need a few ingredients from Gilbert's store."

"Sure," said the tall witch as she marched out of the kitchen.

"Let's go, Hildo." The black cat leaped up on Ruth's shoulder and curled around her neck like a fur scarf. Still wearing her apron and covered in flour, I watched my barefoot tiny aunt hurry out of the kitchen and down the hallway to catch up to her sister.

"You really have a talent for drama," said Iris, a smile on her pretty face, just as we heard the front door open and close again. "Why is it that other people's drama is just so much more exciting than our own?"

I let out a long sigh. "I take it they told you?"

The Dark witch nodded. "Well, her version of the events. I'd like to hear yours. You raced out the door last night. I just thought you were really horny."

I smiled. "There was that. But there's more." I watched as Iris's eyes rounded when I gave her my version of the story. "The guy is a creep, and I'm going to prove it to her *and* them."

"Urgh. I can't believe he kissed you. What an ass. The nerve of that guy. He thinks because he's rich, he can do whatever he wants?"

I shook like I was trying to remove the kiss from memory. It didn't work. "It was vile. Wrong. I almost threw up in his mouth."

"Maybe you should have." Iris's face scrunched up in thought. "And you think he's pulling some sort of glamour on himself?"

"Oh, there's something, all right. Whatever he is, he doesn't want us to know. He's working really hard to keep it hidden."

"Maybe it's just a glamour to make himself better looking. More desirable. Maybe he's a troll, and he's trying to attract women who would have never thought twice about him before. It wouldn't be the first time."

I thought about it. "It's more than that. I felt him try to pull some magic spell on me too. Like a love spell or something? But it didn't work."

"You think Beverly's under a spell?"

"It's the only thing that makes sense and why I'm not slapping the crazy-stupid-love out of her. She's obviously not herself right now. He's done something to her. I know it."

"Hmmm." A frown creased Iris's forehead. "Love spells are not that complicated. And they usually don't work on witches. Beverly's a seasoned witch, and she'd never fall for a simple love spell. It's gotta be something else."

"Like what? Any ideas?"

"No. Sorry." She made a pout. "But I just don't think it's a love spell."

"Well, whatever it is, I'm going to figure it out. And I'm going to find out his secret."

"Here." Iris pulled a white message card from her bag and handed it to me. "I hope you don't mind, I grabbed it from your room last night. I'm sorry, but we couldn't get the locator spell to work. There isn't enough residual magic from the sender."

I flipped over the card, and unease gnawed at my belly as I stared at those two words: HELP ME. Without a location, I didn't have much to go on, but I wasn't about to give up. Not when I knew whoever had sent it was real and was in dire need of help.

When I looked back at Iris, she had a frown on her face, like there was something else she hadn't told me, but she wasn't sure about it.

"What is it?" I asked curiously.

Iris blinked. She opened her mouth and closed it. "The thing is… Ruth and I both could sense magic coming off that card."

"Yeah, I know. We all felt it."

She shook her head. "A *different* sort of magic. We both felt it after our third attempt on the locater spell."

"Like what? Like a spell or something?"

The Dark witch shook her head. "I don't know. Possibly. We tried a revealing spell to unlock whatever magic was hidden, but nothing happened. It's hard to explain, but it's like… it's like there's magic, but it's silent. Like it hasn't *woken* yet."

"Woken?" Interesting. I'd never heard of magic that could do that. "And something needs to *wake* it to make the spell come alive? Maybe turn it on, like a switch?"

"That's what we think," answered Iris. "Or maybe it'll switch on after a while. I'm not sure. But it's clear that whatever magic or spell is in that card will only activate when it's good and ready."

Huh. It only made me want to find the person who sent the card even more.

"Thanks for trying anyway." I stuffed the card in my front jeans pocket, my nerves stretched as tight as violin strings. "I'm not giving up on that person. But right now, I need to do something first."

"Like what?" asked Iris, and then her eyes narrowed at me. "Where're you going?"

My heart pounded madly, but I struggled to remain calm.

"To the Netherworld."

CHAPTER
9

I moved to the basement door and yanked it open. "Dad? Hey, Dad, I need to speak with you. It's really important. Like Lilith important. Can you come here, please?"

I leaned back and cast my gaze at Iris, who was looking at me like I had a few screws loose. Maybe I did.

The stairs to the basement creaked, and when I turned back, my father stood on the threshold. A pair of luminous silver eyes stared back at me, set inside a handsome face with dark graying hair and a meticulously trimmed beard.

"What's she done now?" asked my father, his voice stern with a trace of worry as he stepped into the kitchen.

"I want to hear this," said Iris as she came to join us around the kitchen island.

I swallowed. "I paid Lilith a visit. I mean, she paid me a visit." It was coming out all wrong.

"You're not making any sense," said my father.

"I've been made aware of her plans," I corrected. "Her plans to kill Lucifer."

My father studied me for a moment. "And what does she want from you?" I could tell by the worry in his voice that he knew, or he guessed at something equally bad.

I looked at Iris and my father. "She wants to use my blood as a seal to trap Lucifer."

"That doesn't sound so bad," ventured Iris. "I mean… it's just blood. Right?"

"That's what I thought at first. But here's the thing," I said. "I have to *be* in the Netherworld for it to work."

"No way," exclaimed Iris.

I nodded. "Way."

My father pushed away from the kitchen island, muttering in dark, guttural tones that could only be demonic, though I couldn't be sure. He paced around the kitchen, his fists clenched and unclenched like he was trying to keep it together but was losing that battle.

The air in the kitchen shifted and filled with pressure. It rippled and thickened until a dark cloud formed above my father, literally matching his mood. The air grew colder, dropping, like, ten degrees in a few seconds.

He halted.

And then all the cakes on the table exploded.

Whoops.

Chunks of cake flew in every direction, smacking against the walls, the cabinets, the ceiling. It was a bloody miracle we didn't get hit. Beverly was going to kill me.

"Dad, calm down," I said, before he blew up something else or House threw him back to the Netherworld. "Nothing's happened yet," I added, trying to soothe my father's tension.

My father looked at me. A glimmer of emotion swelled and then died in his eyes. "Not yet. But it will." The pressure in the air lifted, and so did that dark cloud as the temperature rose.

"I wish I had better news," I said. "I knew this day would come. I just never expected that day to be *in* the *Netherworld*."

My father was silent for a moment, and then he shook his head grimly. "Sorry about the cakes. I'll take care of it."

I rubbed my arms to try and get some warmth back. "Forget about the stupid cakes. Can I survive in the Netherworld or not?" Let's face it. That was really the only question I

114

wanted answered right now. Was I going to die trying or could I actually survive the trip?

"I've been in the so-called *pocket* dimension of the Netherworld," I said, "when my buddy Jack, the Soul Collector, took me. Remember? You were there. You saved my life. I'm kinda hoping that's a clue that I'll be okay. That if I could survive there, I can survive the Netherworld. Right?"

My father said nothing.

"I need to know if Lilith is sending me to die," I tried again, studying my father's face for any clues. My stomach twisted with the sudden sickening understanding that this might very well be how I died. It was crazy just thinking about it. And it was crazy that I had no choice in the matter.

My father stared at the floor. "Can you change her mind? Talk her out of it?" His voice was harsh like sandpaper.

I gave a short laugh. "This is Lilith we're talking about. There's no changing anything with that crazy goddess. She gets what she wants."

"Yes, you're right." He made an exasperated sound. "The truth is… I don't know. In theory, it *should* work. You have enough of my blood that should sustain you… at least for a while, but not permanently."

"But you're not sure. So you're saying there's a chance I might die." I wasn't about to gamble my life on a maybe. But what choice did I have? None.

"Death is a possibility," answered my demon father. "Just like it's also a possibility you might survive."

I gave him a thumbs-up. "I love great odds."

"Well..." My father rubbed his beard, deep in thought. "There's only one way to find out," he said. "We'll have to try it first."

Oh goodie.

Have you ever been to hell? Yeah, me neither. The better question was, have you ever been to hell and come back? Nope. But I was just about to find out.

I rubbed my hands. "Okay. How do we do this?" I couldn't believe I was going along with this. I was insane.

If Marcus were here, he'd never let me do this. Knowing him, he'd probably attack my father for trying. Good thing he wasn't here.

"Tessa, are you sure this is the right thing to do?" Iris's face was pale, and she wrapped her arms around her middle like she was cold. "I mean... you might die. You might not come back at all."

"Yes, I might die," I answered. "But better to be with my father than with Lilith and her cronies." I exhaled some of the tension in me. "I'm kinda hoping I won't die."

"There's something else," said my father.

I stared at him. "More than the 'might die' part?"

My demon father nodded, his eyes everywhere but on me. "Once you cross over—"

"And *survive*," I offered.

"It'll feel different: the air, the pressure, the smells, everything. You might have difficulty breathing at first. Try not to panic."

A nervous giggle erupted out of me. "I doubt I won't panic. I'm thinking I'll be doing all kinds of panicking. Colossal amounts of panicking."

Worry etched my father's brow, creases showing around the corners of his eyes and his mouth. "You'll have to tap into your demon side, your demon heritage."

"My demon mojo?"

A smile formed on my father's face. "Exactly. You see, here, on this plane, you're tapped into your witch part. You probably don't even realize you're doing it, but you are. It's your connection to this plane. But in the Netherworld… you've never been there, so your connection will be…"

"Nonexistent."

My father nodded. "Remote." He was silent for a while, and I could see the worry lines on his forehead deepening. "You have to keep tapping into your demon side. Because if you don't, if you let your witch side gain control…" He trailed off.

"I'll die." I looked at him, the fact that he didn't answer didn't fill me with courage about our little trip.

Obiryn tilted his head at me. "It'll be extremely difficult… and painful."

"Nice," I said.

My father was stiff with tension. "It'll be like trying to breathe underwater."

"I've always wanted to be a mermaid."

A laugh escaped Iris, and my father glared at her. She sobered up in a flash and mouthed a "sorry" in my direction.

My father flicked his silver eyes back to me. "This isn't funny, Tessa. This is real. It's no joke."

I licked my lips. "I know that. Just trying to have a little fun before I die. There's no harm in that."

Obiryn shook his head. "You're too much like me. This is going to be a disaster."

"But it's our disaster," I told him with a smile.

My father sighed. "I just wish we had more time. I could have better prepared you for this."

"We don't have that luxury. Lilith can snap her fingers and pull me with her into the Netherworld at any moment. We need to do this now. I have to know." If my father was certain the trip would kill me, I doubted he would be willing to take me with him. I had to believe I had a chance, though smallish, that I'd make it.

"So be it." My father walked over to the basement door and pulled it open.

As I followed him, my heart started to pound, and fear danced over the back of my neck. "So, how does this work, exactly? I've never seen how you"—I made hand gestures—"appear from there." I had always been curious about how that connection between Davenport House and the Netherworld worked, the portal. I peered down the stairs to the empty and very white basement below.

"It's like a portal," said my father, echoing my thoughts. "You need to draw on your demon side and tap into those energies. Once you do, the portal will appear."

Interesting. And scary as hell.

"And where will it take us?" I hated the tremor in my voice, but there was no hiding it now. I was terrified.

"To my home," answered my father. "Where you'll be safe. And then I'll bring you right back."

I swallowed hard, trying to calm my nerves, my blood pressure soaring and making my head spin.

I turned around and met Iris's wide, frightened eyes, and I nearly backed out at seeing that on her face.

"I'll see you later," I told her, my voice high, like I'd had too many glasses of wine.

Iris, seemingly unable to formulate words with her fear, merely nodded.

I whirled back around. "Okay, I'm ready."

"Don't forget how powerful you are," said my father. "Tap into that. Use it."

I nodded. It seemed as though no words would come. My lips were glued together.

I felt a pulse of magic rise, thrumming next to me: cold, familiar, powerful—my father's demon mojo.

"Your turn," instructed my father.

Doing what I was told, I reached out into that source of my power. Cold surged up, and my fear pulled up with the power. As my demon mojo awakened, I let the icy, wild magic rush through my veins, waiting to be released.

And when I looked back down the basement stairs, I started.

A rectangular shape, if I could even call it a shape, wavered. The size of a regular door, it was more like a shimmer, like a heat wave, as though the space had a liquid quality to it. I could see right through it to the bottom of the stairs. Tiny, black electrical currents danced in and around the portal.

I extended my witchy senses, and I could feel the quiver of energies moving through the air and around the portal like a hum of electrical wires.

"Take my hand," instructed my father. I reached out and grabbed his hand, realizing it was the first time we'd ever held hands. His silver eyes flashed as he said, "Whatever happens, don't let go."

"That's just great." Yeah. Now I was really panicking.

Following my father, we stepped down four basement steps together and faced the shimmering portal that would take me through to the Netherworld—or kill me.

No biggie, right?

My thoughts fluttered to Marcus. He'd be livid if he knew what we were about to do. And my heart ached at the idea, the possibility I might never see him again.

I felt a yank on my hand as my father took a final step forward.

Holding on to his hand like a lifeline—with a force of will and possibly a tiny nervous fart—I stepped through.

CHAPTER
10

My body sped forward.

I was wrapped in darkness. It was everywhere and swallowed me as I drifted in silence, floating in nothing but endless night and infinite nothing.

If I had to describe it, I'd say it was similar to traveling with the ley lines mixed with the times I'd traveled to that pocket dimension world where Jack, the Soul Collector, had taken me before.

I could still feel my father's hand around mine, but I couldn't see him. It was the only comfort I had at the moment. Without it, I'd seriously lose my mind.

Especially when the pain hit.

I felt a searing and crushing kind of pain, like every bone in my body was shattered and every cell was on fire. I felt like my body was being pulled apart and then put back together, only to be torn apart again. And again. And again.

Tessa…

Someone called my name. My father.

I heard his voice. I strained my eyes, looking every which way, but no matter how hard I tried to see, there was only an endless blackness.

Then I felt a sudden tug and a tear, like the cutting of a rope. The next thing I knew, I couldn't feel my father's grip anymore.

Fear of the unknown chilled me, and I felt an iron-cold band of dread wrap around my neck.

A second later, I hit solid ground hard, like I'd fallen from a second-story balcony. Maybe I did. I still couldn't see anything.

But pain was a good thing. If I felt pain, I was still alive.

On my knees, I took in a breath — but nothing.

No air. I couldn't get any air into my lungs. They burned as though I'd swallowed a bucket of acid. A ribbon tightened around my chest, but I still couldn't breathe. That, or all the air in the Netherworld had disappeared. I rolled onto my stomach, writhing in pain. My sight went gray at the pain, and I nearly passed out. My face rubbed onto the hard surface as I coughed the acid-like air every time I was able to take even a small breath.

My father wasn't kidding about the breathing part. If I didn't start breathing somehow soon, I wasn't going to make it.

I don't know why I did what I did. I just went with my gut. Call it the faint whisper of self-preservation, but I pulled on my magic, my will, going deep into that cold part of me. I reached into my demon mojo.

Boy, did it answer.

Power soared into my body, into every cell, soaking me with strength. The pain vanished, and my lungs opened up, letting in air.

Except the air was different. It was colder and heavier, like breathing in mist, but it helped.

I licked my dry lips and took another breath, wincing at the burning in my lungs as though I was breathing the fumes of a mixture of bleach and ammonia. It was toxic. The Netherworld was poisonous to mortals.

Good thing I was part demon.

Once the foul air filled my body with oxygen—or whatever it needed—my vision started to clear. I reached out and touched my arms, legs, and chest. All there and in one piece.

"So far, so good."

Still on my knees, I looked around. A dark alley stared back at me. Several empty cardboard boxes and metal garbage bins littered the ground. The air smelled of bile, piss, and rot—the aroma of the Netherworld. Nice.

Tall buildings soared into the sky above, blocking everything else. They weren't unlike those you'd see in a large city—aged and weathered. Every building, even the garbage bin, had physical stains and energies like they were covered in a shivering power of the Netherworld.

I didn't know what to expect. Maybe a burning world with lost souls moaning in forever torment? Yeah, I'd watched too many movies.

I stood up slowly. The alley was cloaked in darkness like a giant drape had blocked all the light from the street and neighboring buildings. I listened, but I couldn't hear the hum of traffic. Maybe no cars were in the Netherworld.

I looked up into the sky because any sane person would know that when you're in another world, you look for some normalcy.

The sky was... odd. Dark, yet no stars or moon were visible, nothing. Heavy clouds raced along the sky in a windless environment. It felt artificial, like they were going for the Earth's night sky but gave up halfway because it was too complicated.

I felt as though I'd just been dropped in another country, where the language and the customs were foreign to me.

I knew one thing. I was lost in a demon world without my father.

A chill that had nothing to do with the icy air scuttled up my spine.

"Dad?" I called out as loudly as I dared. The last thing I needed was to attract the attention of some demon. "Dad!" I spun on the spot, waiting, part of me expecting him just to pop in like he did back in Davenport House.

I'm not sure how long I waited, but I couldn't just stand here. I had to get home. But I had no idea *how* I was going to do that. I needed a portal or a Rift or something, but how the hell was I going to find one of those? My father was supposed to be here with me, and he was supposed to take me back home.

My only option was to try and find where my father lived. He was probably looking for me too.

With my mind made up, I started forward. I could see where the alley opened up to a street and heard my steps echoing loudly.

I made it to the end and cursed.

"Okay. That was unexpected."

What I thought would be a street, or maybe even a large lot was, in fact, an endless desert of gray sand. It was vast and looked like it went on forever. I was in a city surrounded by a vast ocean of sand.

"H'ac q'in tete mele," came a guttural voice behind me.

I jerked and spun around.

Two demons faced me. They were humanoid in appearance, more or less, gaunt and skeletal with gray skin stretched tightly over muscle and bone. Smallish heads sat above broad shoulders. Their eyes were white and burned with some hellish flame. Greasy, thin hair hung from their heads. Overly long limbs tipped in long, dark talons peered from the sleeves of their dark jackets. It was as though their creator had tried to make them look human but didn't get the measurements quite right. They reminded me of the demon I met in Lilith's boardroom. Maybe they were cousins.

Fear shook me. "I don't speak demon," I told them, recognizing a predator in this place like any other. "But I'm pretty sure that wasn't friendly." I coughed, the air suddenly feeling toxic again. A tiny voice inside my head urged me to run. To flee. But where would I go?

Their faces watched me eagerly, burning with what seemed to be an unsatisfied appetite.

"You must be lost, *human*," said the one on the left in perfect English. His fishlike teeth were oversized, cutting into his lips and causing black blood to ooze from the cuts.

"Human?" I scoffed and coughed again. "I'm not a *human*. I'm a demon," I said, hooking thumbs at myself as though somehow it would help. "A hundred percent D-E-M-O-N." No idea why I felt the need to spell that.

"This human female thinks she's smarter than us," commented the demon on the right. Though his English was comprehendible, it was harder to understand than the one on the left.

"Females are stupid," said the demon on the left, his features stretching grotesquely, which caused a slight sinking of his eyes.

"Especially human females," snickered the other. "Tiny brains for tiny heads."

I frowned, not appreciating their condescending tone. "Hey. This female happens to be very clever." I just didn't feel it at this very moment. I felt lost and vulnerable.

The demon on the right shared a look with the other demon. "Which part do we rip out first?"

"We can try the head. But arms are much more fun. They pop. But the screaming is what you really want. If you take the head off first, you don't get the screamin'."

At that, both demons laughed with a stream of hacking wet sounds, guttural and unnatural, that set my teeth on edge.

I clamped my jaw, trying to calm my breathing. "You're not ripping out anything," I growled, though they weren't paying any attention to me.

The demon on the right eyed me and cocked his head to the side, like he was still debating which part of me he wanted to tear out first. "We'll take your light now, human."

"I don't have a light. I don't smoke." I started to feel light-headed, my lungs burning again with every gulp of foul air.

"See? I told you she was dumb," sneered the demon on the left. "She doesn't even know about the light."

"It'll be easier to take it from her," laughed the other. "The stupid ones are the easiest to kill."

I scowled, tired and irritated. "Fine… what *light* are you talking about?" I had to get out of here and find my father.

"The one that's in you," laughed the same demon.

I looked down at myself. Now that my vision was clear, I could see what they meant. The skin on my hands was *glowing*—not kidding—like my blood was made of LED lights. I was a freaking Christmas ornament.

Uh-oh. "How the hell did this happen?"

I was a damn lighthouse, alerting all demons that I was here. Great. And then it hit me. This was my soul, my aura—well, at least the witch part. My inner witch was glowing.

I had not been prepared for this. Still, I realized two things. One, that in my fear I'd let go of the hold of my demon part, my demon side, and had given way to my witch side. And two… that's all I had.

I'll admit, I didn't know much about this world and its inhabitants, except for my father and now Lilith. What I did know was some demons traded human souls. And by the looks of hunger in their creepy white eyes, they were after mine.

My light was my soul.

I looked back at the demons, trying to push down my fear so I could reach out to my demon mojo again. But it was like trying to grab a rope covered in oil. It kept slipping away, so I just couldn't hold on to it. "You're not getting my light," I croaked, my throat burning. "My soul is staying right where it is, thank you very much."

"Oh, but we are," said the demon on the right. "Why else did you come here? Either you are a gift from the master or the stupidest human that ever was."

"Call me stupid one more time," I growled.

The second demon smiled a nasty smile. "Dumb enough to come to the world of darkness in your light suit, your soul for us to take."

"My what suit?" I watched them. "This is getting weird. I didn't come here to argue. I suggest you let me pass and I'll be on my way." I doubted it would work, but I had to try.

They both laughed.

Yeah, thought so.

The demon on the left took a step forward before he angled his head and sniffed. "I smell witch. She's a witch. A stupid human witch."

"Ruzar's been busting everyone's balls for a witch soul," said the other. "Bet he'll give us double for it."

"How about I give you the finger," I said, holding up both hands. "And you can tell Ruzar to shove it." Probably not the smartest thing, but they were starting to really piss me off.

At that, the demons' talons extended into cruel, knife-length claws, ready to do some serious damage to my jugular or elsewhere.

And then they burst into motion before I had time to blink.

Oh shit.

CHAPTER

11

I didn't come here to have my soul taken. I still had work to do, people to save, and a wedding to crash. I didn't plan on running away hiding either. That wasn't my style. Did I even have a style? I didn't think so.

Planting my feet, I let fury surge through me so scarlet and bright that I could hardly believe it was mine. I drew in my will, focusing on that familiar cold power in my core, the same power that enabled me to be here.

The demons came at me in a blur of gangly limbs and talons.

Fear. Pain. Anger. The surges of my emotions fueled my magic, and I would use it. My demon power coursed through me again, feeding me with much-needed strength, and I released it.

Twin black tendrils lashed out of my palms and shot at the two demons.

I had the aim of a three-year-old, but the demons were close enough that even *I* couldn't miss.

My magic hit. I straightened, grinning, expecting to hear screams and maybe even a little thrashing. But all I could hear was the throbbing of my heart pulsing in my ears.

Both demons stumbled back, and my black tendrils snaked around their bodies once before dissolving into nothing.

Apparently, my demon mojo wasn't as effective as I thought it'd be.

Both demons stood unscathed, not a single burnt mark or lesion, not even one goddamn burnt hair on their ugly heads.

I swayed on the spot, the acrid air burning my nose and throat, with my skin sheathed in a cold sweat. And when I turned to look at my hands, my mortal aura was shining again.

Fantastic. I might be part demon, but in their realm, that part of me was harder to control and yield to spindle anything.

The face of the demon on the right wrinkled into a malicious smile. "You had your shot, Witch. And I have to say, it was weak and pathetic. But that's what you are. Isn't it? The sad offshoot of mixing demons and humans. It should have never happened. And we're about to correct that mistake." Glee simmered in his white eyes, evil and absolute. And then he raised his hand. Sparks of black electrical current—same as mine—wound along his fingers like black rings.

Damn. These were the moments where it was perfectly acceptable to panic.

"Wait!" I held up my hand, surprised when they halted. "It's not exactly a fair fight."

The demon on the left snickered. "Who cares."

"Fine, fine," I told him. "Okay, you hit first, and I'll hit firster."

The demon scrunched up his face like I'd just hurt his brain. "What did you say?"

"Kill her," ordered the demon on the left.

The demon on the right grinned and hurled a jet of his black tendrils at me.

Fear welled, and I pitched sideways on the ground, throwing my arms out to protect my head and forgetting about the other parts of my body. Pain gushed as my knees and hip made contact with the hard ground, but it was nothing compared to the agony that followed.

The sharp strike through my body was like an electric shock. Believe you me, being electrocuted hurts like a sonofabitch.

I screamed as a cold, rushing force invaded my body, until every nerve was on fire, burning me from the inside. My stomach twisted, and I

134

panted to keep from vomiting. The undulating surges of demonic power grew and grew until I felt a band tighten around my chest, and I couldn't breathe.

Okay, that's not good.

The demon's power pushed me down, making me crumple to the ground in agony while I struggled and screamed uselessly. My mind was too full of terror to focus or defend myself.

The pain vanished, and I took a gasping breath, regretting it immediately. That foul air burned my lungs.

But I wasn't going to lie here like a victim while these demons attacked me with their tendrils of black demonic power. I was going to get up and probably do something stupid. Better to do something stupid standing up.

Jaw gritted, I reached out and pulled myself up. With my anger growing, I straightened. Okay, so I hurt everywhere and felt like I'd been trampled by a herd of bison, but I could still spindle some magic. I wouldn't go down like a coward. I was a Merlin—a Shadow witch, damn it. I could do this!

The same demon that hit me with his magic came forward, moving with a predatory gait. Black vines of magic coiled around his arms like snakes, and he snickered at what he saw on my face, probably a combination of fear and exhaustion.

I could still feel the pain of using my demon mojo coursing through me, though much less. I focused, trying to call it forth again, but it was faint, and I couldn't reach it, like trying to grab hold of an echo.

My mojo was gone.

I rolled my shoulders, smiling and trying to pretend I was in control when my insides were scattering around like frightened mice.

The demon grinned at my obvious pain, ticking me off all the more. "What do you think you're doing? You can't beat us. We're going to kill you, Witch, and then we're going to take your soul."

"Hmm… let me think about it… *no*."

The demon laughed. "What did you expect? A witch in the Netherworld is an easy target. If you didn't want to die, you should have stayed in your mortal world. Safe."

Behind him, his buddy came forward to join him. They were going to gang up on me.

"Come to think of it," continued the demon. "How *did* you manage to get through? There are no Rifts here. How did you cross over?"

I thought about it. "Your mama." Yeah, I had nothing.

The demon raised one eyebrow. "You're a strange witch."

"I've been called worse."

"Your soul's gonna make us rich."

"Yeah," said the other demon as he joined him. "We're gonna be rich. This is our lucky day."

"You're not getting it." I needed to get out of here, but my escape options were running dry. The fact was, I was screwed. I had no idea where I was and how I was supposed to find my father to get back home.

The demon's face went still. "Oh, yes we are." Rings of black energy burst from his outstretched hands, and my face flamed from the heat of his magic.

"You can't touch me," I proclaimed suddenly, feeling both brave and stupid all at once.

The demon's mocking laughter rang out through the alley. "Yeah? Why's that?"

"Egon, kill her before her soul starts to deteriorate," said the other demon. "Look at her. She's already dying. It won't be worth much if we wait too long."

I didn't know what they were talking about, or why they thought I was dying, but it only renewed my sense of urgency. I had to get away, but I needed to think of a plan first.

"You're right," agreed the demon called Egon. "Its value will diminish the longer she stays here."

Anger returned to me in full force, making my head pound. If I wanted to survive, I had to step up my game.

Adrenaline was flowing, and the pain I felt didn't matter. It wouldn't matter if I was dead in the next few seconds.

Egon's white eyes focused on me, making all the hairs on my body stand. His hands dripped with black demonic magic, and then he raised them.

"Wait!" I hollered. And again, he stopped, confusion crossing his features. These demons were strange or very simple.

"Last words?" Egon's smile was just as creepy as his white eyes.

"Kill her. Kill her now," growled the other demon. "Or I'll do it."

Egon lifted his hand—

"Obi-Wan Kenobi!" I cried out. It was the only thing that popped into my head. "My father's Obi-Wan Kenobi," I repeated, remembering that was the name he'd given to my buddy Jack the Soul Collector demon. I was hoping it had some weight around here.

Egon dropped his hand, and his magic retreated. "Your father is Obi-Wan Kenobi?"

Success. "He is," I said, feeling some confidence coming back. "Obi-Wan's my dad." I kept going, watching the two demons closely. "And I don't think he'd be pleased with you if you tried to harm me."

Egon and his pal looked at each other, or I think they did, but without irises, they could still be staring at me while their heads were turned. So creepy.

"So, if you don't mind," I said, brushing the dirt from my shirt, "how about you let me pass. Or better yet, how about you go and fetch him for me." Yeah, my dad was some sort of demon boss. I was sure of it.

Both demons burst out laughing, which sounded like the screeching of hyenas.

Maybe not.

"Why are you laughing?" I really heated these bastards.

Egon straightened, his white eyes widening. "Obi-Wan Kenobi is a joke. He's a mad fool. Everyone knows that."

"Didn't he die a few years ago?" asked the other demon.

"My father is alive and well, thank you," I growled, feeling the sudden need to defend him.

Egon flashed me a mouth of his sharklike teeth. "Now that we've had our entertainment, it's time for you to die."

He had me there. "I don't think so," I said, trying to match his smile but not feeling the muscles of my face at all. I probably looked like I needed to use the bathroom.

"Goodbye, Witch. Thanks for making us rich." Egon smiled, his demon magic back once more, coiling around his wrists and his arms. Now he was just showing off.

Egon's face morphed into an evil sneer, and he thrust his hands at me—

"Tessa!" someone called out. "Get down!"

I knew that tone of voice. I didn't have to be told twice.

I dropped to the ground as low as I could, flattening myself just as I felt a hiss of Egon's demon mojo take a bite out of my hair.

A second later, a discharge of kinetic force rocked the ground I lay on, two feet away from my face.

The demons weren't so lucky.

Egon and Legon (he needed a name) were blasted off their feet and sent sprawling twenty feet away. They rolled to a stop and didn't move.

"Tessa." My father appeared next to me, his face twisted in worry. "Are you all right? Did they hurt you? Where were you?"

I blinked. "Me? Where the hell were you?"

He shook his head. "It doesn't matter." His face screwed up with concern. "You're glowing. Every demon in the Netherworld can see you now."

"No shit."

"Up you go." He grabbed me and hauled me to my feet. "You look terrible."

"Thanks, Dad."

He pressed his lips together. "Get ready."

"For what?"

He pointed to Egon and Legon. The two demons were slowly getting back on their feet, their faces strained and full of anger.

"They won't be down long," said my father. "We need to get you out of here. Let's go."

Not waiting for me to answer, my father pulled me with him into a run. We charged into one of the buildings that looked like an apartment complex. Once inside the lobby, my father spun around and locked the front door.

"You think that'll hold them?" I asked as a series of coughs shook me. I took a slow breath, trying to ignore my burning lungs. Hell, at this rate, it felt as though they were liquifying.

"No, it won't." My father's worried face made me feel anxious. "You're running out of time. I need to get you back."

A slight chill went through me, and I tried to keep it off my face. "That's what they said."

My father grabbed me by the arm and pulled me across the lobby to the elevators. He smacked the button on the control panel, and with a ting, the elevator doors slid open.

A crash sounded behind us. I whirled around as the building's front door blasted inward, taking the frame with it. Glass shattered. Egon and Legon walked through, and our eyes met.

"Oh shit."

My father hauled me inside the elevator, none too gently, and pushed one of the buttons on the control panel. Then he smacked what I assumed was the Close Door button.

The doors stayed open.

"Uh… you better hurry," I said, my heart thrashing as the two demons came barreling toward us. "'Cause here they come."

With my father still pressing the button, a thick coil of demon magic sprouted from his other hand.

Egon and Legon charged. They were about ten feet away, hissing and gurgling in a language I didn't understand. Eight feet. Five feet. Three feet.

The doors to the elevator shook and slid shut.

Boom!

I jerked back as the doors rattled, sounding like they were about to collapse. I held my breath, but the elevator shook and started to rise.

"That was close," I said with a smile, but my father was eyeing the floor numbers as we climbed. "How far up do we have to go?"

"The twelfth floor," answered my father. "It's the last floor." He turned around and faced me. "When the elevators doors open… we run. We don't stop until we're inside my apartment. Got it?"

I nodded. "Okay." Adrenaline was pounding. My father's nerves were making me more nervous.

A ting came from the elevator, and the doors swished open.

"This way." My father grabbed my arm once again and pulled me into a run. I didn't object. I was glad of it. My legs were starting to feel like my bones were gone and I was going to lose control of them at any given moment.

Together, we flew down a well-lit hallway, which I didn't have time to admire.

I flinched at the sudden crash that reverberated in the building. "That sounded really close."

"They're in the stairwell," confirmed my father. "They're almost here."

"They ran up twelve stories this fast?" My answer came from another blast.

There, down the hallway from which we just ran, stood Egon and Legon.

These were some fast bastards. Simpletons maybe. But fast.

"Come on!" urged my father as he practically yanked me off my feet. I think I was floating now, or he was carrying me.

A moment later, he pushed me inside an apartment and quickly locked the door behind him.

He stepped back, chanting in a low voice, steady and vigorous. Power rolled through the apartment, and pressure throbbed against my ears. Sigils that framed the door blazed to life, like burning red coals. I'd never seen them before, but they were similar to the wards my aunts used for protection. My father had just warded his door.

Obiryn turned from the door. "This way." He gestured with his hand, his voice high with urgency.

I followed him, looking around, my legs shaky and stiff. "This is where you live?" The apartment was large, with high ceilings. Large Oriental rugs designated each space, complete with a comfortable living room and dining room. We passed another room, and I glanced inside. The room was framed with tall bookcases packed with books. A long desk covered in books and papers sat in the middle on another comfortable rug. Three mugs sat on the desk with plates of discarded food. It looked like he lived in that room.

He gave me a short smile. "It's got amazing views."

"Of sand dunes." It might not be the view of the ocean or even mountains with vast greenery, but it was pretty in its own way.

"In here," directed my father as he pulled me into that same room with the books. But when I walked in and turned around, I halted.

There, nestled between two bookcases, was Davenport's basement door. Or an exact duplicate. It even had some of the scratched paint near the door handle.

"Uh… this is weird and fascinating at the same time," I said, turning to look at my father, who had a genuine smile on his face. "Is this our basement door?"

"It is."

"This is how you travel to Davenport House?" I looked back at the familiar door. "How did you do this? Or… did Davenport House create this for you?"

My father sighed with a sad look on his face. "I'll explain it all to you someday, but right now there's no time."

As if on cue, a massive blast sounded from somewhere in the apartment. The floor shook like the building had been hit with a bomb.

My father's eyes narrowed in anger. "They're in. There's no time."

"They know now that you saved me," I said quickly, my heart hammering painfully against my chest. "They'll come back for you. I'm so sorry." I didn't like that I'd put my father's life in danger.

"Don't worry about that now," he said. His silver eyes flashed, his gaze so intense they could start a fire. "I'll handle it."

Without another word, my father reached out and pulled open the basement door. I stared in disbelief at the stairs, *our* Davenport basement stairs.

I blinked. "This is a trip."

The rest of my sentence was lost as my father once again pulled me with him. He spun around and shut the basement door behind us.

Together, we rushed down the stairs. Energy thrummed over my skin and my scalp like tiny electrical currents. Cold power surged, and a burning magical strike hit me next, like I'd just stepped into a cold shower.

And then we were going *up* stairs. Another door stood at the end of the stairs. Okay, now I was totally mystified. My stomach rolled with nausea, and I gritted my teeth. It was like I was going up and down a roller coaster after a helping of Ruth's vegetarian lasagna.

My father reached the door first and opened it. In my haste, or just my pure exhaustion, my foot slipped on the last step, and I fell forward on the hard ground, taking my father with me.

"Obiryn? Tessa? What the hell is going on here?" hollered a voice I knew all too well.

I looked up and blinked into the dark eyes of my mother. "Mom. Your timing is perfect."

146

CHAPTER
12

A size-eleven black, flat shoe came into my line of sight. "Tessa?" questioned Dolores as I looked up at her. Her face twisted and her nostrils flared as she breathed in. "That smell? Were you just... were you just in the Netherworld?"

Damn. I was hoping to have done it incognito. "Yes," I said, no point in lying.

"Are you crazy!" hollered my tall aunt, and for once, I was glad I was on the floor and not face-to-face. I believe some spit might have been involved. "You could have died! You could have been killed! We have no idea how your mortal body would have reacted in that realm."

"I'm alive." I looked over at my father, who was still on the ground. He caught my eye, the muscles in his face twisting like he was trying hard not to laugh. I flashed him my teeth. My dad was awesome.

Not only did he prove to me that his theory was correct, and I *could* travel to the Netherworld, though I couldn't stay long, now I knew going forward with Lilith's plans wouldn't kill me. I'd call this a success, sort of. If you didn't factor in Egon and Legon.

"What possessed you to do something like that?" continued my aunt, her scowl even more frightening from this angle.

I was not about to go into the whole Lilith debacle. Especially with my mother here.

"We tested a theory," I said finally.

Dead silence rang through the kitchen, though I knew it wouldn't last.

"A theory?" My mother's face stepped into view again. "You crossed over to the Netherworld to *test* a *theory*?"

Wait for it…

"Are you out of your mind!" she screamed. See? Told ya.

I looked over at my father. "A bit," I said, making my father laugh. Yeah, we were both in major trouble.

My father leaped to his feet and then pulled me up. "Nothing broken?" He looked me over like an overly concerned parent. I'd seen real fear on his face and regret that perhaps he'd been wrong about my stay in his home world. But I was fine.

"Nothing broken, Obi-Wan," I answered, and we both started laughing again. All the fear, the nerves, and the pain from my trip came out of us in a rush of emotions. It was exhilarating, and it felt amazing.

"Are you two finished?" Dolores appeared next to us, wearing her bulldog expression, with her fists on her hips. Her face darkened, and she looked mad as hell. "This isn't a laughing matter, Tessa. You could have died. And for what?" She poked me in the chest with her finger, hard. "To test a theory? Are you so selfish? Did you even think about what would have happened if you didn't make it back? Did you for one minute think of your *family*? What this would have done to us?"

I opened my mouth. "It's not like that. I had to do—"

"And Marcus? Did you think about him? What would he think of you now if he knew how easily you threw your life away?"

It was my turn to frown. "Of course I thought about him. It's kinda hard not to. Have you seen what he looks like?" I grinned. She didn't.

My father cleared his throat. "This was my idea. Your anger should be pointed at me, not her."

I stared at my father, surprised he would take the fall for my plan.

Dolores turned and pointed her long finger at my father. "And you," she seethed, poking him in the chest with the same finger. "I'm not finished with you."

My father pressed his lips together and leaned back—from fear of Dolores or from trying not to laugh, I couldn't tell.

I took a moment to look around the kitchen. My eyes found Iris. She was staring at me with big, worried eyes. I gave her my version of a covert thumbs-up, and I saw her visibly relax. I had no idea how long I'd been gone, though it had felt like about a half hour or so. But from the looks of the darkening sky, I realized I'd been gone for a lot longer than that.

Beverly sat at the kitchen table, her hands shuffling through the RSVP stack. She looked somewhat relieved that I was okay, but I could still see traces of anger in her beautiful green eyes. And the fact that she was hanging back and not joining her sisters in my crucifixion said it all. She still didn't believe me.

When my gaze found Ruth, she was fidgeting on the spot, a bowl to her chest and stirring what looked like another cake mix, faster than necessary. When she caught my eye, she beamed.

"What was it like?" asked Ruth with round, eager eyes. "Did you meet any interesting demons? Oh. Did you bring back any mushrooms?"

I smiled back. "Actually—"

"Ruth," snapped Dolores. "Don't encourage her. What she did was reckless and selfish and stupid."

I sighed. "I can do without the name-calling."

"There's a lot more name-calling for you, missy, after what you've done." Dolores glowered down at me. I hated that she was taller. It kinda gave her an edge when we argued, and she knew it.

"Do you mind saving them for later?" I asked. "I'm kind of tired from my trip."

My tall aunt's eyes narrowed as she surveyed me. "You don't look like there's anything physically wrong with you. Mentally? Well, that's a whole different matter."

I smiled. "I know."

Dolores leaned forward. "But that doesn't mean you're out of the woods. It doesn't mean that in an hour or later tonight, you might start feeling excruciating pain while your body starts to compress, decompress, or starts to fold in on itself until you melt away and disappear completely."

Nice. "You've always been really good at cheering people up," I told her, though I couldn't help but feel a bit of fear. I hadn't thought about the repercussions of my trip.

151

"How are you feeling?" Ruth joined us, her bowl still resting against her stomach as she mixed. Concern creased her features. "I can whip up a fresh batch of my healing tonic if you want."

"That sounds great," I told her, feeling tired and still a bit nauseated. One of Ruth's potions was exactly what I needed.

My phone vibrated, and when I yanked it out of my jeans pocket, four text messages arrived at once on the screen along with three missed calls—all from Marcus.

Marcus: Hey. You busy? I could use your help with the new bed situation.

Marcus: Sorry about last night. I thought I'd lost you. Call me.

Marcus: Got a bed. Floor model. Now I need us to try it

Marcus: Call me.

My chest swelled with emotion at the memory of the fear I'd seen on his face last night, but I was going to make up for it later tonight. First, I'd drink some of Ruth's fantastic tonic, and then I'd take a shower because I could still feel that acrid air on me from the Netherworld. Then I'd go test his new bed—over and over again.

Smiling, I texted him back.

Me: Sorry I missed your calls. I got caught up with some stuff. I'm ready to test your bed whenever you want.

152

I stuffed my phone back in my pocket and caught Iris watching me. She mouthed, "I want to know everything."

I smiled at her. I knew she and Ruth were probably the only ones truly interested in my voyage to the other realm.

I felt eyes on me, and I turned to find my mother's dark eyes, my eyes, staring back. "When did you get here?" I asked, wanting to change the subject. I could feel Dolores's brain working all the while, thinking up more ways to make me feel bad.

"About an hour ago," answered my mother, proving my point that I'd been gone a lot longer than it had seemed. I'd have to remember that on my next trip. Because, let's face it, I was going back.

My mother looked good in her fitted jeans and modern black top under a black jacket. We had the same dark hair, which she had let down. She was beautiful, maybe not as sexy as Beverly, but it was close.

I glanced around the kitchen and dining room. "Where's Sean?" I had no idea if the guy ever stepped foot *inside* Davenport House. I wondered if House would actually *let* him in.

My mother looked away. "He's very sorry he couldn't be here. He's out on tour again. He's a very busy man, you know. So many obligations to his music and his fans. He can't disappoint them."

"Right." It was just like Sean to miss something as important as Beverly's wedding. Creep. A quick look in Beverly's direction, and her tight-lipped expression said it all. She was pissed that he didn't make an effort to be here.

I glanced back at my mother. "I don't get why you're still with him. He's not a nice guy. He's not even a decent guy. So what if he can play music? Big deal. Any monkey can play music if you give him a guitar."

My mother's head spun around so fast, I was sure it was about to come right off and hit me in the face. "You show him some respect. He was like a father to you."

"Nope and nope," I told her, a frown forming between my brows. "My father is right here. Have you even said hi to him?" I'd just noticed how he'd kept to the shadows, not wanting to cause any more grief at my expense, no doubt.

My mother's face went a few shades redder. "Hi, Obiryn," she said, looking past me to him. "Thank you for bringing her back to us. Though I can't say I'm happy about it."

"It's my pleasure, Amelia," said my father, his voice filled with a kind of emotion I'd never heard before. "I'd do anything for our daughter."

My mother sucked in a sharp breath, and then she looked away, her face strained, and seemed exceptionally uncomfortable. Her eyes darted everywhere at once but at him. That was strange, even for her.

"Dinner is almost ready," Ruth announced. "Will you stay, Obiryn?"

My father glanced at my mother, but she wouldn't look at him. "Thank you, Ruth," he said, "but I don't want to intrude on your family."

Ruth laughed and waved a spatula at him, sending clumps of yellow batter to the floor and hitting the kitchen cabinets. "But you are family, silly. You're Tessa's *father*," she added as though this was news to all of us. "We have more than enough for everyone."

I'd only just noticed that the evidence of the exploded sample cakes had been cleared away. I hoped Iris hadn't been alone to clean it up. I'd owe her if she was.

"Thank you, Ruth," my father was saying. "Means a lot. But I really have to go."

Alarm swept through me. "Go? Go now? You can't go now?" Only moments ago, two demons were chasing us. They were probably still there waiting for my father. I didn't want to think about what they might do to him if he went back.

"I must go, Tessa," answered my father, his eyes on my mother. "I can't stay here." I knew he was referring to my mother not wanting him here. But she didn't get a vote.

"You have to stay. You know what's waiting for you over there," I said, my voice a little high.

"What's waiting?" My mother had turned her attention back to us.

I lowered my voice. "They'll *kill* you."

My father gave me a warm smile. "They won't. Besides, they've gone by now." Apart from the smile, he showed no fear or anxiety.

But my anxiety was going through the roof. "This is all my fault."

My father placed a hand on my shoulder. "Stop worrying. I've been at this for a very long time. Egon and Swat are just thugs."

"Swat? That's his name?" I couldn't help but smile.

"Yes," answered my dad. "And don't worry. I can handle them."

Something occurred to me. "Why were we separated? How come I didn't turn up in your apartment. You *did* appear in your apartment. Right?"

"Yes. I think the gateway's link was interrupted. Could have been just from a lack of practice. Fear is usually the culprit. The energies weren't concentrated enough. Thankfully you landed at a close proximity to my place."

"Yeah—"

"Obiryn," called my mother suddenly, and we both stared at her. "You should stay. Please stay." She glanced at my father one last time and then looked away quickly again.

My lips parted as I stared at the woman who couldn't possibly be the same one who birthed me. The same woman who'd hidden the truth of my real father's identity for most of my life.

I glanced at my father. His silver eyes were so wide, they practically fell out of their sockets. Guess he was just as surprised as I was.

"Here you go." Ruth appeared at my side, a mug of steaming green liquid in her hands. "And drink it all up, please."

"Yes, ma'am." I grabbed the mug and took a large gulp, ignoring the cabbage smell since I knew this was going to make me feel loads better in a matter of minutes. I had no idea how she managed to brew a new batch in the blink of an eye. Ruth was a miracle worker.

When I glanced back at my father, I nearly dropped the mug.

He was staring at my mother, his jaw clenched with emotions. My heart nearly shattered at the longing in his eyes. Sentiments crossed his face: pain, regret, and love. I saw a hell of *a lot* of love right there.

I knew that look. The way he was staring at her now was the same way Marcus stared at me.

Almost in tears, I blinked fast.

My father was still very much in love with my mother.

CHAPTER
13

Dinner was a strange affair, to say the least.

First, well, I'd never had dinner with both of my parents before—my birth parents. And second, was the way they were exchanging polite conversations accompanied with civil looks across the table. Last, was the way my aunts were all acting normal, like my father having dinner with my mother and us was just a routine thing, like we'd done this a million times before.

Part of me wanted to join a certain sexy wereape, naked, waiting for me to test his new equipment—I mean bed—and the other part, well, I just couldn't miss this dinner.

Plus, the longer Marcus waited, the more spectacular the sex would be.

I'd called him just before dinner. "So, you see… I can't miss this," I'd whispered in the phone, standing in the hallway.

Marcus laughed. "I know. I think it's nice."

"Nice? It's a bloody phenomenon."

The chief laughed again, making my smile reach my ears. "You're nuts. You know that? Have fun. There's a new bed waiting for you when you get here."

"Can't wait to try this new bed." My man was so incredibly understanding. I was the luckiest woman alive.

"But Tessa," growled the chief, his voice deep and sensual, making my lady bits thump in time with my heartbeat.

Heat rushed to my face, and I swallowed. "Yes?"

"Hurry." And then he hung up.

I needed a few minutes to calm down after that. The man had panty-melting superpowers.

Ruth had prepared a fantastic and delicious dinner. "We're tasting this to see if we'll serve it at the wedding," she'd explained as she packed my plate with a serving of yummy stuffed poblano peppers, vegetable quinoa, queso, and spicy tomato sauce. Dinner was mushroom ravioli served with a cream sauce, which had my taste buds doing a jig.

As I devoured my mushroom ravioli, I watched said show of my mother and father.

They sat across from each other, each avoiding the other's gaze, but kept throwing covert glances whenever they didn't think the other one was looking. It was like watching two teenagers who had crushes on one another and were too embarrassed to do anything about it.

It was all kinds of weird but incredibly romantic. And I had the best seat in the house, to see it all unfold.

Although this was all foreign to me, I knew something for sure. Something still sizzled between these two. I could see it. Hell, I could *feel* it.

Iris kept throwing me *oh my God* looks from her seat next to me, so I knew I wasn't imagining it. Something was definitely still going on between them.

Ruth sat on the edge of her chair, her knees bouncing while eyeing Beverly as she twisted her apron in her lap. "And? How was it? Do you like it? Do you think your guests will like it? Was it overcooked? I can't serve soggy ravioli."

Beverly tasted another piece of ravioli and chewed as Ruth watched the whole time without blinking. "This is really good, Ruth. You've outdone yourself. Yes, I think we'll serve this at the wedding."

"Oh!" Ruth bounced in her chair and clapped her hands once. "I'm so happy you like it."

Everything Ruth baked, cooked, stewed, or brewed was terrific. It didn't surprise me that her mushroom ravioli was superb. Her comment about the mushrooms from the Netherworld came back to me. If she could, I was pretty sure Ruth would have used them in her ravioli. Yeah, my Aunt Ruthy was wild.

"I never thought you'd be interested in a man like Sean," my father was saying to my mother, and I snapped my attention over to him.

My mother cut into her mushroom ravioli. "Really? And why's that?" she asked casually, keeping her voice neutral and void of emotion. Damn, she was good.

"He's weak." My father lifted his glass of red wine and took a sip. "He's as intelligent as that guitar he plays. He's selfish. Arrogant. Fake. And he treats you badly."

Color flashed on my mother's cheeks. "You don't know what you're talking about. Sean is an amazing husband. He's fun and exciting. Women all over the world throw themselves at him. But he picked me," she added with a false smile.

"And *that's* why you're with him? Because he picked you over a bunch of idiotic humans?" countered my father, frowning at her.

Iris, sitting at my left, gave me her wide eyes. Translation: This was some good stuff — definitely worth staying for.

161

My mother raised her chin, her eyes burning with defiance. "So what if it is? What do you care? You call him selfish, but you're no better."

Obiryn placed his glass of wine back down on the table. His eyes fixed on her. "I am better. Much better than that cheating human you call a husband." He hesitated. "But you never gave me a chance."

Ouch. I think my heart just cried a little.

I cast my gaze around the table, seeing Beverly's angry frown aimed at my mother. She might not like me at this moment, but at least we shared the same sentiments when it came to my mother.

Dolores leaned over the table, watching my parents like she was the judge from some debate team. And Ruth, well, she looked like she was in hell and kept caressing poor Hildo with hard strokes, making his head dip to his paws with each one.

My mother dropped her fork, her face wrinkling as she tried to keep the emotion from showing on her face, but she failed. "I think you should leave."

"He's not going anywhere," I told her and smiled when her eyes moved my way. Besides, I wanted to hear this. I needed to hear this.

"Your mother is right," announced my father, his eyes burning with turmoil beneath his calm features. "I should leave. This was a mistake."

I whipped my fork in his direction. "Stay where you are. This conversion is long overdue. Now, you two need this. We all need this. So, come on, out with it. Get it out of your systems."

The table went silent, though tensions rose.

Finally, my mother spoke. "Sean is not perfect," she said, her face a storm of raw emotions as she glared at each of us. "I know you all hate him." Her eyes focused on my father. "And you can criticize him all you want. But unlike you, he's never lied to me. He never pretended to be someone he's not."

Oh… damn.

Ruth looked uncomfortable as she shoved an entire large ravioli into her mouth. It was so large that she could barely chew, and some of the pasta came spurting out from the corners of her mouth.

"Cheating on your spouse is lying," I added, winning a glower from my dear mama. What? I couldn't resist.

"You told me you were a witch," accused my mother, her gaze back on Obiryn and her eyes blazing with anger. "All that time we spent together, you never once told me you were a demon. You lied to me from the very beginning. Our entire relationship was built on a lie."

"I was going to tell you," said my father. His voice was a cocktail of emotions that sent a pang in my chest. "But I lost the courage. I was a

163

coward. It was a mistake, a grave mistake, not telling you from the beginning. I was afraid."

My mother scoffed. "Please."

"Afraid that you wouldn't see the man but only the demon."

My mother and father stared at each other for a moment, neither of them saying anything.

My mother blinked fast. "I was devastated. Don't you get that?"

"Because I was a demon." Sadness crossed my father's face, and I felt my eyes burn.

"Florence dated a demon once," exclaimed Ruth as she continued to stroke Hildo's head forcefully. "But then he ate her."

"Not really helping, Ruth," snapped Dolores.

"I don't know why we're having this conversation." My mother folded and unfolded the napkin on her lap. "You can't have a relationship without trust. I could never trust you. What you did was unforgivable."

My father's jaw clenched, and his silver eyes flashed with anger. "You kept Tessa from me. Why didn't you tell me I had a daughter?"

Iris and I both shared a glance. Damn, my life was a total soap opera.

"You never told him about Tessa?" expressed Beverly, looking perplexed. "But… no? That can't be? Surely, you must have told him? Amelia?"

"Is that true, Amelia?" asked Ruth, looking upset for the first time tonight.

"Quiet!" shouted Dolores, making Iris and me jump in our seats. "I want to hear this." Her eyes were glued on my mother and father as she gestured with her hand for either of them to continue.

My mother's eyes filled with tears. "I... I couldn't... I thought I was doing the right thing..."

"By keeping my only child away from me?" Obiryn's face contorted with rage.

A tear leaked from her eye. "A mother will do anything to protect her child. Anything." She shook her head. "How could you take her to that place? You know you've put her in danger. You know what they'll do to her when they find her. How could you, Obiryn?"

I raised my hand. "It was my idea, not his, to go to the Netherworld." All eyes snapped to me. "You can stop blaming him. It was all me. I asked Obiryn to take me to the other side. I wanted to see if I could survive. I did. And we're both fine, as you can see." No point in telling them about the two demons.

My mother jumped up, threw her napkin on the table, and rushed out of the dining room with tears spilling down her face.

Oh dear. Now I felt like an asshole. Sure, my mother and I didn't get along on most days, and there was the fact she'd tried to keep me from doing magic, but she was still my mother. And in her own way, she had thought she was doing the right thing. She thought she was protecting me. Which, when I thought of it, she did. Knowing what I know now of the Netherworld, of Lilith, of Lucifer, and the other demon leaders, they either wanted me dead or wanted to use me.

I looked over at my father. He sat with his head down, looking defeated and just as miserable as her. Maybe this hadn't been such a great idea.

The ringing of the doorbell cut through my morbid thoughts.

"Oh, it must be Derrick." Beverly stood and grabbed her purse. "He's taking me out for cocktails on his boat."

"Derrick has a boat?" I asked, but Beverly continued to ignore my existence.

After checking herself in her compact mirror, she rushed out of the dining room to the front door.

I'd been so preoccupied with the whole "I think my dad still loves my mother" thing, I'd forgotten about Derrick the creep. And with Lilith, and my trip to the Netherworld, I hadn't had the time to come up with a plan to cancel the wedding. But I still had three more days.

Iris leaned over. "Your father looks miserable," she mumbled. "He looks like someone shot his dog."

I cringed at her statement. "He looks like someone broke his heart." That was exactly what was happening. My father still loved my mother and painfully regretted his choice of concealing his true demon identity for fear that she would leave him. But she did in the end, so maybe he'd been right to hide it.

In a swift movement, my father stood. "I think I should be leaving now. Thank you, Ruth, for a delightful dinner, as always. Your culinary skills are unmatched."

Ruth's face reddened. "Oh, you." She batted a hand at him and then continued to molest poor Hildo with her hard strokes on his little head.

"You won't stay for dessert?" I stood, knowing perfectly well that he wanted some time alone, and I completely understood that.

"Not tonight." Without another word, my father moved away from the dining table and walked over to the basement door.

I hurried after him. "You sure you'll be okay. Tweedledee and Tweedledum won't be there?"

A smile crossed my father's face. "No. Don't worry about me. Okay? I'll be just fine."

"Easy for you to say."

My father pulled open the basement door. "Tessa? Can you do me a favor?"

"Anything."

He turned and said, "Look after your mother, okay. She needs you right now."

I nodded, surprised. "Okay. Sure." Not sure how that would go down, but I'd do anything for my demon father.

Without another word, Obiryn stepped through the threshold and closed the door behind him.

I stared at the door, feeling sad for both of my parents. Some serious history was there, and I didn't know if it could ever be mended.

"It's a *yacht*, not a *boat*," I heard Derrick's voice correcting Beverly behind me.

"Yes, yes, sorry, a yacht," she said, her voice taking that high note again that I hated.

I balled my fists and marched into the dining room. Only Ruth remained sitting, feeding Hildo some of her mushroom ravioli. Everyone else had gathered in the living room. It was going to be really hard to refrain from punching Derrick in the throat. So I stayed standing behind the invisible line that separated the living room and dining room, debating with myself.

Derrick's eyes moved to me. "Ah, Tessa. How nice to see you."

"Can't say the same about you," I growled, making Iris spit into her glass of wine. See? I could be civilized.

Annoyance flashed on Derrick's face, but he quickly smoothed his features into a pleasant smile. "You should come on my yacht sometime. All women love a little luxury."

"I'd rather stab myself in the eye, thanks."

"Tessa, stop being so rude," snapped Beverly.

I gave her a look. "Oh, now you're speaking to me? How nice of you." I shook with rage. If I stayed any longer, my temper was going to get me into trouble. I didn't have a plan yet, so I didn't want to mess that up. I needed some release and distraction.

I needed Marcus.

With my mind made up, I crossed the living room and made my way to the foyer.

I jerked as heat singed my skin, so much so that I halted right in the middle of the living room, right next to Derrick.

What the hell was that?

Again, the heat pulsed and singed, growing like my pocket was on fire. I stared down at myself. I wasn't on fire, so why did it feel like something inside my pocket was.

And then it hit me.

The message card. The card that had the words HELP ME was in *that* pocket, the one that felt like it was scorching my skin.

I knew at that moment *this* was the hidden magic working, the secret magic Iris had told me about. And I also knew it had come to life the moment I had stepped in front of Derrick.

My pulse thrummed with excitement as adrenaline pounded through me.

Derrick. The message card was about Derrick.

That sonofabitch was hurting someone.

CHAPTER

14

I stared at the white message card resting on my desk with the black letters that read, HELP ME, hoping somehow it would show me more, now that its magic was activated.

"And it just started to burn when you were next to him?" Iris leaned in toward me, inspecting the card like it was the next best thing in all things magical.

I nodded. "Exactly. Like it was *telling* me that bastard is involved somehow. He's doing something to someone… and they need our help." I knew one thing for sure. Whoever had sent it was clever, very clever.

"Well, this is complex magic," said the Dark witch, her eyebrows high. "Whoever sent it is experienced with high-level magic."

"I agree."

"It turned on as soon as you were close to him. Its magic's been activated. Wow. That's really impressive."

"I know." I leaned over and bent forward. "Can you tell me where you are?" I asked the card, hoping it would tell me. "What's your name? Where do you live?"

"Uh… what are you doing?" laughed Iris.

I kept my eyes on the message card as Iris's shoulder bumped against mine. "I'm thinking now that it's activated, maybe this card, this magic, will show me. Like… maybe it'll write out an address or something. Like a message card version of a Ouija board."

"Good." Iris nodded. "Yeah, that's good. Maybe."

Both of us waited for a while, staring at the card until the words blurred, and black spots started forming in my eyes.

I leaned back and rubbed my eyes. "Urgh. Why won't it tell us? I mean, it told us Derrick is involved. Why can't it give us more clues?"

"I don't know," said Iris as she let out a sigh. "But it's a hell of a start. We got him, Tessa. Think of that. It could have taken us *forever* to find out who was linked to this card. Maybe we'd never have found out, but now we know."

172

My blood pressure rose. "Yeah. And I have a feeling whoever sent it also knows Beverly is engaged to him, which means they sent the card hoping it would work. That the magic would work because they knew he'd be here."

"That makes sense." Iris hesitated a moment. "I'm sorry about your parents. It's tragic."

I looked at her. "My mother loves to perform."

"I don't think she was performing," continued the Dark witch. "I think she still loves him… and he definitely still loves her. We all saw it."

"I know."

"I think it's cruel to keep two people apart when clearly they should be together."

I sighed. "It was strange to see them together in that way. I grew up thinking Sean was my father, even though my gut told me something was off."

"They've been miserable for years. It's written all over their faces," said Iris. "Maybe it's time for them to get all those years back. Wounds heal. They deserve to be together. They deserve to be happy."

I looked at her, my chest swelling at being blessed with such a caring friend. "I can see your mind whirling through your eyes. What exactly are you trying to say?"

"I'm saying we should try to get your parents back together."

I stared at her. "I'd be lying if I said I hadn't thought of it, but there is the issue of Sean."

Iris shrugged. "So we get rid of him." She said it with a finality, like it was obvious she wanted to throw the noose around Sean's neck.

"You want us to kill him?"

"Kill him. Curse him. Send him to the bottom of the ocean in a coffin. Everything is possible with a little imagination."

I laughed. "Well, I have thought about killing Sean more than once, but I don't want the human police on my ass."

"Curse him, then," said Iris happily. "I've got my hands on a new tree-man syndrome curse, which causes huge warts that look like tree bark. He'll never be able to leave his apartment for the rest of his life. Let alone play his music."

"Sounds painful."

Her face pulled into a smile. "Oh, it is."

"Excellent."

We both laughed, the wonderful sounds cascading over me and releasing more of my anxiety and tension. Sean deserved to be cursed and worse, but I didn't want it traced back to my mother. We'd have to think of something else.

"Let's deal with Beverly's dirtbag fiancé first. Then we'll deal with Sean," I said, looking over the card again. "Find out what he's hiding," I said, my heart throbbing with excitement, "and we find the person who sent that card."

Iris nodded. "So, where do we look?"

"If this person knew my aunt's fiancé would show up in this house, that tells me they know my aunts or at least know *of* them. Which means… maybe someone from this town or somewhere close? But without much to go on, without a name, it'll take us forever."

Iris bit her lip. "The locator spell didn't work before, but maybe now that the magic is active, it's worth another try."

I beamed. "Let's do it."

Both White and Dark witches had their own versions of locator or tracking spells. Iris's Dark witch version was excellent, but it required hours spent on pre-spells and aura-detecting spells—not to mention adding some sort of compass linked to the card. But she'd gotten better over the months. With tracking Lilith, her abilities had vastly improved.

I hauled the heavy hardcover book called *The Atlas of North America* across my desk next to the card and flattened the map of Maine.

Iris leaned over the card and placed a red marble on the map. "Tenebras voco potestatem ad pariendum mihi daemones dare," she chanted.

Energy crackled in the air, and I moved back to watch in awe as my friend conjured up her locator spell on a whim.

A burst of dazzling light flashed before our eyes as magic tore through the room. The

175

bedroom lights flickered off and on again as power soared.

Iris closed her eyes and cried, "Veni ad nos et apud quem vocant! Veni ad nos, et habitatores hic!"

I felt the energy from Iris's magic flow around us like a breeze, settling around my bed, my laptop, my books, the piles of paper, and into every floorboard until the entire area was immersed in the spell, along with me.

And then the power settled.

Both Iris and I stared at the map. The marble sat at the exact same place.

Iris sighed. "Sorry, Tessa. It's the same as the last time I tried. I can *feel* the magic inside that card, but somehow, I can't break through and pinpoint where it came from."

"You tried. And without Gigi this time. How did you manage that?" I asked, impressed. Dark witches usually borrowed their magic from demons, which meant they first had to summon a demon. Gigi, the cute tiny demon with orange fur, had always been her go-to demon whenever she needed to do some serious magic.

Iris gave me a mischievous grin. "Yeah. I've picked up a few tricks."

I cocked a brow. "I'll say."

"See," said the Dark witch, "your power words gave me the idea."

"Really?"

"Instead of calling up a *physical* demon, I used a different spell—which I designed myself—and called to the demon's power without having to conjure it here. Like a back door. Too bad it didn't work."

"Still very impressive, my friend."

Iris looked away, embarrassed. "Thanks."

I stared at the card as a thought occurred to me. "It's magical, and magical objects are not so easily destroyed. Right? Maybe we just need a different kind of magic to wake it up. To reveal itself."

"What do you have in mind?" asked Iris.

"Maybe all it needs is a little push," I said, my adrenaline flowing.

I tapped into my will, pulling on the energy of the elements around me and holding them until I had just a tiny amount.

"Accendo," I breathed.

A tiny burst of fire shot from my hand and hit the card. It rose an inch before settling back down, the right corner ablaze in yellow flames.

Whoops.

"Oh shit!" I slapped down on the card hard until the flames went out and then looked over at Iris. "I just almost destroyed my only evidence. Guess that was a bad idea."

She laughed. "Hey. We have to try everything. Now we know that the card is not indestructible."

She was right. "We better keep it safe." I rubbed at my temples. "I don't get it. Clearly, it wants us to know about it. Otherwise, it wouldn't have revealed itself to me. And the person who sent it wouldn't have sent it." I shook my head. "Why can't you tell me?" I stared at the card. "What am I supposed to do?" I waited, though I knew nothing would happen. And it didn't.

I rested my hip on the corner of my desk. "I really hate that guy."

"After what he did to you, I'd hex him with the tree-man syndrome curse. Just saying."

I crossed my arms over my chest. "Maybe I'll ask my father what he knows about magic cards. Now that I know I can visit him."

Iris pressed her hands on her head, her eyes wide. "Ohmygod. I still can't believe you did that, you crazy witch. You could have died. I'm *so* envious. I wish I could go."

I smiled. "It took some getting used to, not to mention the demons who tried to kill me, but I'll get the hang of it." Hopefully before Lilith came calling. "I'm still going to figure out a way to stop the wedding and show my aunt he's a douche. I swear. I will find out who the real *Derrick Baudelaire* is."

The message card jerked and started to spin on its axis on the desk like it was possessed or something.

"What the hell?" I stared at the card as it spun one last time before finally settling.

"Ooooh! Something's happening," said Iris excitedly.

"No shit."

The ink glowed brightly on the card for a second and then vanished as though it was sucked into the paper. The words on the card faded until all that was left was the blank, white surface.

And then something really happened.

My heart thundered with anticipation as dark ink oozed back out through the card. First, it was just a blotch, and then a line. I leaned forward, barely able to contain myself.

Thick, dark black lines seeped through the surface until all the lines took shape and spelled a name.

EVELYN STAR

Holy crap. We had a name.

CHAPTER
15

"Evelyn Star? You've never heard of her? Are you sure?" I asked Dolores sitting across from me at the kitchen table the following morning.

Dolores peered at me over her reading glasses. "I'm sorry, but no. I've never heard of a witch called Evelyn Star. I think I would remember a name like that. Sounds like a prostitute. She's not from Hollow Cove, if that's what you're asking."

Iris and I had stayed up until two in the morning searching the internet for anyone by that name. And after hours of us both looking, we came up with nothing.

Iris had gone to Ronin's after that, and I'd collapsed in my own bed, too mentally and physically exhausted to do anything else. I'd even canceled with Marcus, though again he'd been so understanding. I realized my trip to the Netherworld had done a real number on my body, and even with Ruth's healing tonic, nothing was better for the body than sleep.

However, I still woke with a feeling like I had the hangover of the millennium.

"And you got that from the card?" asked Ruth, busy at the kitchen sink as she washed some dishes. "How exciting. I wish I'd been there with you when it happened." I could hear the longing in her voice.

I'd decided not to tell them the card had revealed its magic in the presence of Derrick and then again when I'd used his full name. I still believed he was using a fake name. I had to choose the right time, and now wasn't it.

Beverly was already gone by the time I came down for breakfast, or an early lunch, seeing it was past ten in the morning.

Evelyn was the proof I needed. Beverly didn't believe me now, but if I could reach Evelyn, if I could find her, Beverly would have no other choice than to believe me.

Derrick was doing something to Evelyn, and I needed to find her fast.

Dolores pulled her glasses from her face and used them to point at me. "I told you. This is the work of the Wanderbush witches. This is just the sort of thing they'd do—make you go out on a wild-goose chase while they executed their master plan."

I rolled my eyes. "Which is what? To rule the world?"

Dolores glowered at me. "To take over Davenport House. Haven't you been paying attention? This is all they want, what they've always wanted. But let me tell you… it'll never happen. They'll never get Davenport House. Never."

"Okay," I answered, watching that manic glee in her eyes closely.

"What else did the card do?" asked Ruth, her blue eyes round and sparkling. "Did it say anything else?"

"It *wrote* something. It didn't speak, you half-wit," snapped Dolores.

Ruth made a face. "I still would have liked to have been there. Magic cards are really rare, and not many witches can manage them. The only witch I know who could work them is Susan Woodward. It's kinda like potion making. Some witches work potions, and some witches work magic cards. The skill takes years of practice and control. I've always wanted to learn how to do it," she added with a bit of a pout.

She was so cute. I was tempted to go over there and pinch her cheeks. "Where's Hildo?" I asked, only now noticing the black cat was nowhere to be seen.

"Out hunting," answered Aunt Ruth.

"Hunting? Hunting what?" The cat was practically spoon-fed, he was so spoiled. And seeing as he was a witch familiar, I didn't even know if those feline instincts were real.

"Mushrooms," answered Ruth. "I need more mushrooms for the ravioli I'm serving for the wedding. He's got a really good nose. He could have been a sniffer cat for customs. You know, detecting all that cocaine and the bad people."

"Right." Not sure what to say to that. "Thanks for breakfast, Ruth," I said as I leaped to my feet and downed the last of my coffee.

My aunt beamed. "Oh, you're welcome, Tessa. You sure you don't want more waffles?"

I rubbed my belly. "I look four months pregnant. Thanks, but I'm stuffed."

"Where are you off to?" inquired Dolores with a skeptical sparkle in her eyes.

I set my mug down. "Well, since you don't know anyone called Evelyn Star, I'll see if Marcus has that name in his database. Maybe she's from a neighboring town."

"Tell him to check the escort services," said Dolores, flicking a finger at me. "She sounds like she's a working girl."

I didn't buy that. "Okay, Sure."

"What about your RSVP duty?" Dolores's face took on a severe expression. "Cards are still coming in. You're abandoning us?"

"I'm uninvited, remember? See you later!" I called from the hallway and hurried out before they ganged up on me for card duty. Besides, all they had to do was grab the cards coming in. No big deal since they were physically in the kitchen and next to the toaster.

I grabbed my jacket and rushed out the door. Two strides onto the stone walkway, and I halted.

Three witches stood in my way. Three Wanderbush witches.

"You?" I said, surprised at how I hadn't even seen them when I came out onto the porch. It was as though they'd just materialized from thin air. Could they do that?

"Amelia's spawn," said the witch I recognized as Davina, the one who reminded me of Dolores.

"Don't call me that." I eyed them each in turn. "What are you doing out here?" This was private property, though I didn't mention it.

The three sisters standing outside, loitering like that, made them out as shady characters in the bright sun. It gave me the creeps. They were up to something; that was for sure, like thieves checking out the house in daylight before returning to rob it that night. I had a feeling they were contemplating their next move. Perhaps Dolores wasn't wrong after all.

Belinda winked at me and flashed me a perfect smile when I looked at her. Reece's face was stretching and pulling, still trying out which expression to wear at the moment, which was still all kinds of creepy. It was hard not to stare.

Davina sneered down at me, her face cold and unpleasant. "Not that it's any of your business… but since you live here and will be affected, you might as well know."

"Know what?"

"We're going to secure our family home once and for all."

"Uh-huh."

"You'll see, Amelia's spawn," continued Davina. My face reddened with that word again. "Soon, it will be Wanderbush House and not Davenport House."

I snorted. "Yeah. Good luck with that. Doesn't really roll off the tongue as well. Does it? Wanderbush House? But good luck anyway. I mean it. Good luck." I sidestepped and moved away from them as fast as I could without running. I thought of tapping a ley line, but then I didn't want them knowing anything about me. Dolores had been very clear.

The houses on Stardust Drive rushed past me as I speed-walked down the sidewalk. I really needed to speak to Marcus, but I also really needed to see him.

I'd walked for about seven minutes until I spotted the gray building of the Hollow Cove Security Agency. Crossing Shifter Lane at a jog, I hit the sidewalk and made a beeline to the chief's building.

I pulled open the front door and made my way inside, blinking into the harsh white lights. As I crossed the lobby, I spotted an older woman with short white hair seated behind the front desk. She wore a white pressed shirt and a critical look, making the wrinkles around her face sharper.

She looked up as I marched past her. "Tessa Davenport? Where do you think you're going? Do you have an appointment? Stop! You can't just walk into his office!"

"Watch me," I muttered.

Most of the time, Grace, Marcus's administrative assistant, ignored me. So I chose to ignore her too.

Down the hall, I turned the corner to Marcus's office and came face-to-face with the chief, Allison, and a woman I'd never seen before.

Marcus's eyes tracked me as I approached. A brown leather jacket fell over his broad shoulders, hitting him around his trim waist. He oozed confidence and strength, and he was smoking hot. Maybe I was just horny. His intense gray eyes pinned me, making my stomach erupt in delicious batting butterflies.

Allison, the pain in my ass, stood with her arms crossed over her ample chest, looking beautiful with her high blonde ponytail and restricted in her stupid black pencil skirt. I really didn't get those. Her full lips were pressed tightly, her smile so fake it might have been a mask. She looked… she looked constipated. I'd never seen her look this uncomfortable.

When I spotted the new deputy, it all made sense.

Wearing a small black bomber-style jacket and black pants, she had the body of an athlete and the face of a supermodel. Hell, she looked like a younger Cindy Crawford. Wow, she was a showstopper. The small pulse of magic I got from her said werewolf.

I looked over at Allison again, her lips practically pulled into a snarl as she eyed the new deputy. That fake smile she was holding looked painful. Yeah, this was Allison's version of hell.

It made me all giddy inside.

If I had the space, I would have broken out into cartwheels. Instead, I did what any good girlfriend would.

I walked up to the new deputy and raised my hand in a high five. "Give it here, sister," I told her, grinning as our palms smacked loudly.

I winced inwardly. Damn, she was strong.

"Thanks," she said, her hazel eyes sparkling. "I've heard you're pretty awesome yourself."

A stupid smile crept over my face. I liked her immediately. "I'm Tessa."

"Scarlett," answered the deputy. "Nice to meet you."

"Likewise."

"Tessa? Did you need me for something?" asked the chief, his handsome face so deliciously hot and sexy, I wanted to high-five myself.

"Yeah. Can we talk? In private?"

"Sure." With his hand on the small of my back, Marcus steered me toward a door with the name MARCUS DURAND stenciled on the window in black letters with the words CHIEF OFFICER written under it. "What's going on? Does this have something to do with this Derrick guy?" he asked as he began to shut the door to his office.

I got a glimpse of Allison's constipated expression. I waited for her to see me and flashed her a thumbs-up with a smile just as the door closed.

Marcus's office was as tidy as his apartment. To the right of the door was a wall lined with filing cabinets, and rows of bookcases occupied the wall next to the desk. Sitting in front of the only window, his desk was stacked with papers next to a laptop.

"It does." I quickly shared what the message card had done inside my pocket and then how it gave a name once inside my bedroom.

Marcus crossed his arms, his face creasing in a frown. "Evelyn Star? The name doesn't sound familiar. And it happened when you said the name Derrick Baudelaire out loud?"

"Yes. He did or is doing something to that witch. She needs my help, Marcus. Can you see if her name comes up in your database?"

"Sure."

I settled myself in the chair facing the chief's desk as he sat on the other side and began typing on his computer.

"I like your new deputy," I said after a while.

A smile tugged at his lips. "I noticed."

I exhaled long and loud and leaned back into the chair. "Allison looks like a wet cat. I love it."

"I noticed that too."

"It's like… a gift from the goddess," I said, pleased with myself as though it was my idea to hire that new hot deputy. I wished it had been. "No spell or curse can even come close. Scarlett is my gift from the gods."

Marcus laughed. "Yeah, well, I'm not very fond of one goddess at the moment."

Lilith. Right. "About her," I started, and once I did, everything sort of flew out of my mouth. I told him about how Lilith planned to kill Lucifer and my part in it. Specifically, me going to the Netherworld.

Marcus stilled for a second, his fingers hovering above his keyboard. "Tessa…"

"There's more," I cut in. Might as well tell him about my trip with my father. So I did. I sat back and watched as his face went through an array of emotions. When they landed on what I could only describe as white-hot fury, and he was *very* hot, I started to regret my choice of being completely honest.

The wereape took a breath, his shoulder muscles bulging as he strained to hide his tension and maintain the practiced calm of a chief.

"I can't believe you did that," he said after a moment, anger and fear straining his voice and making my own tension creep along my spine. He wasn't looking at me, instead staring at his computer, like if he looked at me, he'd lose it.

Shit.

"But I'm fine. I survived. I made it back."

When he finally turned to look at me, fear lay deep in his gray eyes. "You could have died."

"But I didn't. And now I have an edge over this Netherworld thing. I know I can travel there and survive. So, you see, Lilith's plan won't be too bad."

"Won't be *too* bad?" Marcus rose from his seat.

Uh-oh.

Muscles twitched on Marcus's jaw. "How can you say that when she wants to *use* you to kill her husband? Even if it means you'll die?"

I pressed my lips together. "That's not what I meant. I mean, I'll *survive* the trip."

"You think it'll work?" said the chief, the muscles popping along his neck. "You think Lucifer can be killed that easily? The king of hell? Really? The most powerful being in that world?"

He had a point. I shook my head. "The truth is… I don't know. But she has thought it through. I don't think she'd put it in motion if she didn't have a chance of success." I hoped.

"And then what? Let's say her plan works. You think she'll let you live after that?"

I hadn't thought of it. "Yes. She won't hurt me."

Marcus shook his head at me. "You can't be that naïve, Tessa. She doesn't care about you. She's *using* you. That's what gods and goddesses do. It's all a game to them. She's playing you."

"I get it. But after this is over, I won't owe her any favors. Don't you see? I can get back to my life and forget she ever existed." Highly doubtful, but if I kept telling myself that, maybe it would come true.

Marcus didn't say anything after that.

I shifted in my seat, feeling a lot less sexy and a lot more anxious. "Anything?" I asked after a moment, unease staining my senses.

Marcus sat back in his chair. "Nothing. I have no record of this Evelyn Star ever existing. But it doesn't mean she doesn't exist. I just don't have any documentation."

"That's weird," I said, deflated. "And really not helpful." The fact that we knew she could do magic meant she was a paranormal, a magical practitioner. Her name should have been in those records.

Still, I had one place left I could look for answers.

"Thanks." I leaped up, moved around the desk, grabbed the chief's face between my fingers, and kissed him.

A stab of desire flew to my middle as a moan escaped him. My breath came fast as he slipped his tongue into my mouth. It was hot, and he tasted like coffee and pastries. I couldn't get enough. His warm lips and hot tongue were intoxicating.

The chief excelled in the mating department, and he was also a fantastic kisser, making my eyes roll into the back of my head.

I pulled him against me, my hands drifting under his shirt and rolling over his hard back muscles. Where my hands touched his skin sent delicious slivers of heat to my fingertips. I moaned as his rough, manly hands slipped under my shirt, his fingers tracing up and down my back. Waves of demand pulsed from his touch, and my skin flared up in goose bumps.

He growled low and cupped my ass to pull me against him. I could feel the hardness in his pants, telling me how much he wanted me.

But it would have to wait.

He pulled back, his gray eyes flashing with desire as he let out a little growl that had my lady regions pounding. If I stayed, I would jump on the chief and take him right then and there on his desk.

But I had a job to do.

"I gotta go," I said, moving back and keeping a safe distance from his intoxicating smell. He really did smell amazing.

"Where?" said the chief with a loud sigh, his eyes still blazing with hunger.

"I'll tell you later," I told him and watched his skeptical brow rise.

I turned around and left his office before I got into trouble.

I wanted to tell Marcus about my sudden plan, but I couldn't because I knew the chief would never agree to do what I was about to do.

Because tonight I was breaking into Derrick's house.

CHAPTER
16

"**A**nd you think this Evelyn is here?" asked Ronin, leaning against the stone wall. The exterior lights cast dark shadows around his eyes.

"It's the only place that makes sense," I told him as I peeked around the corner with my eyes glued on the front door. I yanked out the message card with the name Evelyn Star and held it up, waiting for a sign that she was here. But the card didn't so much as flicker or heat up. Nothing.

I stuffed it back in my pocket. "Even if she's not, I'm pretty sure we'll find something about the lying bastard. I'm not going back empty-handed." My relationship with Beverly depended on it.

Derrick's property stood at the top of the hill on Serenity Row, the only place in Hollow Cove with sprawling mansions. The ten-thousand-square-foot homes perched on the steeply sloped lots, looking down on the rest of us. Okay, so Derrick was loaded. The kind of loaded that if he had grandchildren, they'd be loaded too.

I glanced around the front yard. The massive, three-story red brick manor had tall, gaudy Roman pillars with windows of every size at the front, all arranged around a central courtyard. It lacked any clear architectural style as though many different designs were all jumbled together. It didn't have the quaint country feeling and comfort of Davenport House and wasn't inviting either. The longer I stared at it, the more it gave off a cold, trapped feeling, like a prison.

Splashes of yellow light spilled from the exterior of the house. It was well-lit for ten at night, which wasn't ideal with what we were about to do. Good thing Derrick's neighbors were too far away, hidden mainly by thick wooded areas on each side.

"So, Derrick owns a McMansion," commented the half-vampire. "Does that make him McDreamy?"

I snickered and then turned around and smacked him on the arm. "Don't make me laugh. This is serious business. Very serious."

"And why couldn't Marcus be here?" voiced Iris.

"Marcus would never agree to break into someone's home without a warrant or something," I told her, which I knew was true. If he did, he'd probably lose his job. But then again, he was ready to commit murder on Derrick was he was feeling possessive, so who knows.

"And you're sure it's empty?" Ronin peered at the large home.

I nodded. "Derrick and my aunt went to his yacht. They're sleeping there too... I think. Maybe. But just in case they're not, let's just give ourselves twenty minutes tops to search the house."

Ronin whistled. "Not sure we can do the first floor in twenty minutes. Have you seen the size of this thing? It's practically a hospital."

"I don't want to stay too long. Just in case. We go in, look around for Evelyn, grab some evidence, and get out. Let's go."

My pulse quickened as we crossed the front yard and made our way toward the large home. My boots crunched on the gravel path that separated a garden of boxwoods, lilies, and crabapple trees before leading to the main doors of the house.

I reached the front doors first, quickly followed by Ronin and then Iris. I went for the door handle and froze.

"Is this thing spelled or cursed, you think?" I did not want to end up a fried witch just when things were getting interesting.

"Get back," instructed Iris as she placed herself before the doors. "Let's check for curses first." From her bag, she produced that magical magnifying glass she'd used to find Lilith's hair on my bed. Instead of one single glass component, this one had three, all with a yellow tint.

"If there's a curse, I'll find it." Iris mumbled a few words and rolled her magical magnifier over the large double doors.

Ronin watched her like he wished he was alone with her at the moment, preferably with no clothes on.

After a minute or so, Iris leaned back. "Clear," she announced, raising her hands like she was using a defibrillator. "No curse. No spell. No residual magic particles. No magical energy deposits of any kind. We're good."

Ronin let out a playful growl. "God, you turn me on when you speak geek magic," purred the half-vampire, making Iris blush under the lights of the columns.

I laughed. "We're the worst breaking-and-entering perps in the history of breaking and entering."

"At least we're something." The half-vampire smiled.

I bit my lip, thinking. I wasn't sure if the fact that no magic protected the entrance was a good thing or not, but we were already here so we might as well keep going with the plan.

"Okay then." I reached out to the door handle again, and to my surprise, the knob turned. It wasn't locked.

I pushed in and stepped inside, waiting to see if an alarm would go off, but all I heard was a whole lot of nothing and the beating of my own heart in my ears.

"No spells, no lock, no alarms," came Ronin's voice behind me. "Anyone else think it's weird?"

"Like he *wanted* us to come inside?" said Iris.

Ronin stiffened. "It's a trap."

"No," I answered. "I think he's just arrogant enough not to care if he gets robbed. He wants everyone to know he can always buy back whatever was stolen."

"That guy's a dick," said Ronin, loosening up a little.

Soft light spilled into a large foyer from a bronze sconce on the wall. It was enough illumination for Iris and me to see our surroundings. Ronin had that annoying vamp night vision that I secretly envied.

Miles of crafted wood paneling extended in every direction, all polished and glowing, and a grand, double-sided staircase split the house in half. The walls were decorated with paintings and warm wainscoting. All the furniture looked like a nineteenth-century design, elegant with lots of wood detail and practically screaming luxury.

I glimpsed inside a room right off the staircase. It had a very masculine feel with lots of brown leather sofas and chairs accented with dark polished wood, which stood out handsomely against the white walls. An antique Persian carpet in deep shades of wine, blue, and gold contrasted boldly against the dark wood floors. At the end of the room sat an enormous limestone fireplace, which was empty at the moment but could have been suitable for roasting a deer.

I saw no framed pictures and no photo albums, nothing that would suggest someone lived here.

"Weird," I muttered.

"What's weird?" Ronin sauntered into the room.

"I was expecting to see a massive naked portrait of Derrick over the fireplace mantel. You know, the ones with the rose in the teeth and the extremely small penises. Looks like I brought my black marker for nothing."

Ronin's white teeth flashed in the dim light. "You never know. We haven't checked the bedrooms yet."

I laughed. "There's hope yet."

We continued in silence and found a two-story library lined with bookshelves and designated reading spots with writing desks and comfortable chairs, but the shelves lay empty. Next, we checked a formal dining room connecting to a kitchen three times that of Davenport House with a butler's pantry that would have left Ruth drooling.

The last room we inspected was a massive family room, resting at the back of the house with two enormous fireplaces on opposite ends. Shrubbery and trees peeked through the tall windows, most of which were covered in darkness.

I pulled my eyes from the windows. "Nothing. There's nothing here." No clues or evidence that would help find Evelyn or even just some intel on Derrick.

"Where do we go next, boss?" asked the half-vampire as we stepped out of the room.

"Basement," I ordered, knowing from experience that crap usually originated in the bowels of an establishment.

Look at me being an experienced breaking-and-entering witch. So, what did that say about me?

The basement entrance was located at the back of the enormous staircase and just as massive as the first floor. With the message card in hand, we checked the wine cellar, which had me drooling with envy, the cinema room, where we had to *physically* pull Ronin off the row of reclining chairs, the gym, and the four bedrooms with connecting bathrooms.

All the while, the card gave no sign of life or any clues. Nothing.

"There's nothing here," I said, frustrated. "No evidence that anyone's even been here since it was built. It's too…"

"Clean, way too clean," said Iris, who rolled her magical magnifier over a black leather couch. She wrinkled her face like her nose was just assaulted with a disgusting odor. "It doesn't feel lived in. More like a model home or something."

"It's something, all right." I bit my lip again, ticked that I didn't find anything about who Derrick was and worried that Evelyn wasn't here. But we'd only seen the basement. Like Ronin had said, the house was huge. We still had lots of ground to cover and rooms to discover.

"Hey look, an elevator," said Ronin, and I turned in time to see him walk into a waiting elevator across from me. "All aboard!" he called.

Together, Iris and I stepped into the elevator. I thought of my father, and my stomach clenched in worry. I should have checked up on him before coming here, and I made a mental note to do so once we got back. I would make sure my father was okay before I did anything else.

"Floor?" asked the half-vampire.

"Second floor," I answered, since *I* was the captain of this ship. "Let's check the other bedrooms."

After a few seconds, we found ourselves in a plush hallway decorated with Oriental rugs and large landscape paintings.

"It's like a hotel," noted Iris. "But I like hotels. I don't like this place. Feels… uninviting and cold. It feels… off."

I agreed with Iris. I blinked as an icy feeling settled into my gut. The place felt cold and stale, like a laboratory instead of someone's home.

I glanced around, my eyes settling on the doors that lined the long hallway.

Ronin walked forward and turned. "There must be at least twelve bedrooms. Who has twelve bedrooms?"

"Derrick does." He probably had a woman in each room. My imagination ran wild as I pictured women tied to beds while he experimented on them.

I followed Ronin and checked the first bedroom on the right. A single bed was pushed against the wall beneath the only window. It only had a mattress: no sheets, no pillows. It was strangely empty of anything that would suggest Derrick lived here or ever had guests.

We checked four more bedrooms, which were all equally empty and creepy stale with ordinary and unremarkable furnishings that looked like guest bedrooms.

"Why buy a big house if you don't fill it with people and stuff?" I shut the drawer from a dresser in bedroom number five, having found it empty just like all the others.

"To show off," said Ronin. "To impress and intimidate. The guy's loaded. He probably has ten other houses like this all over the country."

"I'd be lonely in a big place like this," said Iris, her eyes narrowed. "It's a sad, depressing house. I *hate* it."

I let out a very unattractive snort at the conviction in her tone. Thank the cauldron Marcus wasn't here.

"I think I hate it too," I said with a smile.

"Who the hell are you?" barked a voice behind us.

I flinched and my smile vanished.

CHAPTER
17

The three of us froze, and then one by one our gazes searched for the source of the new voice.

A short overweight man in his late sixties stood in the doorway of bedroom number five. His receding white hair was cut short, and his pale blue eyes were hard as he took us in. He held himself with confidence. His long, hawklike nose and permanent frown were cemented to his wrinkled face, and his protruding gut hung over the elastic of his navy pajamas. The pulsing of energy coming from him revealed that he was some sort of witch or mage or something, though I couldn't tell which.

Yet he looked familiar… and then it hit me.

He reminded me of Gilbert.

The card in my pocket didn't so much as give me a warning about the new guy. It didn't tell me if this was a friend or a foe. But that didn't mean he wasn't involved with whatever Derrick was doing to Evelyn.

"What are you doing here? This is Mr. Baudelaire's residence," said the man. By the tone of respect mixed with the inherent arrogance, I figured Derrick was his employer. This guy had to be a butler or bodyguard, though bodyguard was a bit of a stretch considering the size of that belly.

"Where's Evelyn?" I demanded as I took a step forward.

Butler-Gilbert's eyebrows went up. "Excuse me?"

"Evelyn," I said again. "I know she's here somewhere. Let her go, or you'll be sorry." I had no idea if she was here or not, but when in doubt, lead with confidence and bullshit. Then see where it got you.

Butler-Gilbert stared at me with the air of casual contempt. "*Evelyn?* You're looking for Evelyn?"

My anger grew, overshadowing my other emotions. Clearly, he knew who she was. I'd been right to come here. "Yeah, Pajama Man. Evelyn Star. Hand her over. We're not leaving until you do." I had no idea if Evelyn was here, but I was really hoping she was.

Butler-Gilbert laughed softly. It was high-pitched, wicked, and even sounded like Gilbert's laugh. The man's pale eyes narrowed, clearly unafraid and unperturbed. "You have no idea. Do you? You think you have everything figured out, yet you're nothing but mindless miscreants who had no business coming here tonight. Big mistake."

"Did he just call me a miscreant?" asked Ronin.

"He did." I stared at the little butler, frowning. I didn't like his tone or the poised smile on his face, like he was privy to some secret information. "Then how about you tell us? I know Derrick has Evelyn. And I happen to know that he's not who he says he is."

Butler-Gilbert made a face. "He's claiming that he's *not* Derrick Baudelaire?"

"Derrick Baudelaire is playing himself, but he's disguised as *another* Derrick Baudelaire." Yeah, that didn't come out right.

The butler snorted. "Well, well, well. Did you use your witch superpowers to figure that one out?" he mocked, looking at me like I failed my math test for the fourth time. Yeah, he was even as snotty and hateful as the real Gilbert.

I narrowed my eyes, thinking I just about hated this guy as much as the real Gilbert. "You know who I am? Funny. I don't remember us meeting. 'Cause, trust me, I would remember those pajamas," I said, wiggling my finger at him.

"I know who you *all* are," answered Butler-Gilbert, looking smug. "You're Tessa Davenport. And these are you friends, Iris and Ronin."

I heard Iris's intake of breath beside me, and Ronin stiffened, clearly surprised. His fingers unfurled, and I could see his restraint, controlling his own vamp beast.

I kept my face blank, trying to keep from showing the surprise I felt. I hated that this guy knew who I was when I had no idea the little turd existed before this very moment. It gave him an edge over us and gave Derrick an advantage too. Why did he tell his butler about us? Because he wasn't just a butler.

"Well, I'd love to swap stories," I said. "Okay, not really. We're really just here for Evelyn. Tell us where she is, and you won't get hurt." I didn't know how involved he was in Derrick's affairs, but I was willing to bet he was all in, pajamas and everything.

At that, the butler bent over forward in a laugh. "You three are truly the stupidest people in this pathetic little town. Evelyn?" He laughed harder. "Oh dear. You're all clueless."

I was really tired of being called stupid. "Then educate us," I said through gritted teeth, trying to keep my temper in check.

KIM RICHARDSON

His face wrinkled in a vicious grin that had the hairs on the back of my neck rising. "You shouldn't be snooping around in Mr. Baudelaire's home either," he added with a sneer. A ripple of energy cascaded around him. He was pulling some magic.

Okay, I, too, could play that game. "What are you, his guard dog? Mr. PJ? Mr. Wiggles?" My heart pounded as sweat broke out on my forehead and my upper lip. I tapped into my will, filling it with the power of the elements.

A smile curved over the butler's lips. "Something like that." He pulled the elastic of his pajama bottoms away from his middle and then let it go with a snap. "I'm a bit rusty, but there's nothing like the removal of murderous intruders to get the magical juices flowing again." He lowered into a squat and then raised his arms and did a few stretches. And I shit you not, he threw in three jumping jacks.

"Is this guy for real?" asked Ronin, leaning over.

"Maybe we're all having the same dream," said Iris, gawking at the large, bouncing gut as the butler jogged on the spot. "More like a nightmare."

I stared at the butler. "You're not touching anyone."

The butler did a final squat and straightened. "Oh, but I am. After I'm done killing you, I'm going to call the sheriff. I'm going to tell him it was self-defense. That you came at me, and I had no other choice. That's the narrative he'll hear when he sees your bodies since this was a breaking and entering."

"First of all, it's *chief* not *sheriff*," I corrected him. "And second, he'd never go for that. He knows us." No, if he saw me lying on the ground dead, I was pretty sure the butler would be turned into butler jam.

"I guess you'll never know." The butler's lips moved in a chant, his voice low, steady, and strong.

"What's he doing?" asked Ronin, squinting. "Is he pulling some magic crap on us?"

"He is," I answered.

A ripple of cold energy stirred the air, swirling around and forming a constant, intimidating pressure over me as pinpricks of power rolled over my skin.

Every fiber of my attention went to the butler.

"For the record"—Ronin held up a finger—"he started it." A fierce light backlit the half-vampire's eyes. He blinked, and they were completely black. His posture shifted to predatory, and talons sprouted from the ends of his fingers. He placed his body in front of Iris, shielding her, which was—let's be honest—super romantic.

"It's time to teach you a lesson," hissed the butler. "You should have stayed away."

A wicked smile spread across his face as he waited, and anticipation brightened his expression at the thought he was going to fight us all.

That either meant he was delusional to fight two witches and a vampire, or he thought he was stronger and more powerful than the three of us.

We'd see.

Guttural words spilled from the butler, and I felt a cold pulse of magic rippling in the air, dark and powerful as it wove around us. It reminded me of the Dark wizards we'd faced barely a week ago. He snarled, and wisps of blue energy dripped from his left hand. Yeah, he was a wizard.

"I really hate wizards." My power grew, solid and steady, seeping into me with a sort of hungry eagerness and replacing uncertainty with nothing but strength and ferocity.

"You just hate wizards because you're envious of our immeasurable power that witches can only dream of," said the butler, breathing heavily as though just summoning his power took an enormous amount of energy. His face reddened with the sudden beading of heavy sweat on his brow, and moisture trickled down his temples.

"You look like you should lose some weight," I told him. "A man your age and with that gut, it screams heart attack. You should cut back on the cheeseburgers and beer."

The butler snarled. "I'm in perfect health." A smug grin still marred his face as coils of his wizard magic spilled from his outstretched hands.

"You can't even call up your wizard mojo without looking like you're about to cough out a lung."

Ronin snorted. "Dude, she's right. Maybe you should back down before you give yourself a stroke."

Anger flashed over the butler's face. "I might not be young like you," he said and then raised his chin, "but I'm in my magical prime."

"Magical prime?" I looked at Iris. "Is that even a thing?"

The Dark witch shrugged. "First time I've heard of it."

Ronin raised a taloned finger and dragged it from me to Iris. "So, if he's in his magical prime... what does that make you two?"

I looked at Iris and said, "Magically delicious?"

The butler's face twisted in fury. "You know nothing—"

"Jon Snow," interjected Ronin. He eyed the wizard's confused face. "What? Not a *Game of Thrones* fan? I couldn't resist."

Iris and I laughed. The butler didn't.

The butler's eyes became patronizing before he leaped in the air and landed in a crouch.

"Uh… what's he doing now?" asked Ronin.

I sucked the air through my teeth. "I don't know if I should be scared or if I should laugh. This is all really confusing."

With a flick of both hands, the wizard hurled blue energy at us.

But this wasn't our first magical rodeo.

"Declinare!" I hollered.

White energy blasted from my outstretched hand, batting the blue energy like I had swatted away annoying flies. The wizard's magic hit the far wall with a thundering boom and proceeded to burn a chunk of the drywall.

It was a new power word I'd been practicing, and it worked better than I thought.

"Nice," complimented Ronin.

"Thanks." I straightened and rolled my shoulders. "I'm here all week."

I slipped my focus back to the butler-wizard, a new rush of adrenaline pouring into me. "I wouldn't try that again," I told him. "You might get hurt."

"Argh!" shouted the butler-wizard as he flicked his wrists in my direction.

"Argh!" I shouted back at him and quickly added, "Inflitus!"

Flinging my hands at him, a kinetic force blasted out of my palm. It hit the butler-wizard in the chest, sending him crashing against the wall. Then he slid to the floor and was still.

Whoooops.

"Oh shit. I just killed the butler. I think I just killed the butler. Who kills the butler?" I cried. Cauldron be damned. I just killed an old man. I'd used too much power.

"Apparently, you do," said Ronin, and I glared at him.

I flung a finger at him in warning. "Shut it. Or you're next." I was wired tightly, and my nerves were shot.

"I'd like to point out that he did *try* to *kill* us," added the half-vampire. "Just saying."

Iris rushed over and pressed her fingers on the man's throat. "He's alive." She looked back at me. "I think he's just unconscious."

I let out a sigh. "Thank the cauldron." But something occurred to me. "When do you think he'll wake up?"

Iris shook her head. "I don't know… a couple of hours. Maybe less? Why?"

"He's going to blab when he wakes up," I said. "That's a guarantee. It doesn't give us much time to try and find Evelyn. When Derrick gets back home, he'll know we were here. He'll know we're onto him. We'll lose that advantage."

"Maybe not." Iris pulled out Dana, her DNA album she lugged around. "Here… we'll use this." Between her fingers she held a piece of red tape.

I frowned. "You want to tape his mouth? I don't think that's going to work. And you're going to need a lot more tape if you want to tie him up."

"Bondage has a bad rap, but it's really exciting when done right," added Ronin, and I raised my fist at him.

Iris slipped Dana back into her bag. "It's a memory-spell tape," she said and kneeled next to the unconscious wizard. Then carefully, she pressed the two-inch piece of red tape to his forehead and stood back up.

I watched, impressed, as the tape dissolved into the butler's skin. "He won't remember us?"

"No," answered Iris. "He won't remember a thing. All he'll remember is going to bed and waking up here."

"You're a genius," I told her, wishing I knew a spell like that. And the fact that Iris could transfer the spell into a piece of tape, well, that was incredibly clever.

I let out a sigh and walked toward the door. "We'd better go in case Derrick comes back. We've been here way too long."

The three of us took the elevator back to the first floor and rushed out of the house.

Frustration and nerves hit as we scrambled into Ronin's black BMW 7 Series parked a bit farther down Serenity Row.

After yet another breaking and entering, I hadn't learned anything new. I still didn't know who and where this Evelyn Star was. And I needed to crash a wedding. But I wasn't going to give up. I still had a few ideas.

However, first, I needed some sound advice from a hot, uber-sexy male who'd just bought a new bed that still needed testing.

CHAPTER
18

"**T**hat's all of it," I told the chief, recounting the night's events. I set my glass of red wine on the coffee table and leaned back on the sofa. "And then I came straight here."

"*After* you broke into his house and attacked his… *butler*?" inquired Marcus, sitting next to me.

"The butler attacked first. Just… FYI."

"Because you broke into his house."

"His *boss's* house."

Marcus narrowed his gray eyes. "You know what I mean. He wouldn't have attacked you if you hadn't broken into his *boss's* house."

"You're pissed. You're pissed at me."

The chief shook his head. "Why didn't you tell me what you were planning? You told me you weren't going to keep secrets from me."

"Because you would have stopped me. I know you, Marcus. You would've never let me go if you'd known. You would have talked me out of it or something. Or you would have come with me, and then, cauldron forbid, we'd have been found out, and you'd lose your job."

Marcus sat on the edge of the sofa, his eyes flashing with barely controlled anger. "I would glue your ass to that sofa," his voice slid into an icy calm. "You have no idea who this Derrick guy is. You told me yourself that he has strange magic that keeps the real him hidden. That's shady. To me, that's dangerous. Guys like him have ulterior motives, and they're never about sunshine and rainbows. They're always about money and power."

"Probably."

"If something had happened to you, no one would have known where the three of you were." His jaw clenched in anger over the words. "It could have ended badly for you. By the time I found out where you were, it would have been too late."

He had a point. "But nothing happened," I said with a smile. At the deep frown creasing his pretty forehead, I added, "I had to see if Evelyn was there." I eyed the card I had showed him earlier, still sitting on the coffee table. "Derrick and Beverly were out on his yacht, so I jumped on the opportunity. Stupid? Probably. But it's done. He did something to Evelyn. Maybe she's dead? I don't know. But I'm not going to let him do the same to my aunt. I *have* to stop him. But without proof, without Evelyn, it's his word against mine. And we all know how that went."

Marcus picked up the card and studied it. "And you're sure this butler won't remember you?"

I nodded. "According to Iris, he won't remember anything." And I was counting on it. I needed more time to find Evelyn. "Evelyn asked for our help. She's in danger. I have to believe she's still alive, and I need to find her."

Marcus set the card back down, his gaze fastened on me. "I kept looking after you left. I even called the New York office to see if maybe they had a record of this Evelyn Star."

I leaned forward anxiously. "And?"

"And nothing," answered the chief. "They've never heard of her either. Have you considered the possibility that she doesn't exist?"

"She does exist. That card didn't appear out of thin air," I told him, though it kinda did… through the toaster. I grabbed the card off the coffee table and stuffed it in my pocket. "Someone sent us that card. Someone with magical knowledge who knew Derrick would be around. She's real, Marcus. And she needs my help."

The big chief sighed, visibly upset that I had done something stupid without telling him. Yeah, it was stupid when I thought about it. Marcus was right. Derrick had some serious magic, and I'd just stalked into his lair thinking that my badass magic would be enough. Maybe it wasn't.

We'd been lucky.

I traced my eyes over the large, muscular male—from his square jaw and perfectly straight nose to his broad shoulders and his abs of steel that his snug T-shirt did nothing to conceal. It was hard resisting the urge to run my fingers through his tousle of black hair that Ronin admired so much. He did have great hair.

Tension rolled off his shoulders and neck. He'd been worried. That gorgeous specimen of a man needed to release all that stress.

Good thing I knew how to do that.

I stood up and bumped my knees against his. "Let's go, big boy," I teased and grabbed his hand to pull him up with me.

He smirked. "Big boy? Which big boy are you referring to?"

A smile twitched my lips. "Oh, you know the one." I dragged him with me away from the coffee table. The idea of his naked body on top of mine sent pools of warmth to my core.

Marcus's eyes flashed with desire as he let me lead him away from the living room, his eyes rolling over every inch of my body—from my breasts to my toes—very slowly.

I pulled his hand to my lips and kissed it, sucking on the tip of his finger before letting go. "Don't you have a new bed in there?" I gestured with my head toward his bedroom and then sucked on another finger.

Marcus let out a little growl. "I do. Wanna see it?"

"Mmm-hmm," I murmured, pulling his hand from my lips. Trust me. I couldn't care less about the bed. The pounding in my lady bits was way too distracting.

We stepped into his bedroom, and I pushed him onto his new bed. Again, I barely noticed the bed.

It didn't help that Marcus had already ripped off his T-shirt and jeans and was lying there in his tiny black boxer briefs.

I eyed the tent with a smile. "You better take that off if you know what's good for you—"

Then I bent over in excruciating pain like my insides were liquifying.

"Oh, not this again." I gasped.

I met Marcus's worried gray eyes, and the last thing I saw was a big, muscular body leaping toward me before my world shifted.

Marcus's bedroom vanished, and after another volley of pain and darkness followed the feeling of weightlessness before my feet hit solid ground.

I was dizzy, and the pain came in buckets at a time, but I was too angry to care.

I'm going to kill her!

Balling my fists, I glanced around my new surroundings and found who I was searching for.

Lilith stood facing the only window of a large room with cold, boring white walls and the same colossal bed I'd seen her in before, which was the only piece of furniture. Only this time Lilith wasn't in the bed entertaining a few paranormal males. She was alone.

"Seriously? You've done this to me *twice* now. Twice! And Marcus just bought a new bed!" I shouted. I realized that shouting at a deity wasn't the way to go, but I was ticked. And twice she'd pulled me away from some much-deserved sexy time with my wereape. At least, this time, I wasn't naked in front of strangers. But still. Enough was enough.

I waited, expecting a reaction, but the goddess just stayed there with her back to me, staring out the window.

Granted, since this kidnapping had happened once before, I was hoping Marcus wouldn't go all wild and crazy and destroy the new bed and mattress.

"Hello? Lilith? I'm talking to you," I called. "If you think you can snatch me away anytime you want, well, I'm here to tell you that you can't. I'm putting my foot down." I actually stomped it like an idiot. "Lilith? Did you hear me? Lilith?" Why wasn't she looking at me? I took a moment to look her over.

A red silk robe hung on her tall frame, her red hair loose, and she had a tangled knot at the back of her head like she hadn't brushed it in weeks. Her arms were wrapped around herself, her shoulders tight as she stared out into the city below. Her posture suggested she was worried, maybe even waiting for something or someone?

"Lilith? What's going on?"

The goddess finally turned around. The hair on the top of her head stood at odd angles like she'd spent a great deal of time scratching her scalp. Her red eyes expanded at the sight of me as though she just realized I was there.

"Did he find you?" she asked, her voice hurried and high. Unlike the times I'd spoken with her before, she sounded out of control, very unlike herself.

I frowned. "He who? What are you talking about?"

Lilith's face creased in worry, and I was shocked at the sight of it. Who knew she was capable of that emotion?

"Lucifer," said the goddess, panic sliding behind her red eyes. "Has he come? Did you speak to him? Did he talk to you?"

My lips parted, and I did nothing to hide my utter surprise. "Ah… yeah… no. He didn't. Lilith? What the hell is going on?"

"Are you sure?" pressed the goddess. Her head jerked in a nervous little shake. "Think. Did he come to you?"

"I think I'd remember if the king of hell came to dinner. I never saw him. And no, I didn't speak to him."

The goddess began pacing around her room barefoot, and then a cigarette appeared between her fingers. She took a long drag and exhaled, mumbling words I couldn't understand. I didn't even think it was English.

"He knows… he knows," I heard her mumble as she paced back and forth, this time staring at the ground like there was an imaginary line. It was disconcerting.

Damn. The goddess was even crazier than before. That was a really bad sign.

"He knows? Lucifer knows about your plan?" I guessed, watching her pace without stopping.

Lilith nodded and took another drag of her cigarette. "He knows. He knows. He knows."

I stepped closer to her to see her face better. "He knows what, exactly?"

"He knows. He knows about my plan. Everything. He knows what I was going to do to him. All of it."

Shit. That means he knew about me too. Great.

My stomach clenched, and a panicked fear slid through me. "Who told him?" It had to be one of the three I'd met in the boardroom. My money was on the male Dark witch. They were always looking for ways to increase their power. What better way than to make a bargain with Lucifer and give him all the details of his wife's plans so he could climb up the magical power ladder.

The goddess halted. She looked up at me, her gaze drifting over me like she couldn't focus or even truly see me.

"A conduit," said Lilith, pacing again. "Blood spilled upon its surface will take life with it. You must see to understand. The blood. The blood. It takes all."

A chill crawled up my spine at the monotone of her voice. She was talking gibberish. She was losing it, which made me realize this was possibly a glance at what she was like inside her cell, her prison. It was a horrible visual. And she'd been captive in there for *so* long.

I felt sorry for her, which was surprising, considering that she'd just taken me away from Marcus—*twice*—and had forced me to take part in her plot to kill her husband. However, Lilith had also given us back Davenport House after the Dark wizards had burned it down to the ground. She didn't have to, yet she did.

I'd felt that the goddess was a complicated creature, and there was more to her than she let on. That I knew. She had good in her, though perhaps in only small doses and only on rare

224

occasions. Still, it was there, and that was saying something.

The conversations I had with my father had shone a different light. He had sided with Lilith over Lucifer, as had many. That told me if my father thought she was worth fighting for, Lilith couldn't be all that bad.

Yes, she was unhinged and scary, and torturing mortals was her favorite pastime, but maybe that was just on her bad days. We all had bad days, and I could think of a few people I'd like to torture.

Perhaps tonight was one of her bad days.

I wasn't staring at an evil, powerful, supreme being with the attention span of a three-year-old. Right now, I was staring at a broken woman.

Lilith sniffed and wiped her nose. "Trying to keep me. He overpowers them. His hunger against theirs. I take it all. There is no mercy," she prattled on. "I'm not going back… not going back… not going back…" Lilith flicked the cigarette butt away and lit another one.

She looked so fragile and damaged. I felt a pang in my heart at the fear and desperation in her voice. I also felt anger for her. I couldn't believe it, but the fact was, Lilith had been wronged by her husband. Yes, her methods were questionable, forcing me to help her in her scheme and all, but I wasn't about to let him do that to her again.

I exhaled slowly, shocked at myself for what I was about to say. "You're not going back. I won't let him take you," I said. Damnit. I was going soft in my old age.

Lilith froze. She blinked at me, and her lips twitched as she thought through the ramifications of what I'd just said. "What did you say?"

Damn. I was a fool. "I said you're not going back in that damn cage. You hear me? And I'm going to help you."

Yup, I was definitely going to get myself killed.

What had I gotten myself into now?

Chapter

19

It was Wednesday morning, the day of Beverly's grand wedding.

And it was raining.

No, it was *pouring* like the goddess herself dumped her bathwater all over Hollow Cove. The entire town was drenched, the lawns soaked, and tiny rivers flowed through the streets to the sewer drains. It seemed the goddess didn't want Beverly to marry Derrick the Douche either.

Worse, I was still nowhere near a suitable plan to stop the wedding, and the whereabouts of Evelyn Star were still unknown.

Every time I looked at that card with her name, I felt like a failure. I was failing *her*. I don't know how I knew, but somehow I knew she was running out of time.

When I finally got up this morning, my mind still buzzing about the state in which I'd found Lilith, I went in search of some coffee and breakfast—

"Well, spank me cross-eyed." My mouth opened wider than if I were yawning.

Not because of the hurricane of nerves that was Beverly, standing next to the kitchen window as she hysterically cried over the rain outside or the mountains of food piled on the counters, table, and chairs that Ruth had prepared. But because of my father, who was sitting at the kitchen table with my mother next to him, both engaged in what appeared to be a genuine, happy conversation.

Last night I'd come back home by ley line. Lilith was too distraught to send me back, and I really didn't want her to in case she sent me somewhere else by mistake, like the Netherworld or Antarctica. During a quick stop at Marcus's place, I'd found the chief on his knees trying to repair what appeared to be another massacred bed frame and mattress.

"You need to work on that temper," I'd told him, though inside I was thrilled that my disappearance had that effect on him. Yeah, he was totally mine.

228

Leaving the chief to try and salvage his bed, I'd gone to Davenport House, only to find my father and mother sharing a bottle of wine.

I'd been surprised, *really* surprised, but glad he was okay. I'd worried about his return to his apartment with Egon and the other demon, whose name I'd already forgotten, but seeing him here soothed my fears.

Yet, finding my father here again this early in the morning was even more surprising.

I stood in the kitchen halfway to the coffee machine, gawking at my parents.

I flicked my finger in their general direction. "Are those the same clothes you were wearing last night?" I asked my father.

My father's silver eyes darted over to my mother. Two dots of color marred her cheeks.

Yeah, he had definitely stayed over.

I was too restless from everything going on to think about my estranged parents doing the hibbety-dibbety, right now, but I'd definitely ponder it later.

After pouring myself a large cup of coffee, I sat next to Iris, who was intensely watching my parents across from her, like she was viewing a real-life reality TV show and having a hell of a good time.

She met my gaze and raised her brows. "Isn't this amazing?" she whispered and then mouthed, "Wow."

"I'll let you know later." I had no idea how to feel about the fact that my father had stayed the night. It really wasn't any of my business, but seeing how happy they both seemed… well, I was not about to interfere with that. My mother kept tugging the same strand of hair behind her ear, which I'd learned she did when she was nervous, and my father had that goofy smile that spread across his face.

"Why is the goddess punishing me?" whined Beverly, looking radiant in her white silk bathrobe. She threw her hands in the air dramatically. "Look! Just look at this weather! I don't *do* rain…" She caught herself, a slow smile spreading over her face. "Well, yes, I've done *it* in the rain." She giggled. "More times than I can count, but this is my wedding day." She continued to grumble, her face red and in obvious distress. "I checked the forecast last night. It's supposed to be sunny and warm."

"Rain is considered good luck on a wedding day," encouraged Ruth, turning from the pot she was stirring on the stove. Hildo sat perched on her shoulders, his yellow eyes fixed on whatever my aunt was mixing.

"I don't think they meant a downpour," said Dolores, her gaze glued to what looked like a bill of sorts. "At this rate, we'll be asking Noah for a ride on his ark."

Beverly's shoulders slumped, and she crossed her arms over her chest. "Maybe it's a sign I shouldn't get married?"

I looked up. "It's definitely a sign. You shouldn't get married today." Maybe Beverly was finally coming around. Maybe she'd finally come to her senses and had seen Derrick for the prick he truly was.

Beverly's eyes found me, and then she glowered, looking like a really pissed-off but really pretty pit bull. "Of course I'm getting married today. Why wouldn't I?"

Maybe not. "But you just said..."

"Ruth," said Beverly, whirling around, "how are you with the overlay spell? Will it be ready soon? I can't have rain on my wedding day. I just can't. Beverly Davenport can't get married in the rain."

"Don't worry. Should be ready in about two hours," said Ruth over her shoulder. She sprinkled an orange powder into the mix. "That's plenty of time before your wedding."

"Good. Good," answered Beverly. "Did Gilbert come through with the seating arrangements?" she asked Dolores.

Dolores looked up from the bill. "I'm still going through it, but yes, it appears we will have enough chairs," she answered in a businesslike manner. "But the bill doesn't add up. It's not what we agreed on."

"Why am I not surprised," I said and took a sip of my coffee, enjoying the heavenly aroma of the freshly brewed beans.

"Do you have a new dress for the wedding?"

I looked up to find my mother's dark eyes on me with an expectant expression. "No."

She frowned, her face shifting to a bewilderment. "*No?* What do you mean, no? You need a new dress," she said each syllable clearly and precisely, like not having a new dress was a capital offense. "You can't be seen in something you've worn before."

I rolled my eyes. "Because what would the neighbors think?" From the corner of my eye, I saw Iris trying to form a curtain of her hair to hide behind, but when I glanced at my father, he wore a smirk.

My mother stared at me like I was five years old and had painted her favorite dresser with red and blue markers. "We'll go to Boutique Maddalena after you've finished your coffee and get you a new dress. My treat."

"I don't need a new dress."

"Why do you always have to disagree with everything I say? You're being obtuse."

"Well, you did drop me on my head when I was a baby, so you told me. Sometimes I find it hard to cohesively formulate the words coming out of my mouth."

My mother sighed, irritation coloring her cheeks. "You *will* look presentable at my sister's wedding. And I'm not taking no for an answer. Tell her, Obiryn."

My father flinched like he'd just been slapped in the face. "Ah… well… I'm not entirely sure…"

"We're going to go shopping together, and we *will* have a wonderful time," continued my mother. "That is all there is to it."

I took a gulp of my coffee. "Cute. I'm all for the mother and daughter bonding and all"—I raised my fist—"but the fact remains… I'm not invited to the wedding. I've been *uninvited*."

"Stop kidding around, Tessa. We're going shopping, and we're going to find you a new dress."

"I'm not joking. Ask her."

My mother's pretty mouth fell open, and her eyes darted to Beverly. "Is that true?"

Beverly looked up from the pile of bills next to Dolores. "Yes. Derrick and I don't want her there," she said as she gracefully moved to the coffee machine, her robe swaying gently like a movie star from the 1940s.

My mother leaned back in her chair and crossed her arms slowly, though her anger was absolute. "Beverly. You can't do that to my daughter."

Surprised, I shared a look with Iris. *Go, Mom.*

Beverly grabbed her coffee mug and took a sip before saying, "I can. I will. I already have. This is *my* wedding, and I choose who I want to be there. I don't want Tessa there." She held her head high, still clearly furious at me.

My mother shook her head. "Not this nonsense again. Give me a break, Beverly. I don't think that happened at all. It's a misunderstanding. You're overreacting."

"I saw what I saw," snapped Beverly, roughly adjusting her robe.

"Which was Derrick on the floor after I nailed him in the balls after he jumped me," I said, burning off some angst.

Coffee dribbled out of my father's mouth. "Excuse me," he wheezed, his face taking on a darker contrast.

"Tessa's been a little tense lately," my mother continued, and it was strange seeing her defend me like that. "She's adjusting to her new powers. Her new life. She's jumpy. She's not a whore."

I grinned. "Awww… thanks, Mom." I was touched.

"You're welcome, dear."

Beverly's anger doubled at our joint smiles and casual attitude. "You don't know what you're talking about. You weren't there, Amelia. Derrick told me everything." Her rage sizzled as she met my gaze. "I don't want her there, plain and simple. She's going to ruin everything. This is *my* day. *My* wedding. And I don't want her there."

"I'm right here," I said, annoyed that she was talking about me as though I wasn't sitting right in front of her. It was astonishing how she'd changed for a man.

"You're different. You know that?" commented my mother, echoing my thoughts. "Don't think we haven't noticed. We all have. We've all talked about it."

"Hey," growled Dolores. "Don't you bring me into this."

"Yeah," echoed Ruth. "Into what, exactly?"

"It's like you're a whole different person," said my mother. "When he's around, I don't even recognize you. My sister wouldn't treat her family the way you're treating Tessa."

Beverly scoffed. "Give me a break. When have you been so interested in this family? Never. You've been too preoccupied with that loser husband of yours, following him like a sick little puppy."

My father stiffened at the comment, clearly still having issues with the fact that my mother had left him and chosen Sean the Douche.

"I'm still part of this family," my mother hissed, "and so is Tessa."

Beverly waved a red manicured finger in my general direction. "She's not invited to my wedding, and that's final. The bride decides, not the sister."

"It's fine, Mom," I said, not wanting them to fight about me. "It doesn't bother me. I don't want to go anyway." The last thing I wanted was for this family to split apart, especially when things were finally going in the right direction.

My mother shook her head, clearly not wanting to give up. "I can't believe you're doing this. You, of all people, have been in very similar situations, if I remember correctly, Beverly. I don't know where you get off acting like this and telling my daughter off."

Beverly let out a fake laugh. "And *you*," she seethed, her green eyes darting from my mother to my father. "Who are you to judge me? A married woman sleeping with another man. This is an old house with thin walls. We *all* heard you last night."

Oooooooh.

Dolores looked up just as Ruth spun around, sending clumps of green goo to the floor and kitchen island.

My mother's dark gaze leveled with her sister's. "We all know who the real slut is in the family."

Oh crapola.

I think we all froze at that point. Too afraid to breathe. Too scared to do anything but blink.

But my dear mama wasn't afraid.

She stood up. "If you're not going to invite my daughter to your wedding," she seethed, "then I'm not going either."

"Fine!" shouted Beverly. "Consider yourself *uninvited*!"

"Fine!" my mother hollered back, her hands fisted as she marched out of the kitchen. I could hear her heavy steps as she climbed the staircase.

"Fine!" cried Beverly again, bending at the waist for more volume, as though we didn't hear her the first time.

"Okay, this is bad." I let my head fall into my hands. This was not what I wanted to happen. They were both acting like teenage girls fighting over the same guy.

"Don't worry about it," said Ruth as she turned around with a massive smile on her face. "It's just wedding jitters."

Dolores snorted. "Sounded more like wedding hysteria."

Beverly pressed a delicate hand to her forehead. "I'm feeling the effects of a headache coming along. I can't have a headache at my wedding. I'm going to lie down for an hour. Wake me if Derrick calls. Okay?"

"Okey dokey," answered Ruth, returning to her overlay spell.

My tension rose. I couldn't just sit here and let my aunt marry this sonofabitch. I had to do something.

And I had to do it now.

I watched Beverly exit the kitchen and waited until I heard her climb the stairs to ask my next question.

"So, is Derrick getting ready at his house?" I still had a couple of hours before the wedding—plenty of time to get Plan B rolling. And I had one card left to play.

I was going to seduce Derrick even though the thought made me want to vomit. I was pretty sure he'd take the bait—me—and I was going to get everything on video.

His unusual magic was still an issue, but I couldn't think of that right now. I'd figure it out later when I had more time.

At that moment, I noticed my father had conveniently slipped away and disappeared. Sneaky bastard.

Iris was watching me with a quirked brow. She knew I was formulating a plan. She just didn't know what it was. Yet.

"No, I believe Beverly said he was on his yacht," answered Dolores, still eyeing Gilbert's bill.

His yacht.

I'd completely forgotten about his stupid yacht. I was going for a boat ride. And maybe I'd drop Derrick in the middle of the ocean.

I glanced at Iris. "Feel like going for a stroll in the rain?"

Iris grinned, giving me a knowing look. "I'll get my umbrella."

Okay then.

CHAPTER
20

I stole the Volvo station wagon.

Okay, well, *technically*, I borrowed it without asking permission. Any sane person would have done the same once they looked outside. A stroll in the rain? Did I mention it was pouring outside? It was a freaking deluge.

Heavy gray clouds raced across the dark sky, bringing forth a cold wind from the north. Hard rain fell like bullets. Davenport House's gutters gurgled and spouted streams of water. Screw that. I wasn't walking anywhere.

I'd grabbed the car keys from the wicker basket that was wedged between bite-sized appetizers and bottles of wine on the table.

Dolores was so preoccupied with Gilbert's bill that she never even noticed. And Ruth? Well, Ruth was humming the wedding march as she stirred her potion with Hildo cheering her on and swinging his tail like a conductor.

I drove past Sandy Beach, my windshield wipers on high, but it was still hard to see through the downpour. I felt like I was trying to see through the bottom of a thick glass. Except for my headlights, the streets were gloomy, and the heavy clouds cast a premature darkness, making it feel like it was night when it was only half-past ten in the morning.

"You drive like an old woman who's blind in one eye," laughed Iris. "I think I can run faster than this. No. I *know* I can run faster… and in heels."

I shot her a look. "You try to drive through this. I can barely see anything. It's like driving through the bottom of a lake in a storm."

"I know, sorry," said the Dark witch, though she didn't sound sorry. She leaned forward and squinted. "I think I see it. Yeah. There is it."

I'd driven past the Hollow Cove Marina many times, but I'd never really paid much attention to it. I didn't have a boat, because, well, boats were expensive, though I'd always wanted to learn how to sail.

The marina was conveniently located next to the town beach. It was hard to see, but I could just make out the giant bowl of the ocean and the blurred bodies of boats bobbing in the harbor as giant waves crashed over each other and rolled up on the beach. I could barely see the faint outlines of a building at the entrance.

Following the signs, I drove to the parking space closest to the entrance and parked, right next to a huge, black SUV. It was the only other vehicle in the lot besides the Volvo and most probably Derrick's.

I killed the engine and leaned back with a heavy sigh, trying to calm my nerves. My heart thrashed, mixing with a heavy dose of adrenaline. A plethora of emotions ran through me—mostly about Beverly's animosity toward me and Lilith's odd behavior—which made it extremely hard not to lose control.

Iris turned to face me. "So, what's the plan?"

I gripped the steering wheel and stared at the rain hitting the windshield. "I'm going to find Derrick and seduce him." God, that sounded lame, and I had to force the bile from rising in my throat. "He wants me. That part was obvious." I swallowed hard, the words disgusting me. "And you stay in the shadows and record the whole thing on your phone."

Iris made a questioning sound in her throat. "You think he'll fall for that? He doesn't strike me as the stupid kind."

"Oh, he'll fall for that. And yes, he's the stupid kind." I'd gotten all kinds of pervy vibes from Derrick. I was certain the moment I showed him a bit of flesh as an invitation, he was mine.

Then guilt hit hard. It had been constantly eating away at me, but I'd done my best to ignore it. I knew this would hurt Beverly, maybe even destroy the last bit of affection she had for me, but I couldn't let her marry this bastard. Even if it meant she'd hate me forever.

I was really hoping she'd see it my way, but I doubted it.

"I'm texting Ronin," said the Dark witch as she pulled out her phone. "To tell him where we are. You know... in case things don't go as planned."

"In case we don't make it back?" Yeah, that was a possibility. I still wasn't sure about the extent of Derrick's magic. But I'd left in a hurry, not thinking it through properly. We were running out of time, and I just wanted this guy away from my aunt.

"That's not what I meant." Iris's fingers glided over the screen of her phone. "But you know how these things can go."

"Extremely bad?" I was being a little dramatic and morbid. I blamed it on the weather.

She looked up at me from her phone. "Well, someone should know. Does Marcus know? Did you tell him?"

I let out a small laugh. "About me going to seduce Derrick? Yeah, I don't think so. He'd probably rip apart the boat and murder Derrick. There'd go his career as chief. He's a tiny bit possessive."

Iris giggled. "I noticed. It's kinda hot. All that overprotectiveness. You have to admit… you *love* it."

I nodded. "God, yes."

We both laughed. It released some of the anxiety, but only a tiny part, as unease strained my senses.

Here I was again, breaking the promise to Marcus that I wouldn't keep secrets from him while doing something stupid without telling him. Hey. I wasn't perfect, and this was my last shot. The chief hadn't found any dirt on Derrick. So now it was up to me.

My heart pounded as my unease grew. "But I'm going to call him as soon as we're inside Derrick's boat," I told her, making up my mind. "By the time he gets here, I'll have what I came for." Hopefully. "He's been out of sorts since Lilith started beaming me out of his apartment."

"Twice," the Dark witch reminded me. I'd filled her in on the drive here. "Did you talk to Ruth about the glamour potion that could help conceal you from the big bad guy?"

"No. I completely forgot." Marcus had mentioned it to me. I'd discussed it with Iris, but then life got in the way, and I hadn't thought of it since. "I guess it's worth a try, but I have a feeling he already knows who I am and where I live. Glamour or not, there's no hiding from the king of hell."

Iris flinched and cleared her throat, trying to disguise her unease. "I still think it's a good idea. I have a few glamour spells we could try too. You know, I could make you look like Allison," she added with a sly grin.

I laughed hard. "You're crazy, but I like the way you think."

"Wish I could have been there when the new deputy showed up," said the Dark witch. "Just seeing Allison's face, I would have snapped a picture and framed it."

"I've got it frozen in memory," I told her, pointing to my head, and she laughed.

Iris was the best friend anyone could wish for, and I was putting her in danger.

"Listen, Iris," I said as I turned in my seat to face her. "If you're not comfortable with this, I can go in alone. I'm not afraid of this bastard. I can just have an audio recording. It's almost as good."

"Not on your life." The pretty Dark witch narrowed her eyes. "I'm not letting you go in there by yourself."

"I won't force you to do something you don't want to do."

The Dark witch blinked. "I know that." She slipped her phone back into her bag. "And you're not forcing me. I wouldn't be here if I didn't want to. This guy's bad news. The card proved it. Now we only need to prove it to Beverly. Trust me. She'll thank you later."

"Not so sure about that." I was pretty sure attempting to seduce your aunt's fiancé was crossing all kinds of boundaries.

"She will," said Iris. "I know she will." She looked out her side window. "Which one is his boat? There're like… fifty boats out here? Which one is Derrick's, you think?"

Good question. "No idea. Knowing him, it's probably the biggest boat in the harbor." I was willing to bet my life on that given how much he liked to show off. How better to show off than by buying the biggest yacht?

Iris's gaze found mine. "And if it doesn't work? What if he's suddenly not interested in you? What do we do?"

I shrugged and smiled. "We could just kill him and throw his body in the water."

Iris laughed. "In a storm like this, his body'll wash up somewhere in Florida."

I let go of the steering wheel and leaned back. "I know this is a pretty crappy plan, but I've got nothing else. I don't know how to make Beverly believe she's about to marry a scumbag."

Iris patted my hand. "It's a good plan, Tessa. And we're going to nail the bastard. Just you wait and see. We'll get him."

I was counting on it.

I opened my car door carefully as the strong winds tugged on it. Straining with effort, I finally got it closed and blinked through the sheets of heavy rain. Forget umbrellas in this weather. They'd just be swallowed up by the winds.

Iris shut her car door and joined me, both of us bent against the strong winds as cold rain slapped against our faces. We hurried forward, pushing against the storm toward the harbor.

White wharves stretched over the water with yachts and smaller boats moored to them like a floating parking lot. The air was filled with the scent of dead fish, algae, and motor oil.

Together, we hit the pier and started forward. I squinted through the rain, searching for the most extensive boat here.

My eyes immediately found a source of light.

Only one boat had yellow light spilling from the upper level. "That one," I cried over the wind and rain, pointing to it. It was the largest vessel in the harbor. I hated being right.

"It's huge," said Iris, squinting in the rain.

I shook my head. "Who does this guy think he is? Jeff Bezos?"

We hurried along the pier until we arrived at the yacht that was most likely Derrick's.

My eyes traced the massive yacht as I looked for stairs or something that would take us aboard.

The yacht was over a hundred feet in length and three stories high with separate sun decks and balconies overlooking the water. It was like a mini cruise ship. The port side of the vessel was white with navy trim.

And there, across the bow, stenciled in navy letters, was the name *EVELYN STAR*.

Chapter
21

Okay. *That* was unexpected.

The huge stenciled name stared back at me, and it took a few beats for it to register that I was actually *seeing* what I was seeing. My stomach twisted, feeling like I'd been sucker punched in the gut.

Evelyn Star had never been a person. She'd always been a yacht. Derrick's yacht.

It explained why his butler laughed in our faces when I demanded he hand her over.

"Evelyn's a boat?" Iris said next to me, looking like she'd gone for a swim in the ocean.

"She is." I stared at the letters, feeling as though the puzzle pieces didn't fit anymore.

"Whoever sent the card was talking about the boat. He or she—she, I'm pretty sure it's she—is in there. I know it."

"The boat's huge." Iris wiped her face. Black mascara spilled down her cheeks, making her look like she was crying black oil. "Where do we look?"

Iris was right. The boat was massive and intimidating. "We'll have to separate to cover more ground more quickly." I wiped the water from my eyes. "It'll give us more places to hide, though."

"Right," said Iris, but she didn't look convinced.

"I'll text you if I find anything, and you do the same."

Iris nodded. "Okay. So, I guess you're not seducing Derrick anymore."

"Change of plans," I told her, feeling marginally better at the idea of not having to throw myself at that creepy man. But it didn't help settle my nerves. In fact, I was jumpier than before. My body shook with adrenaline because now I was positive that Derrick was holding someone in his boat. The sheer size of it explained why Beverly never knew. You could hide lots of dead bodies on a vessel of that size.

"If we find that witch, she's the only proof we need." Iris was right; I was going to nail Derrick with real, twelve-inch nails. Then, I was going to drop him in the middle of the ocean.

My gaze traveled the length of the boat and settled on a short ladder with stairs connected to the side. It looked like a temporary staircase, but it would do to get us in.

"Stairs." I pointed. "Let's go."

Together, we made for the stairs. I went up first, seeing as this was my plan, and if I fell through to the water, that was my own damn fault. The stairs were slippery, but I managed to make it to the top and stepped onto the first floor of the yacht with Iris right behind me.

A three-foot roof jutted out from the top, so we were mostly out of the rain but not out of the wind.

I stared at the dark windows of the yacht, not seeing much. The entire first floor looked deserted. The light I'd seen came from the top floor, probably the main living areas or Derrick's quarters.

Iris looked at me expectantly.

"Let's find a door."

I didn't have to look very far as a door was right in front of us.

Iris immediately went to work with her magical magnifier, rolling it over the doorframe.

"We're good," she said after a moment and stuffed her instrument back inside her bag. "No wards or curses. There's nothing."

I took that as a good sign. Derrick obviously wasn't expecting any unwelcomed visitors.

I grabbed hold of the first door I found and pulled it open. We stepped through and found ourselves in semidarkness. Immediately, I was hit with warmth and the smell of leather and luxury, if that was even a thing. As my eyes adjusted, plush cream-colored sofas and chairs surrounded a living room area nestled below huge windows. It was probably very nice in sunlight, but now it was just as gloomy as the outside.

"Okay, now what?" whispered Iris, her pretty face set in determination.

"I go left, and you go right," I told her, keeping my voice low. "I think Derrick's upstairs where we saw the light, so let's avoid that floor for now. We'll start on this floor and then go down." Basically, I had no idea. "There doesn't seem to be anyone here, no crew or anything. That's a good thing. It means we can probably search the boat without being discovered." Hopefully. And I was also hoping Derrick, being the narcissistic ass he portrayed himself to be, was getting ready for his big day by trying on dozens of different tuxes and would be there for a while.

"Good luck," I said. "And be careful."

Iris tapped her bag. "Dana will keep me safe."

I gave her a tight smile. "Text me if you find anything."

"Will do."

I watched Iris move off to the right, and then I was moving.

Excitement pulsed through me as I made my way around thick chairs, wet bars, and rows of seating that lined the side of the vessel. Getting rid of Derrick would bring joy to my heart. It was tough not to smile despite the dreary situation we found ourselves in.

I let my witchy senses go, trying to get a feel for anything magical, even Derrick's presence, but I got nothing back. Weird. But it didn't mean there wasn't any magic here.

I hurried along the yacht, as fast as I dared and as quietly as I could, stopping every now and then to listen and send out my magical senses.

I found myself at the back of the boat after a few minutes, staring at a staircase in polished wood. The stairs went up a level and down a level, and I saw a soft light coming from the upper level. When I stared down the stairs, the steps ended in darkness and shadow.

Well, you know me and dark basements. So, of course, I decided to go down into the belly of this metal beast.

I reached the bottom and looked around. I stood in a narrow corridor with doors lining each side and hallways branching out. My first impression was that it was not as luxurious as the first floor, quite the opposite. Small, round light fixtures were placed at intervals every twenty feet or so, giving me enough illumination. It felt more like a prison to me. It had no glossy wood moldings around doorframes, just lots of metal posts, walls, pipes, and barely any windows. I felt like I was in the below-deck level in the *Titanic*, where all the poor third-class souls were crammed.

"Sorry, Jack. But that scrap of wood was big enough for you *and* Rose," I mumbled.

A cold draft wafted over me and seemed to settle into my skin.

I started. I felt a pulse. Weak, but it was there.

A pulse of *magic*.

My heart pounding, I followed the source of the magic, letting my witchy intuition guide me. I passed what looked like a small kitchen area and then what looked like a bathroom with a stand-up shower. All without doors.

The magic grew stronger. The pulse thrummed heavily in the air and coated my skin like a thick mist. Whatever magic this was, it was ancient and powerful.

And then I was running.

As I dashed in between two poles, I felt it— the cold haze of energy that accompanied demons when they came into the mortal world. Only this was different, like the energies were still drifting, not settling. Weird.

Light flickered from somewhere ahead of me. I hurtled around another pole to an open space the size of the living area from the upper level and came face-to-face with what I'd call a hell of a lot of pagan ceremonial magic. I skidded to a stop. There must have been at least a hundred candles placed around an empty space. Spirally letters and symbols marked in blood were painted on the walls, the floors, and everywhere, like poorly drawn graffiti.

The skin at the base of my neck went tight.

In the middle of a circle lit with black candles lay three women, their arms and ankles bound in thick-linked chains. Their clothes were stained in dirt and what I could only guess was blood. Their hair was dull and matted in clumps. I grimaced at the stench of unwashed bodies and what could only be urine.

I'm not sure what I expected to find. Not three women, that was for sure.

The one in the middle raised her head. Her face was gaunt, almost skeletal, like all the fat in her body had been sucked out of her. A brown-stained shirt, which once could have been white, fell around her bony shoulders and frail figure. Her dull, brown eyes widened a little when they found me. Her lips moved, but I couldn't hear the words.

Tears welled in my eyes, and I blinked fast. It was like she'd been exsanguinated. White-hot fury soared through me like a fever, and rage shook me so violently, I nearly lost my footing. I saw red. I saw Derrick's laughing face as he tortured these women.

He was a dead man… or whatever he was.

And then the next thing I knew, I rushed toward the women, trying to think of a spell that could remove their shackles but coming up short.

I kicked a few candles out of my way and dropped to my knees next to the woman who had lifted her head.

"I'm Tessa. I'm here to help you. I'm going to get you out." My fingers shook as I grabbed the heavy chain, knowing that my fire magic could not melt metal. I was willing to bet Iris had a spell or a curse that could, though.

I yanked out my phone and quickly texted Iris, telling her where I was and what I found, not caring about the plethora of spelling mistakes I made. I waited to see the text go through, but it wasn't sending. The service bars on my phone were nonexistent.

"Damnit. There's no reception." Second damnit, my plan of calling Marcus sank to the bottom of the ocean with poor Jack.

"My name…" wheezed the woman, sounding like she hadn't spoken in years, "is… Susan Woodward."

I stuffed my phone back in my pocket and studied the woman's face. Why did that name sound familiar? And then I knew. "You're the one who sent us the card? You're the one Ruth said was skilled in magical cards."

Susan nodded. "Yes." She swallowed hard. It looked painful with her lips all dry and cracked. "I knew… the Davenport witches… would help."

Right. I wasn't about to burst her little bubble by telling her they thought the card was fake.

"Susan. Did Derrick do this to you?" I needed actual proof that the scumbag had done this. I need to hear it from her lips.

Susan blinked slowly. Tears had crusted some of her eyelashes together. "Yes." It was impossible to guess her age. She could have been in her forties, but she looked like she was long past a hundred going on two.

"The card… he knew. He found out."

I realized why Derrick had been in my room. He wasn't trying to seduce me. He was trying to get his slimy hands on the card to get rid of the evidence, and I just so happened to walk in on him.

I clenched my jaw. "Why? Why would he do this?" I looked around, my gaze rolling over the strange symbols but not recognizing them. "What kind of ritual is this? What's he doing to you?"

Susan looked at the woman on the floor to her right, who hadn't moved since I got here. "He's been… draining us of our blood, our witch magic."

I frowned. "To make himself more powerful? That sonofabitch."

"I'm not sure," said the witch, her lips cracking more with every effort to speak. I should have brought water or food, but it's not like I'd known they'd be here. "All I know is that he needs it," she said, her voice stronger, seemingly having gained some strength. "It sustains him. I don't know what he is… but it keeps what he is a secret."

I glowered. "I knew that bastard was hiding something." I still didn't know what it was, but it's pretty psychotic and evil if it meant he was slowly killing off these witches to do it.

"I was the last to be taken," said Susan, her eyes round. "All I remember was going to bed one night and waking up here, chained like Francine and Naomi."

"You know them?" I glanced at the two women who were either unconscious or dead.

"No. Well, I didn't before."

"Witches?" I guessed.

"Yes," answered Susan. "Francine is from Nantucket, and Naomi is from Myrtle Beach."

I thought about that. With his boat, Derrick could easily move from state to state, picking up witches and hiding them in the bowels of his yacht while he drained them of their blood and their blood magic.

I really hated this guy. But if he was after power, why hadn't he done this to my Aunt Beverly? Why wasn't he draining her? Why go through with the whole marriage thing? It didn't make sense. I was missing something important.

I met Susan's hollowed face. "Don't worry. I'm going to get you out of here." Glancing over her body, I knew Susan didn't look like she could walk. And even though she was bone thin, I didn't have the upper body strength to carry her all the way to the Volvo.

Iris. I needed to get Iris. The two of us could manage. And then we'd come back later for Francine and Naomi with backup once we'd found Marcus, his team, and everyone else who wanted to kick Derrick's ass.

"Listen," I told her. "There's no reception down here. I need to go get help. And then we'll get you out of here. I promise."

"You'll do no such thing," mocked a voice behind me, a voice that made my entire body pulse with rage.

I cringed, knowing all too well who'd just spoken.

Still on my knees, I turned around slowly.

Derrick stood in the chamber.

CHAPTER
22

What does a witch do when she's surprised by a psychopath? She pretends she knew he was there all along and acts normal.

"Aren't you supposed to be getting married or something?" What? I had nothing else to say.

A whimper came from Susan, and I turned to see her cower into a ball on the ground, her body trembling. The other two still had not shown any sign of life. Their faces were hidden under clumps of hair and dirt, and I couldn't even tell if they were breathing.

I stood slowly. No way was I going to be on my knees to deal with this asshole. I was going to do this face-to-face, like all women with serious lady balls.

Derrick scoffed, and I didn't like the fact that he didn't seem one bit nervous that I could kill him with my magic—*if* I wanted to. Yeah, I wanted to.

Derrick leered, and my skin erupted in goose bumps. "I couldn't have planned it better myself."

"What was that?"

He swept his arms. "You… here… it's ridiculously perfect."

"More like you're ridiculously insane."

Derrick began to walk around the space leisurely, like his torture chamber was a stroll in the park. "I know you broke into my home. I knew you were looking for something, which told me you were onto me. For a while, I guess. Herbert was very confused as to why he woke up in one of the guest rooms. I'll give you points for the memory charm. It took some minor adjustments to remove it. Hardly complex enough for me to dissolve it."

"So? Big deal." No point in denying it now. "Going to call the chief on me? News flash, he's my boyfriend. Not sure how he's going to react when he sees what you've done here." I shook my head, disgust and anger radiating from my body. "What exactly have you done here? What is this? Why are you doing this to them? You sadistic bastard."

His smile never wavered. "I've always admired your strengths. That inner fire. Your defiance. Your strong will."

"Answer the question, jackass," I ordered, my heart racing, not sure if he would or not. But I wanted some answers before I kicked his ass.

Derrick laughed. "Temper, temper." He flashed me his too-white, too-straight teeth. "I like that too. Relax, Tessa. I'll tell you since you asked so nicely," he said, his voice low and silky.

"Hurry before I throw up."

He cocked a brow. "You see, witches have a unique bloodline, a special magical gene that enables you to do magic. White. Dark. It doesn't matter. As long as they are witches, it works."

"Are we going to get to the interesting part? Or do I have to beat it out of you?"

Derrick waved a finger at me. "See? That's what's so delicious about you."

"Fuck off."

He laughed, and I wanted to kick him in his overbleached teeth. "The thing is, I need it. I need their specific witch blood. I've tried the blood of werewolves, fae, and even vampires, but it just isn't enough to sustain me. I need witch blood. I need their magic. So I took it. Just a little at a time… draining it out of them when I needed it." He gestured lazily with his hand. "These two died in the middle of the night last night. I felt their deaths. Maybe I was too greedy. My bad." He chuckled, chilling me, and I felt like I was going to vomit. "It doesn't matter now. I don't need them anymore. I don't need to pretend."

He was slime. He was a bastard, and I was going to kill him for this. I might not have been able to save Naomi or Francine, but I was going to get Susan out of here if it was the last thing I did.

I gritted my teeth as sweat started to gather at the back of my neck. "You're a monster."

"Touché," he answered, looking pleased with himself, and I wanted to punch that smile off his face. "You see. Their unique blood sustains me in this mortal world, but it also gives me the power of illusion. Without it, well, I couldn't be here. And I wouldn't look like this—attractive, handsome, desirable."

My heart raced, and I narrowed my eyes, stiffening. "What are you saying? That you're a demon?" I would be very surprised if he was since I'd seen him many times in the daylight, something ordinary demons couldn't subject themselves to without suffering their true death. But then again, my knowledge of demons and all things Netherworld left a lot to be desired.

"Incubus," he answered, and I felt a shimmer of cold energy zing through the room.

I laughed. "A sex demon? Really? Well, let me give you a tip. Women don't like the slimy, creepy types."

Derrick darted his gaze to me, his eyes gleaming with a deep hatred that scared the crap out of me. He was not a happy camper. Too bad.

"So that's how you've been manipulating my aunt," I said, realizing it. As an incubus, he could easily make women fall in love with him. "You've got some sort of sexy mojo magic. Because without it… she'd never have fallen for your crap."

He smiled again. "Beverly was so easy, so eager to be with me. I didn't even have to try. The witch threw herself at me."

I gave him my best pageant smile. "I still don't get all the secrets and the pretenses. All this," I said, gesturing to Susan and the other witches, "just so that you can stay here, in the mortal world and get laid? There's got to be a better reason. You're not that smart. I mean, you got caught."

"I didn't."

I hooked a thumb at myself. "*I* caught you."

Derrick watched me a moment and crossed his arms over his chest. "Did you now? *You* caught *me*? How fascinating."

The guy was a bit slow. I wrinkled my face. "Yeah. I did. See, Susan and I are walking out of here. And if you decide to come at me with that

weird, creepy sex magic of yours, I'm going to
kick your ass. It's over. You're not going to hurt
anyone else. Ever. I'll make sure of that." I
moved my finger toward his man bits. "You're
done. I've already called the chief. He'll be here
any second."

Derrick uncrossed his arms and stepped
closer to me with the swag of someone in
control. I didn't like that since I thought *I* was in
control here. "Oh, but you're so, so wrong, my
beautiful Tessa."

I flinched. "Don't make me vomit. It'll ruin
the effect of me kicking your ass."

He closed his eyes and lifted his head to sniff
the air. "Mmmm. Yes. Your blood is unique. The
smell is intoxicating. Like a fine wine. It's why
it was so hard to resist you at the beginning."

"And what's this crap you're yapping about
now?" He was really getting on my nerves. I
wanted him to strike first, so I could call it self-
defense. The sooner he did, the sooner I could
get this show on the road and get Susan the help
she needed.

Derrick opened his eyes and met my gaze.
"You're the one I've been searching for," he
purred, his voice a pleading desire. "You're the
one I've always wanted."

Ew. And ewww. "What about Beverly?" This
guy was really nasty. I might not have the
energy to wait for him to strike first. I was going
to have to shut him up.

"That washed-up, old lady? Please," he said, pulling on the sleeves of his jacket. "I was just using her to get to you."

I scowled. "But you were going to *marry* her."

He took a few steps forward, his stride smooth as he glided effortlessly with the grace of a predator, a killer—strong, supple, and deadly.

"Yes. If it meant I could get closer to you and get my hands on you," he said calmly. "It was always about you, my delectable, fierce Tessa."

Bile bubbled up. So did my fury. "Why? Why me?"

He made a disgruntled sound in his throat. "Despite being as ignorant as a turtle, you're capable of so much power. It's unfortunate that you won't see it happen."

I'd had enough. He hadn't struck at me yet, but I was going to use his creepiness as the intention to kick his ass.

My body shook with adrenaline. With my feet wide apart for better control, I pulled on the elements around me, thinking about which power word I was going to use to fry the sonofabitch.

But then something weird happened.

Weirder than that self-satisfying smile on Derrick's face.

I sent out my will, reaching out to that familiar elemental power that was all around us, to the metals on the ship and the water that surrounded us. All I got was a dull thud—a vast emptiness.

I couldn't reach my elemental power.

I could feel it. I knew it was out there, but my connection to it, my link was cut. It was as though an invisible wall was keeping me from reaching out to my magic.

Straining with effort, I sent out my will again, this time calling out to the ley lines. Instead of the thrumming power of the ley lines answering, I got a lifeless pulse. I couldn't tap into them.

Panting, I staggered with a bit of weariness and tried again. I tapped into my core, to that cold power inside me, willing it to surface, but it didn't answer.

Just like my elemental power and the ley lines, I couldn't reach my demon mojo.

My magic was there, but something was keeping me from reaching it.

Derrick smiled wickedly, seeing the fear in my eyes. "Poor Tessa. You can't use your magic down here. Didn't she tell you?" He gestured toward Susan.

Shit. Susan hadn't said anything, and judging by the amount of shaking, I didn't think I was going to get anything else out of her. She was terrified of this guy, and she had good reason to be.

"The hull is made of a unique brand of aluminum, a metal that I personally modeled and crafted with wards," he said with a cocky grin. "It keeps all witches from using their magic down here. Undetectable until it's too late. As soon as you reach the lower deck, it's over. Any type of witch magic is useless. Think of it like Superman's kryptonite. You're powerless."

Well, that wasn't very good. It also explained why Iris hadn't felt any wards when we'd first climbed onto the yacht. Because they were down here, merged into the metal.

"Wards can be destroyed. They're not invincible." Too bad I didn't know how. I needed Dolores.

Derrick pursed his lips. "Yes. You are correct. It would take a very skilled witch to break through the wards. And she would have to know about them first. But unfortunately for you... you're not in a position to do that. You're still just coming into your powers. And from what I've heard, your magical knowledge is somewhat left to be desired."

"Bite me." I realized it was the wrong thing to say as Derrick's eyes widened, and his smile turned lustful. Gross.

Movement caught my eye behind Derrick.

My breath caught as Iris froze when she stepped in the chamber, her eyes wide as she took in the scene.

"Iris! Run!" I hollered.

Derrick spun around, and the smell of rot and carrion rose. He was pulling his magic. Faster than I thought possible, he threw himself in her direction.

I might not be able to use my magic, but nothing stopped me from using my body.

I hurled myself at him, connecting with him in a hard crash and grabbing him by the legs as I pulled him down with me.

We hit the hard floor, me still hanging on to his stupid legs. That's when his boot made contact with the side of my head.

I let go of the hold I had and rolled over in agonizing pain as I tasted blood. Stars danced in my vision.

"You miserable, intrusive witch!" shouted Derrick as he stood. With a cry of frustrated rage, he kicked me again in the stomach.

My breath escaped me. I crumpled, blinking the stars from my eyes.

"It doesn't matter," I heard Derrick say. "She's not the one I need."

Panting, I opened my eyes and searched for the spot where I'd last seen Iris. She was gone. She'd escaped.

Thank the cauldron.

Derrick laughed. "She left you, you know? She abandoned you. Not much of a friend. Is she?"

My blood pounded in my temples. Instincts demanded I do something, so I pushed myself up and gave him a hard stare.

He leered. "That power of yours is dangerous. I felt it when you were immune to my advances."

"That didn't take magic. That took common sense."

"You should have never been able to conjure that power in your veins. It has created… problems. Lucky for you, I'm going to fix that."

"Go to hell."

He shrugged. "Been there. Done that." He laughed. "You see, Tessa. My kind is not only gifted in sex." He grabbed his groin in a disgusting way. If he whipped it out, I was going to puke. "And though we are masters of illusions, we are also gifted in the consumption of someone's magical essence, or aura, if you will. We take their magic."

I felt him tap into his magic, that creepy, oily magic I'd sensed when he'd thrown himself at me in my bedroom. My skin tingled at its strength and wrongness.

His face split into a disgusting grin. "It's time to take yours."

"My power is useless to you," I told him, my heart thrashing madly in my chest as I tried to figure out a way to get the hell out of this mess. Sorry, Susan, but if I had a chance to flee, I would. I'd come back to get her later with

Marcus and reinforcements. "I might not know much about the whole paranormal world, but I know one thing. Witch magic can't be transmitted to demons unless you're born with a demon and witch parent." Like me.

Derrick stilled, power bristled behind his eyes. "Oh, but it's not for me, darling."

Horror trickled through me, and I screwed up my face. "If not for you… then for who?"

Derrick snapped his fingers with a showman's flair, and the air filled with a sudden hum of power.

I jerked back as the pull of his magic flowed into me like a curse, coating me with the scent of sulfur and something sweet. I strained to move, but it was as though my limbs were made of cement. I was paralyzed.

Dizziness hit, and I blinked, trying to rid the fog from my mind. It was wrong. It was all wrong. Something cold and heavy touched my wrist just as I felt my motor functions returning. When the dizziness finally faded, I gave a little cry of shock.

Metal chains were wrapped around my wrists and ankles, just like Susan and the others.

I was trapped.

CHAPTER
23

*T*his can't be happening.

Panicked, I pulled on the chains as hard as I could, but it was like trying to pull a bus. I wasn't strong enough.

"You can stop fighting. It's over," said Derrick. "You're going to wear yourself out."

"It's not over," I seethed as searing pain erupted from my wrists where the metal had cut into the soft flesh. "You're not taking my magic." He couldn't take it. Right? "You think you can bottle it up and sell it to the highest bidder? That's not how this works." But then again, I had no idea. Maybe that was precisely how it worked.

Derrick let out a moan. "Enough with the deceptions, am I right? Aren't you dying to see the real me?"

"Not really."

"Trying to be someone I'm not is really exhausting." He snapped his fingers again, and I saw a coat of shimmering red and gold descend on him, like someone had thrown a silk blanket over him.

Instead of a handsome, fortyish-year-old man, stood a creature.

The demon's flesh was pale gray, pasty, and wrinkled like a walnut. Something was wrong about his shape—something that just wasn't a part of this world. He was tall, at least seven feet, with elongated arms and fingers ending in sharp talons. His face was somewhat humanoid but too big to be considered normal by our standards; his jaw was just a little too large, his cheekbones too high and protruding, and his nose just too broad and flat. A tuft of gray and black hair sprouted from the top of his head and disappeared down his neck.

Yikes. I raised a brow. "You should have left the glamour on."

Derrick, the incubus, shrugged. "Perhaps. The other shell might be considered more attractive to the mortal females. But the guise interferes with my methods. An incubus must be in their natural form to perform the kiss."

"Hell no." I rushed back as far as I could and staggered as I felt the chain go taut. I knew what it would do. His disgusting kiss would leave me looking like the witches on the floor, like a corpse.

The incubus demon walked toward me. "Oh yes." He laughed, the sound wet and sending a chill wrap around my neck. "You might even enjoy it."

"I'll enjoy kicking your ass," I hissed, trying to sound brave even knowing I couldn't call on my magic to save me.

"I'm sorry, Tessa," came a faint voice from the ground.

I looked down to see Susan watching me, her eyes round with fear and what I could only surmise was regret. I'd felt sorry for her before, but now I was just angry. She knew he'd do this to me, so why hadn't she warned me? I wouldn't be in this mess if she had just said something.

I glared at her, and I saw her flinch and cower like I'd assaulted her. Crap. Now I felt sorry that I glared at her. Wonderful. She looked in a bad way physically, which meant her mind was in an equally abused state. It probably didn't occur to her to warn me about the incubus demon. She was just too messed up.

But I couldn't think about how I'd hurt her feelings. I was about to get my own feelings hurt.

Think, Tessa! Think. How do I get out of this mess?

To think I'd planned to seduce this demon… it made my stomach churn. I needed to come up with a plan to save my ass.

"What do you get in return? Money? I can get you money. I've got about two hundred dollars in my bank account. Yours if you let me go."

The incubus laughed. "I couldn't possibly want anything you have. Other than your magic, of course." He no longer had any beauty in his features, just a twisted malice, as though inflicting pain on others was his favorite thing.

A deep panic rose in me. It was impossible not to freak out in this kind of situation—when a creepy, soul-sucking demon wanted to make out with me. I couldn't even think clearly, and I didn't know whether the incubus was lying or not. No one was here to help me now. No Marcus. No one. I was utterly alone.

I was a powerful witch, but my magic wouldn't save me. Not this time.

"Why do you want to kill me?" My heart thrashed in my chest as a helpless sort of panic took over.

The incubus halted. "Kill you? Oh, no, no, no, silly Tessa. I'm not going to *kill* you. In fact, I was instructed to let you live. He was very clear on that. I just need your magic. All of it… so you can't use it anymore."

My body went cold. "He?" No. It couldn't be. "He who?"

He grinned and said, "Lucifer sent me. He says hello."

I had a brain-fog moment. "Lucifer? But what—"

Derrick, the incubus, grabbed my shoulders, his fingers pressing hard into my flesh to the point of pain. Alarm filled me. I lashed out and pulled at his hands around my shoulders, trying to pry his fingers apart, but it was like trying to bend steel. His grip on me was iron tight.

The demon opened his mouth, and his gray-forked tongue licked his lips. The smell of rot and something I wouldn't even mention assaulted me, making me gag.

I jerked my head back as far as it would go, afraid he was going to kiss me. Kissing a dirty scumbag was one thing, but having those gag-worthy incubus lips touch mine, well, that was no-no.

"Get away from me! Stop!" Desperation filled me as I fought with everything I had, but the demon was much too powerful for me. I couldn't fight off his strong hold, let alone his iron chains.

The incubus pulled me closer as I kicked and lashed out, like a wild animal.

His eyes rounded with excitement and hunger for my soul, my magic. His mouth opened wider, and then a slip of something yellow shot out of his mouth and ripped into me.

The world flipped over, and pain lit through me as the demon's magic, raw and unfiltered, entered my body. I felt a sudden pull, a weakness. It was hard to explain, but I knew he was consuming my soul—my aura, my chi, where my magic came from. He was eating it, sucking it out of me.

Panic surged, and I thrashed, instinct moving in as I tried to get away from the demon. The pain was too intense, and I lost my focus.

I was dying. Soon I'd be nothing but a corpse like Susan and the others. I didn't think there was a cure for that, not once our bodies had reached that point.

I should have told Marcus where we were. My stupidity was going to cost me everything.

I blinked through my tears and saw a thin, yellow veil, like a mist pulling away from my body and into that horrid mouth of the incubus. In my pain, I could see a part of my soul slipping into him, my strength and my magic going with it.

I felt weak and feverish, like I had the flu. He said he didn't want me dead, but if he kept this up, I was a very dead witch.

My thoughts moved to Lucifer. I'd underestimated him. He'd been onto me for a while, it seemed. A lot longer than I thought.

Around the time Derrick started dated my Aunt Beverly, Lucifer had set his plan in motion.

In order to stop Lilith's plans, he needed me out of the picture. My magic. Without me, Lilith couldn't trap and kill him.

I had no idea I was so popular. Too bad I was about to die.

It all made sense. Derrick was Lucifer's man. He'd sent him to take my power away.

I felt my legs give way beneath me. I didn't have the energy to stay upright, but the incubus kept me upright, preventing me from falling on my face.

I was weak. But a faint whisper of self-preservation forced me to turn my head and face him, or maybe I was just crazy and stupid. Perhaps a little bit of both.

My lips parted, but nothing was coming out. My body shook with pain. My head lolled to the side because I didn't have the strength to keep it straight as the incubus kept draining me, killing me softly.

I wasn't sure how much time passed. Minutes or hours, I couldn't tell. I felt the last drop of my magic being pulled away. I had no idea how I knew. I just did. I knew my magic would exist only in memory.

My mind drifted to beautiful gray eyes, a drool-worthy face, and a smile that turned me on, no matter where I was or what I was doing.

Those strong, manly hands were so delicate at times.

Marcus. I wasn't so sure how he'd react to my withering, corpse-like body, remembering how he'd flinched from me when I'd become an eighty-year-old woman overnight. All because of moving back and forth between worlds. I couldn't see myself, but seeing what the incubus had done to those witches, well, it wasn't good for my sex life. Would I even have a life?

A sudden blast shook the ship.

I staggered, and the incubus flinched. His hold on me faltered, but he didn't let go.

I'm here! I called out in my mind, knowing I couldn't speak and not knowing if my savior could hear me.

Iris. Iris was going to blow up the ship!

Another great blast.

The yacht rocked, and for a moment, I thought we were about to capsize. As the boat settled, the air echoed loudly with the sound of screeching metal, like a giant was trying to crush the vessel with its hands.

I had no idea what was happening, but I liked it.

The incubus demon let go of me, and I felt the sudden absence of his pull.

I fell. The world lurched, and I hit the cold, hard floor. A pained sob escaped me as I lay on the floor in a crumpled heap, my breath a whisper and my lungs burning with every intake of air. Fiery pain racked my back and shoulders, biting deeply.

I made contact with something cold but soft. That was either Susan or one of the dead witches. With great effort, I rolled over, looking for the source of the blast.

Words spewed from the incubus in a language I didn't recognize, but it didn't matter. They were words of hate, of malevolence, and death. Words that were meant to destroy, to kill.

He rushed around the chamber, grabbed some candles, and set them around him. Then he moved to one of the dead witches and, with his talons, sliced off her right wrist. Thick blood oozed from the stump. I grimaced as he dragged her body around him, making a circle with her blood. He tossed her when he was done.

The incubus's features were highlighted grotesquely by the dark light flowing up from the circle around him.

He'd just formed some sort of protection circle. If he needed protection, it meant his wards were gone. Someone had obliterated them.

Footsteps sounded. *Lots* of footsteps.

"I thought I smelled a bastard." Dolores's voice thundered around the chamber. "Ladies. Let's get him!"

CHAPTER
24

Bodies rushed into the chamber in a blur of color, motion, and incantations. At the head of the group was Dolores, with none other than Davina at her side. That was unexpected. Next came Beverly, Ruth, and my mommy dearest followed by Belinda and Reece. Coming in last was Iris, with a murderous expression on her face.

It was an impressive arsenal of witches to the rescue—a grand, magical entrance, if ever there was one. If I'd had the strength, I would have applauded.

Instead, I used the only strength I had and propped myself on my elbows for a better view.

My mother's dark eyes found mine. She did a quick scan over my body, like she was looking for injuries, and then snapped her attention at the incubus, her eyes hard with a murderous gleam.

Voices rose in unison, steady chants of incantations and spells and curses, all mixed together with the rumble of soles of boots on the hard floor.

Derrick, the incubus, thought his wards were unbreakable, but he didn't know my Aunt Dolores. If anyone could break his wards, she could.

Go, Dolores!

"You son of a bitch! You'll pay for this." Beverly's voice rose above everyone else's to a fevered pitch. Her beautiful face was twisted in anger and anguish. She was pissed. I would be, too, if I'd been taken for a fool. It appeared his so-called sex magic he'd used on her had been eradicated; she was no longer under his spell. My guess was it broke with the tearing down of the wards or when he removed his glamour.

"Oh, come on, Beverly," came Derrick's voice above the chanting. "You enjoyed it. You asked for more, over and over again. Admit it. You and I had a good time. You were going to marry me, you loved it so much."

"Fooled by your deceitful magic," she spat, a snarl on her face. "But not anymore. Now my eyes are open."

Beverly yelled something I couldn't catch, and heat rose up around me, like I'd stuck my face too close to a fire, as hot white flames sprouted out of my aunt's hands.

Her white fire rushed at the incubus like a rocket. There was nowhere to go.

But he just stayed there, a smile on his grotesque face.

The incubus disappeared behind the wall of white flames as the fire soared to the roof of the hull, and warmth like a campfire sank into my skin.

Beverly straightened as her white fires flared and then receded.

And there stood the incubus with that same winning grin.

That had been a serious hit, but it never touched the incubus, as though he was protected by some invisible barrier, a wall of protection. His circle was a lot more powerful than I would have thought for a mid-demon.

"Is that all you've got? Witches?" laughed the incubus. His lips moved, and I knew he was conjuring more of his magic. The air in the lower deck was thick with the cold prickling of demon energy.

"That should have taken his down his protective circle and vanquished him," yelled Dolores, eyeing the incubus like he was the dog poop she'd stepped in earlier this week.

283

"Lucifer," I wheezed, as it all came to me. When Dolores and the others met my gaze, I added, "He's got Lucifer's magic or something. Lucifer is helping him." It was the only thing that made sense. The king of hell had supplied the incubus with some serious magical resources.

Dolores dropped her head in the incubus's direction. "Is he, now? Well, then. We'll just have to work harder! Come on, ladies!"

Like a storm of wild magic, the witches exploded into motion.

"That's for my daughter!" cried my mother, as she vaulted what looked like a small glass vial with a green liquid inside at the demon's shield. Green flames rose as it hit its mark.

I blinked through my blurred vision and saw Dolores *and* Davina standing shoulder to shoulder, their elemental fire pouring out of their outstretched hands like flamethrowers, and smashing into the incubus's protective shield with everything they had.

Next to them was Ruth and Reece. Large bags at their feet, they kept digging in, pulling out small containers, and throwing them at the incubus. Ruth arched back, lifted her leg like a seasoned pitcher, and let her vial go.

"Ha! Take that, you nasty sex toy!" Yeah, Ruth was ruthless when it came to insults. It sounded more like a broken-down vibrator, but I wasn't about to tell her.

Her vial flew straight and true. The glass smashed on contact, sending walls of blue flames rising to mix with the yellow flames of elemental fire and green and red smoke. An acrid stench rose, burning my eyes. The shield sizzled like it was covered in acid.

My heart thumped. *They got him.*

But when the flames and smoke vanished, the incubus's shield was still intact. The demon was unharmed.

The incubus's laughter echoed around the chamber, resonating in my head like a migraine as it thundered around the walls. "Your bag of tricks won't save you," he said, an ugly scowl on his face. "Nothing will. Who do you think you are? You're no match for the master's power. You're... well... not much to look at. But I can tell you this... you're all going to die."

Beverly stepped forward, her face red and sweaty. "You're the one who's going to die."

Twin mini tornadoes flew from her hands, and a howling wind rose. My hair and clothes lifted around me as a powerful gust of wind filled the chamber, sending debris and papers scattering and me sliding a few feet.

Through my squinted eyes, I saw the tornadoes glide across the chamber, and together they hit the incubus's shield. My ears rang as a loud clap of thunder shook the hull.

But when the winds died, the demon's shield was unscathed.

"Is that all you've got?" laughed the incubus at the fury on Beverly's face. "Pathetic. And you call yourselves witches. Those were the lamest spells and potions I've ever seen. A two-year-old demon could do better. Once the body goes... the mind follows. You're nothing but a bunch of washed-up, old hags."

"How about you lay down your shield, and I'll show you what this old crone is capable of," threatened Dolores, raising her fists like she meant to have a boxing match with the incubus.

Davina swept a finger in the direction of the incubus's groin. "The last idiot who laughed at my age, a part of him was never seen again," she added and widened her eyes for dramatic effect.

"Ha ha, she's funny," I said to myself, apparently.

It's too bad Dolores and Davina hated each other because they made a great team.

"Only impotent males hide behind the power of others," said Belinda, a cold fury in her eyes and a smile on her pretty face. "Without it, they could not perform."

"Ha ha, she's funny too."

The incubus splayed out his arms, his feet planted in a confident stance. Clearly, he didn't think these eight women were a threat. His voice rose in an incantation, the words lost to me again, as he held his spell in readiness for release.

In a rumble I could feel through the hull of the vessel, the incubus's chant took on an edge of viciousness and spiteful satisfaction. I saw tendrils of inky darkness drifting out of his palms, coiling around his hand, and moving up his arm.

And then he let it go.

A wisp of black energy shot forward toward Belinda.

Moving fast, she thew up her hands. A shimmering gold wall of protection rose from her feet and over her head.

The black energy hit and pierced through her shield.

With a cry, Belinda went sailing back and slammed into the vessel's side wall. The back of her head smacked hard with a horrible thud. She slid to the floor and didn't move.

Davina howled a few words I couldn't catch. A flaming red spear soared from her hands and blasted toward the incubus.

Lips moving, the incubus flicked his wrists, and Davina's flaming spear burst into a shower of red particles.

"Like I said, pathetic." The incubus chuckled, but his laugh was cut short.

"Ut ignem!" cried Dolores as she leaned forward with orange flames spewing from her hands. Orange light flooded around her as she hit the demon's shield again and again.

Through the orange light, all I saw were the incubus's rotten teeth as he smiled. He straightened, countering with a shot of black flames.

Dolores waved her left hand and knocked the flames quickly away. Impressive.

I caught a flicker of movement, and my eyes found Ruth kneeling next to Belinda as she helped her up. I felt a massive wave of relief wash through me. She was alive.

Beverly stepped in my line of sight as she came forward, her arms out to her sides and her lips moving in a chant I couldn't hear as lightning blasted out of her palms, aimed at the incubus.

Next to her was Iris, a dark chant emanating from her lips as she threw a small leather hex bag at the demon. My mother and Reece took turns throwing all the vials they could find in those bags.

I smiled. The witches weren't done, not by a long shot.

With a roar of light and sound, a flash of blinding yellow and red sparks illuminated the chamber resembling fireworks as witches flung their magic at the incubus like automatic weapons.

The ground and walls shook under the magical fire. I watched in awe, impressed as the witches took on that slimy bastard. The sounds of battle blared in a combination of cries, shouts, the boom of magic, and the incubus's laugher, making my ears whistle.

The witches threw every spell they knew, putting everything they had into it.

But still the incubus's shield held.

I watched as if in slow motion as the incubus spun his magic, shooting blasts of black energy at the witches. It didn't look like he was tiring either.

Damn. This wasn't looking good at all. The shield didn't even waver, even after such a magical onslaught. Not so much as a hole or even a small crack. It seemed as though nothing could get through.

The incubus laughed and then tsked. "Look at you. You're nearly done in," he said, gesturing at Dolores's sweat-covered face, her tall frame hunched. She looked exhausted. "You're wasting all that energy," he mocked. "*I* can do this all day… I can last all night." His gaze moved to Beverly. "Isn't that right, Beverly?"

"Go to hell." Beverly pinched her side like she had a cramp, her blue blouse stained with sweat down her front and back. Her face twisted like she was about to throw up. I didn't blame her. I would, too, if the guy I'd been sleeping with actually looked like he was wearing his skin inside out.

I caught a glimpse of Belinda leaning against the wall where she'd fallen, her face pale as Ruth stood beside her.

"You don't have much magic left," continued the incubus. His eyes traveled over to Reece, who was breathing heavily next to my mother, their empty bags at their feet. "You're not going to last. You've got what? One spell left? Two? *I* have a fountain of tremendous power at my disposal."

A growl of frustration came from Iris as she angled Dana in her arms, flipping through the pages as fast as her fingers could go. Her pretty pixie face was nearly purple with strain.

He was right. They were exhausted. Sooner or later, their magic would cease. Just like all magic, it wasn't an endless well.

Not like Lucifer's. Apparently, Lucifer's magic had its own replenishing well.

"And you're old and frail and weak," mocked the incubus. "Just like your magic."

"We're not weak," snarled Davina, fatigue pulling at her posture and making her look much older than her years.

The incubus gave a false laugh. "Still, the magic that's left inside you, well, I'll take it."

A wind rose, and so did a darkness around the incubus. His clothes furled around him as he raised his arms slowly. The darkness kept pouring in, gushing through his connection to the Netherworld, his connection to Lucifer's magic. His eyes closed, and he staggered like a drunk, though drunk with immeasurable power.

When he opened his eyes, they gleamed with demonic power, like burning coals, very similar to Lilith's.

"Ztak'uagh!" he cried.

Metal chains appeared out of thin air, and before anyone could do anything, bonds circled around every witch's wrist and ankle, until all of them, until every single witch, including my mother and Iris, were tied.

Just like me, they were prisoners.

We should have never come here.

"Ahhh. This is much more comfy." The incubus's eyes flashed with hunger as he leered. "You're all mine now."

CHAPTER

25

I'll admit. It didn't look good for us witches. It looked like the incubus was going to win. Mind you, he was cowering behind a protective wall, which would have fallen by now if it wasn't for his pal Lucifer's magic. Yeah, the demon was a douche.

But I wasn't going to lie here like a boiled vegetable and not help my aunts. I had to help. I had to *do* something.

First, I had to get up.

Straining with effort, I rolled to the side, my chains rattling as I tried to bring up my right leg. The trouble was, my right leg felt like it was disconnected from the rest of my body. Panting, I attempted to move the left. Nothing.

"This sucks." Unfortunately, my body seemed to have other plans. Said plans were to keep me on the floor in a semi-vegetative state, chained to the bottom of some yacht. Totally undignified.

The effort of trying to move seemed to do me in. I felt worse than before, weaker, as though that failed attempt at moving had used up any bit of effort in me.

I rolled back onto my stomach and lifted my head. It lolled to the side and hit the floor like it weighed more than my entire body put together. Either that, or my neck was gone. How did that happen?

The truth was, I had no idea what I looked like. Staring at my hands, I noticed they looked like my hands, not skeletal like Susan's. I might not look like a corpse, but I felt like half of me was mummified.

"I haven't lived this long to be beaten by an incubus, a bottom-feeder of the Dark world," spat Davina's voice.

Not wanting to miss any of the action, and since I could move my arms, I grabbed my hair from the back of my head and yanked my head up. Next, using my free hand, I made a fist and lowered my head so my chin could rest on my knuckles. Kinda like a hard pillow. It wasn't ideal, but at least I had a view.

The incubus rolled his eyes over Davina and then shivered, his face twisted in disgust. "You're one ugly bitch. If you'd been my mark, I don't care how much power Lucifer promised me, I'd never touch you."

Davina raised a brow. "Beauty is only skin deep, but ugly goes clean to the bone."

She was sooo much like Dolores, it was freaky.

Usually, this was when Beverly would have intervened, but she just stood there, looking mad and a little wild. With her hands up in clawlike position, she looked like she wanted to scratch out his eyes, and rightly so. She probably would have if not for the chains wrapped around her wrists and ankles.

The incubus cocked his head. "Yes, well. Only ugly people say that."

I wrinkled my face. "Did he really just say that?"

"The truth is... well... the truth is you're just a horribly unattractive female." He clapped his hands together once, sending forth a gust of darkness, rippling from him like a wave of death.

Davina's lips moved in an incantation as she lifted her hands—

The darkness smashed into her *and* Dolores.

I watched as both witches were lifted off the floor and thrown across the chamber. Their bodies jerked painfully as their chains went taut. They fell, the darkness enveloping them like coils of black rope. Dolores's voice rose in a chant, her face a mask of pain as the darkness tightened around her and Davina.

A boom sounded, and the darkness blasted from the witches like pieces of rope.

Dolores held on to the wall for support. She glared at the incubus, a mad gleam in her eyes. "Is that all *you've* got?"

Davina pulled the hair from her eyes. "Not bad for a Davenport witch."

Dolores straightened. "Still better than a Wanderbush."

"We'll see about that," said Davina, her focus trained on the incubus across from her. Her lips moved in a chant. A semitransparent white sphere grew in her hands until it was the size of a bowling ball. She held it above her head, words spilling out of her as her clothes flapped in a wind.

She let out a cry of fury, and then she released it.

The sphere struck the incubus's shield in raw kinetic force with a thundering blast like a blazing meteor.

My ears rang, and for a moment, I couldn't hear anything. When I could hear again, there was only the sound of the incubus's laughter.

Davina's face fell with shock and disappointment as she slumped. That spell had taken a chunk out of her energy and magic.

It didn't even ruffle the damn demon's hair.

I saw Ruth and Reece pouring liquid from containers over the chains that dragged behind them. Smoke rose from where the liquid made contact with the metal. I stared hopefully, but when both witches yanked and pulled on their bonds, the chains remained untarnished. Their potions didn't work.

I cast my gaze around the witches—from my mother to my aunts, the cousins and Iris—and I could see their resolve falter as the fear settled in.

Fighting was pointless. They were trapped, just like me, just like Susan and the others. And the incubus was going to take their magic and their life force from them.

It was over.

The incubus snickered. "I've never had so many females fight over me. It's quite exciting. Isn't it? I might have been turned on if the lot of you weren't in the *sagging* stage of your lives. Once gravity hits… it's all over."

"I'd kick your teeth in if I could move," I said as tears fell freely down my cheeks, my voice carrying loudly enough for the incubus to turn and look in my direction.

"Ah, poor little Tessa," he mocked. "You'll soon realize that you're nothing without it. That thing that made you so, so special. Well, I took it." He laughed. "You're finished."

My lips trembled as I opened my mouth, but the comeback wasn't there. I stared at the vile incubus demon, anger bubbling up in me at the realization of what he'd done. Of what he took.

I was exhausted, and part of me just wanted to close my eyes and go to sleep…

Then something extraordinary happened.

A roar echoed that had the skin on my arms rise in a good, delicious way.

I blinked as a magnificent silverback gorilla bounded into my line of sight. Following quickly behind him in a blur of black clothes and talons was Ronin—my resplendent half-vampire friend.

I stared at the glorious yet terrifying beast, *my* beast. The muscles on his chest flexed as he stood on all fours, his front hands resting on his knuckles. His silver eyes rested on me, and I saw the terrible storm that brewed behind them. I knew that look. It was the "I'm going to destroy everything around me" look.

Yay!

Slowly, his gaze landed on the incubus, and something primeval flashed in them. He roared, shaking his head. His lips pulled back, revealing teeth that could chomp through a man's neck— preferably the incubus's. And with a powerful thrust of his back legs, he shot forward and rushed to meet the demon.

And then he did something that surprised me and the incubus boy toy over there.

The gorilla slammed into the incubus's invisible shield, over and over again. He didn't stop. He kept on throwing his four-hundred-pound body of hard muscle against the shield, the vessel rocking at the sheer impact of the wondrous beast's strength.

Yeah, I was so turned on. Too bad I was chained to the floor.

And I shit you not, the shield *wavered*.

For the first time, the incubus looked worried, and a frown crossed his features.

"Ha!" I shouted as loudly as I could, and a fit of giggles took over. "Ha ha ha." I was delirious.

Ronin had placed himself on the opposite side of the gorilla, his black eyes intense. He wiggled his talons in anticipation like a cook sharpening his knives, getting ready to slice into a chunk of meat. He was going to rip apart the incubus when his shield fell.

I smiled. Look at me. I had such awesome friends.

"Quickly, hands," commanded Dolores, and I saw her and the others hurrying to take each other's hands until they were all connected physically and formed a line. The wizard Dragos and his boys had done the same thing before he'd shot laser beams out of his eyes.

I watched the witches hold each other as the air in the chamber was suddenly filled with crackling energy again.

Marcus, the gorilla, never stopped smashing his incredible body against the shield. And each time he did, the shield became visibly weaker. And I mean *visibly* because I could see a silver shimmer and a web of fissures in it. It was going to crack like an egg.

Not only was this hunk of a beast somewhat resistant to magic, but it seemed the incubus's magic weakened in the presence of the wereape's own magic.

Wereapes rule, prick.

A wind rose, following the incantation repeated by the witches.

"In this darkest hour," they chanted in unison, Dolores's and Davina's voices loudest of all, "we call upon the goddess and her sacred power. Join our powers and see them rise, a force unseen across the skies."

I sucked in a breath. I remembered that spell. We'd chanted it together in the Stepford witches' basement as we tried to close the vortex that came after Lilith's release.

I grinned at the sudden outpour of combined magic creeping up from hand to hand as the energy from each witch rushed through them in turn, circling within the confines of their linked hands with a visible shimmer of yellow, orange, and red, spreading and spinning until they were all connected like they'd tied a magical rope around themselves.

It was beautiful.

"It won't work," cried the incubus from behind his wall, though his voice cracked with fear. Yeah, he was scared. He jerked as the gorilla threw himself at the shield again. "Your spells are weak. You're just witches. You're nothing. *I* have the power of Lucifer! Me! You've got nothing. Nothing!"

I smiled at the fear in his voice. "You're the one who's done."

"Hear us, Goddess, in this place and in this hour," recited the witches together, their voices loud over the rumbling winds and the shrieks of the incubus. "Heed our will and vanquish the incubus forever."

The power of the spell exploded out of the witches, like eight beams of blinding lights in combined energies, auras, life forces, and magic.

The beams merged into one and curved—actually contoured around the gorilla—and hit the incubus's shield.

With a flash of light and a thunderous boom, the shield warped and pulled, slewing back and forth in a gushing spout of unearthly flames.

The gorilla pounded his great body on the shield one last time.

And with a pop of displaced air, the shield disintegrated until it was gone, as though it never existed.

"You're mine now, bitch." With his talons flashing in the dim light, Ronin leaped at the incubus.

I saw a sudden rippling effect on the wall of the boat, right behind the incubus, as though the metal had transformed into water. I knew what that was. A Rift—a portal to the Netherworld.

The half-vampire lunged, but it was too late.

With a last cunning, evil smile my way, the incubus leaped into the Rift and was gone.

A chorus of applause and shouts went around the chamber. As the winds settled, the chains that had been bound around our wrists disintegrated, just as the incubus's shield had done.

The hold of his magic had left with him.

The next thing I knew, I was floating in the air as the scent of musk and something male filled me. Heat from a body washed over me like a warm blanket.

"I've got you now," said Marcus, his deep voice rumbling through me as he cradled me in his big, strong arms. "I've got you. You're safe." He kissed the top of my head and the side of my neck, sending tingling warmth down to my core. I let out a sigh, wanting to melt against him and let him hold me forever.

My head fell back on Marcus's chest, and I closed my eyes, breathing him in. He was warm, so warm. And safe.

"It's all right, Tessa," I heard Beverly say as I felt her hand squeeze my shoulder.

"He's gone," came my mother's voice. "You're going to be fine now."

But it wasn't all right, and I wasn't fine.

Straining, I tried to spindle the magic from my core, but I was only an empty shell. The magic I'd felt before was gone, and I didn't have the energy to will it back.

I knew it in my heart, my soul, the core of my being.

My magic was gone forever.

CHAPTER
26

The sky was a perfect blue with tiny clouds peppering it. It was a glorious day.

And perfect for a wedding.

The 109 white chairs Gilbert had ordered for us were neatly placed in rows, leaving ample enough space in the middle for the bride and groom. The chairs were lovely, made of wood instead of plastic, with a comfortable white cushioned seat. The chairs' backrests were decorated with red and white ribbons.

At the end of the row of chairs was a small platform tucked under a white-painted garden arbor and decorated with red roses. A long white drape was placed in the aisle with red and pink rose petals. Each aisle chair had a bouquet of red roses tied to it, fastened with white and red ribbons.

The platform stood empty now, but it was still pretty, and the scent of roses was divine. Garden weddings were, in my opinion, the most enchanting and beautiful. Something was just so comforting and pretty about the sounds of birds chirping and the smell of the great outdoors, the scent of nature.

I wiggled my toes in the grass. I didn't know where my shoes were. I'd lost them somewhere between the ceremony and the tossing of the bouquet—when Martha came out of nowhere and body slammed me like a UFC fighter.

"I've got it! I have it! It's mine! Get away! Move! Ha ha!" the larger witch had yelled, her face red with effort. She looked positively menacing in that pink tulle, a snarl on her face as she held on to that bouquet, eyeing all the single witches like she was about to body slam them too if they got too close to her prize.

I giggled at the memory and took a sip of my wine, casting my gaze around the grounds. Ten large garden pavilions had been stockpiled with tables and loaded with food, wine bottles, and grill stations that were singing meat. Happy chatter filled the air, and Glenn Miller's "In the Mood" blared from the wireless speakers.

I spotted the witch Reece under one of the pavilions, chatting with Iris, who had her trusted Dana in her hands. I narrowed my eyes as Reece handed something to Iris, who then put it in her album. I was going to ask her about that later.

I made my way through the crowds of guests, enjoying the feel of cool grass squishing under my feet. Belinda looked absolutely stunning in a low-cut red dress, her long, dark hair cascading behind her and gleaming in the sunlight. Four men surrounded her, all handsome and all very different, though their common denominator was the clear desire to be her champion. I smiled at the four men competing for her attention. She caught me staring and gave me a wink.

I laughed. She was definitely made from the same mold as Beverly.

Moving on, I spotted Ronin next to one of the buffets, having a conversation with Davina.

"And the name *Wanderbush*…" Ronin was saying as I neared. "Where does that come from exactly? Is there any significance to the words *wander* and *bush*?"

I snorted and moved away quickly before I was hit with one of Davina's murderous glares.

I'd never expected my aunts to welcome their cousins the Wanderbushes on their property, especially after their threats of taking Davenport House. I still didn't know if they had any proper claims to the house. I'd been too busy to look into it. But then again, they had come to my rescue, and they'd fought together alongside my aunts to defeat Derrick the Douche.

A lot had changed, and I was happy about it. Maybe they'd finally put their enmities aside. Though I was still unclear about the allegations the Wanderbushes put forward regarding their grandfather's claim on Davenport House, it seemed they weren't going to push it anymore.

Susan Woodward was on the mend in some paranormal hospital in Upstate New York that specialized in curses and demon afflictions. The healers couldn't tell us if she'd make a full recovery, but she would live. Francine and Naomi weren't as lucky. The two witches had indeed died before we could get them the help they needed.

"They *are* worth the price!" shouted a voice.

I turned in search of the commotion and found Gilbert standing on one of the wedding chairs, his face set in a frown and his hands on his hips.

"They are *not* worth double the normal price!" yelled Dolores, standing next to the row of white chairs, her long, purple dress flowing lightly in a breeze.

"Yes. They. Are." Gilbert started jumping on the chair and waving his arms around to keep his balance. Though in a brown suit and red bowtie, he looked more like a performer from the circus than our town mayor, at the moment.

"See?" he said, a little out of breath. "Can a cheaper chair let me do this?" He kept on jumping. "These are solid. Made of a hundred percent oak wood. I can keep doing this all day long!"

"We didn't need chairs to jump on like lunatics," hollered Dolores. "We needed chairs to put our behinds on them. You charged us *double* for nothing!"

Gilbert stopped jumping. "With a butt like yours, I should have charged triple!"

Oh no.

Dolores leaned forward. "Why, you miserable, cretin; you slimy little shifter! I'm going to boil you in one of Ruth's cauldrons!"

Gilbert held his chin high. "I'd like to see you try! Witch!"

Pressing my lips together to keep from laughing, I turned and made my escape. I spotted Marcus. He was hard to miss in that dark blue suit that made his mesmerizing gray eyes pop and fit his muscular body to a T, contouring every muscle. The man was born to wear a suit. He just was.

He stood with a beer in his hand, conversing with Scarlett, the new deputy, and Cameron, whose voice kept getting louder with every downed drink. The three of them seemed to really be getting along. I did not want to interfere with that. Though Allison was not invited, I hadn't put it past her to show up, trying to oust the new hot deputy, but the gorilla Barbie was nowhere to be found.

Pulling my eyes away from the chief, I saw Ruth behind one of the buffet tables, slicing pieces of the five-tier wedding cake, so I joined her.

The five-tier ivory butter cake was textured with rosettes and Swiss dots on each tier along with sculptured icing red roses and gold ribbons. The bride-and-groom toppers glided over the cake in a waltz, pausing only to toss glitter-like confetti.

Hildo, the black cat, lay on his back, his limbs splayed out to the sides with his belly protruding, like he'd eaten a whole tier of cake on his own.

"Ohhh…" he moaned. "I think I'm going to be sick."

"Nonsense." Ruth waved him off. "It's just gas. Nothing wrong with a bit of gas. I'm a little gassy myself sometimes." She giggled. "Once you pass the gas, you'll be ready for more food. You'll see. Just let it out."

I laughed. I couldn't help it. Talking about gas at a wedding? That was my kind of wedding.

"This is the most beautiful cake I've ever seen, Ruth. Truly. Just wow."

Ruth beamed. Flour spotted her left ear, her cheek, and on her hair, too, but I wasn't going to tell her. She'd braided, what I'd suspected were, some icing flowers in her hair. An apron with the words DON'T DRINK AND FLY covered her pink-and-white dress.

She caught me staring at her hair. "Here," she said as she pulled out an icing rose from her hair. "Go on. Try it. Tastes like strawberries."

I shrugged. "Why not." I took the icing rose, the size of an actual strawberry, and popped it into my mouth. Delicious flavors burst over my tongue as I swallowed. "Mmm. Does taste like strawberries," I said, my mouth full.

Ruth giggled again. "I know." She reached up and picked another icing flower before shoving it in her mouth. "Would you like a slice of the wedding cake?"

"Maybe later," I told her. "I think I'll finish my wine first."

My aunt narrowed her blue eyes in an attempt to look concerned, but it made her look like a she was having trouble with her eyesight. "I know you're upset. I can see it on your face. What happened to you was a terrible thing. But know this… life has a funny way of turning things around, you know."

"I wish I did."

"Usually when you least expect it to," she added and plucked another icing flower from her head. "Whatever life brings you, you can handle it," she said around her mouthful. "I know you can. You're the strongest person I know."

I blinked fast, my eyes burning at her comments. "Thank you." My face warmed at the love and faith my Aunt Ruth had for me. After hearing that, I felt lighter somehow. She'd given me hope that I could face whatever was next.

Ruth grinned, a slip of her teeth showing through her pink lips. "I believe in you, Tessa. Now, here. Have another one. Go on. Take one."

I did as she instructed and took another icing flower, this one a daisy. "I see you've made amends with the cousins," I commented between chews.

Ruth made a face. "Well, I wouldn't call it 'amends,' but we all agreed that it would be rude not to invite them to the wedding. They did help us when we needed them."

"They did. And they also took a beating," I said, remembering both how Belinda and Davina had gotten hit by the incubus's magic. I washed down the last of my icing daisy with a sip of wine. I turned my head and looked back at the three cousins. "Don't you think it's weird that they all look like your doppelgängers? I mean… it's really, really weird. Right?"

"What?" exclaimed Ruth when I turned back around. "They look nothing like us." She laughed as though I was telling her a joke.

Okay then.

"Girls!"

I spun around to see Beverly swinging her hips in a light blue dress that hugged all her curves, a new man on each arm. Yes, that's right. A man on *each* arm.

"What a glorious day to have such a glorious wedding." She smiled radiantly as she neared and gestured with her right arm. "This is Alfonso." Then with her left. "And Sebastien," she introduced happily.

I took them in. Alfonso was a tall, dark, and very handsome forty-something who had all the looks and charms of a vampire. And Sebastien, though not as attractive, had a more rugged, sexy edge to him, like a fifty-something cleaned-up lumberjack. What he lacked in looks, he made up for with his muscle. Their eyes held the same emotion. They both were in serious competition for Beverly. Just like Belinda's men.

Beverly's green eyes flashed at something she saw on my face. "I don't know which one to choose," she said with a huge smile, as though the two men weren't standing right here in front of us. "So, I say… why choose when I can have them both." She giggled and steered her reverse harem across the grounds.

I eyed my aunt sashaying away and giving Belinda a daring smile as she wandered past the other witch. "Wow. She moves fast."

Ruth nodded. "That's what all the men say."

I choked on the mouthful of wine, liquid dribbling down the sides of my mouth. As I wiped my mouth with my other hand, I felt an itch between my shoulder blades, a feeling of someone watching me.

I turned around and met my mother's disapproving glare. Her dark eyes traced down to my feet, my *bare* feet, and she shook her head.

I wiggled my toes and gave her a finger wave. I would have much preferred to give her a toe wave, but then that would have entailed me lifting up my leg and showing everyone my lady bits. I wouldn't do that to her. Well, not on her day, that is.

My mother then smiled at me, which was totally uncharacteristic of her. But then again, she *was* a blushing bride.

Amelia Davenport looked radiant in her off-white, off the shoulder, long-sleeved, lace-draped gown, with a sequin lace bodice that hugged her curves just right. She wore her hair up, and her makeup was tasteful. Add in a thin, white gold chain and matching earrings, and she really did look amazing.

Next to her, holding her hand, stood my father. He wore a beige three-piece suit that fit him expertly. He looked like a model for Ralph Lauren, off to his expensive sailboat. They both looked, well, stupidly happy and in love and *very* married.

That's right. My parents got married today. The world had gone mad.

As temporary officiant, it came as no surprise that Dolores had performed the ceremony. She'd been preparing for Beverly's wedding for the past few days.

"But aren't you already married to Sean?" I'd asked my mother when we came back to Davenport House after Derrick had vanished through the Rift, and I was feeling somewhat better, thanks to Ruth's tonic.

My mother shook her head. "We weren't. Not officially. We never signed any documents or got a marriage license, if that's what you mean. We were, in our hearts, at one time. But the love hasn't been there for years. And I'm older now. I want to spend the rest of my life with someone who loves me and who'll return my love."

It had been one of the strangest conversations of my life. And I've had many, many of those.

I sighed. My father couldn't stop smiling and staring at my mother like she was some precious jewel and he was the luckiest man alive in the worlds.

You wonder how my father was able to be here, at this very moment, under the sun and out of Davenport House? Let me tell you.

Last night, when I couldn't keep my eyes open after a meal of my favorite veggie pizza, I'd climbed up to my room, only to find a red-headed goddess sitting on my bed.

"I'm really tired, Lilith," I mumbled, dragging my feet to my bed, my legs feeling like they were made of wood. "Can you come back tomorrow?" I maneuvered my way to the other side of my bed and climbed on top. I would fall asleep. I didn't care if she was there.

"Is it true?" she asked, her voice empty of emotion.

Maybe if I pretended she wasn't there, she'd go away. "Is what true?" I closed my eyes. She wasn't the broken-down goddess I'd seen her last. She looked more like the annoyingly smug one who had returned. And somehow, I really didn't care.

"That Lucifer took your magic?"

My eyes flashed open. I didn't answer right away. "It's true." I knew why she was here. She was angry because her perfect plan wouldn't work anymore, now that I was useless. Well, tough.

I closed my eyes again and felt the bed shift. "And an incubus working for Lucifer did it." The memory of his horrid face so close to mine brought bile up in the back of my throat. Worse was the feeling of being drained of my magic and not being able to do anything about it. I gritted my teeth against the hot tears that burned my eyes. I was not about to cry in front of Lilith.

"I'm sorry," said the goddess, her voice low.

"Sure you are." I choked down my anger. It wouldn't do me any good to lose control.

"I am." Her tone hardened. "I never expected him to do that."

"Well, he did. And now I can't even conjure up a tiny little flame or the ley lines or even my demon magic. It's all gone," I said bitterly. Part of me wanted to kick her off my bed and shout at her that this was all her fault. None of this would be happening if I hadn't let her out of her damn prison.

"I'll make this right," said Lilith. "I will."

I scoffed. "Can you give me my magic back?" My heart thrashed as part of me, just a small part, filled with hope that somehow the goddess could restore my magic. I took Lilith's silence as my answer. My chest tightened, the tears resurfacing again. "There it is, then. You can't."

The silence that followed became uncomfortable. I just wanted her to leave.

"What will you do?" asked the goddess, her voice neutral like she was commenting on my bedroom furnishings.

I sighed. "I can't be a Merlin anymore, so I'll just have to rely on my freelance work, book covers, websites." I'd admit, the regular income from the town had given me a sort of security and comfort, knowing I wouldn't run out of cash. Now that would be gone too.

"I meant, what are you going to *do* about *it*? The no-magic thing?"

"The no-magic thing? Are you serious?" I sat up and glared at her, surprised to find her staring at me. She'd been facing me the whole time. "I've got *no* magic. Nothing. There's nothing for me to do. Nothing magical. And what would you have me do? I can't produce any kind of magic. So, you'll just have to think up another way to kill your husband since I'm obviously out of business." If she thought I was going to help her now, she was clearly delusional. I was tempted to ask House to throw her out the window. The nerve of this goddess. Maybe Lucifer had been right to lock her up.

Lilith's right brow flinched, and I knew I'd hit a nerve. "I heard your parents are getting married."

I stared at the goddess's red eyes. I wouldn't look away. "Yes. Tomorrow night. What do you care?"

Lilith rubbed a hand over my comforter. "In this house?"

"Yes. He can't leave Davenport House. He can't walk under the sun like you. So the wedding'll take place in the living room tomorrow afternoon. It'll be cramped and we can't have too many guests. But there's nothing we can do."

"Maybe I can help," said the goddess, a smile on her face.

"I don't need your help."

"Your father will be married outside under the sun. He will have a proper wedding."

Again, that goddess had surprised me. She surprised me once more when she showed up this morning after my father had just arrived. She'd mumbled a few words, the scent of spices had filled the air, and then she'd touched his shoulder.

We'd still been super careful when my father attempted to go outside into the morning sun. We'd all gathered at the kitchen's back door as he'd stretched out his foot, the sun shining down on his polished black shoe.

When he didn't combust into flames, he tried his knee. Followed by his other leg and then eventually his entire body.

I'd forgotten to ask the goddess if this miracle was just for the one day, or if my father could now go out into the sun any time without detonating to ashes. I guessed time would tell.

I'd expected to see Lilith at the wedding, seeing that my mother had begged her to come, but the goddess was a no-show. She was most probably hiding from Lucifer. He was onto her. He'd found out about her plans, and I was pretty sure he was looking for her.

I tried to stay mad at Lilith, but it was exceptionally hard when I looked into the happy faces of my parents.

A witch stepped into my line of sight, pumping her arms to get to me faster. She wore a long, flowing pink tulle adorned with strawberries with red sequins.

I cringed on the inside, wishing I could make myself disappear.

"Oh, hon, I heard all about it," said Martha, and she neared. The bouquet she'd caught was buried in her impressive cleavage.

"What's that?" I asked.

Martha put her fists on her wide hips and looked at me with pity in her eyes. "Your magic. I heard that you lost it all. *All* of it. Gone. You don't have an ounce of it in you anymore."

I frowned at her, wishing she'd just keep her mouth shut. "Mmmm."

Martha was the gossip queen of Hollow Cove. If she'd heard about my loss of magic, that meant that the entire town knew about it too. Possibly the White and Dark witch courts as well.

Martha pressed her palm to her chest, her eyes rounded dramatically. "I think I'd just *die* if one day I couldn't do my magic. A glitz witch who can't do a beauty spell, a charmed perm, a magical facelift, or butt-lift spell? What a disgrace. I'd be the laughingstock of the town!" She let out a high laugh.

"Mmmhmm."

"We're witches. What's the point of living if you can't produce magic?" She laughed harder, bending over from the waist like this was a great joke.

"Mmmm."

Martha pressed her lips together in thought. "I knew of a witch who lost her powers like you."

I raised my brows. "Really?" That was the first I'd heard of it. I was surprised Dolores hadn't told me. "What happened to her?"

Martha sighed. "The poor dear. She threw herself off Maiden Cliff."

Nice. That's just what I needed to lift my spirits.

"Don't worry, hon." Martha took my hand between hers. "Who needs magic when you have a man like Marcus, eh?" Her head turned in his direction. "I'd give up mine in a heartbeat for some horizontal refreshments with a man like that."

My frown deepened. I wasn't sure I appreciated where this conversation was going. "Mmmm. Right."

Martha spun around, beaming. "Well." She wiggled her ample bosom at me. "I've got to show the bouquet to Maria. Ha! She's going to be *so* jealous."

I watched Martha make a beeline for a short, pudgy witch with red hair and purple highlights. A bad box-dye job, no doubt.

Her comments hurt. I wasn't going to lie. It was hard watching all these witches in their magical prime and all of them capable of some serious magic. Even Martha, though hers was more geared toward beautifying, I'd take it like a shot if it meant I could do magic again.

My heart pounded, and I felt a bit claustrophobic despite being outside on the vast grounds of Davenport House. Dejected, I walked away, wanting solitude. I was happy for my parents, I really was, but their glorious day didn't lift my spirits. I didn't want them to see me this way. The last thing I wanted was to ruin their perfect day.

I found myself walking back to Davenport House and up to my bedroom, not even remembering how I got there. My legs seemed to have traveled without my knowledge.

I stared at my computer, my heart clenching. I knew with certainty this was going to be my lot in life, designing book covers and websites. Not that there was anything wrong with that. I just preferred doing magic.

Because magic, well, magic had made me feel special.

"So, this is where you're hiding?"

I turned to Marcus's voice, seeing him in the doorway. I hadn't even heard him come in. That was very vampish, in a hot, sexy, prowling kind of way.

I force a small smile. "You stalking me?"

"Yes." He smiled, showing me his perfect teeth in that stupidly perfect mouth of his. The intensity of his stare sent a surge of heat through me, sudden and rousing.

I let out a sigh. "I guess I am hiding."

Marcus closed my door and crossed my room. He took my hand and steered me toward my bed. My mattress sank as the large wereape sat on the edge of my bed, his broad shoulders bumping into mine as he pulled me down next to him so our thighs touched.

"I hate seeing you like this," he said after a long moment, his voice filled with emotion. My eyes burned. "It breaks my heart seeing you so sad. Tell me what to do. Tell me what I can do to help."

I blinked the wetness from my eyes and swallowed hard. "You can't do anything. Don't worry about me. I'll be fine."

I was in no way fine. I was in pain, physically, like a heartache, a breakup with the love of your life. Only this time, it was my magic. And my heart ached for that loss.

"You're not fine." Marcus's gray eyes pinched in worry. "I know you're hurting. I feel so helpless. I'm supposed to protect you. To take care of you. And… I don't know how. I just wish I could make it stop."

"Me too." More than anything.

He pushed my hair back over my shoulder, his rough fingers grazing my neck and leaving my skin burning where he touched it. "You could have died yesterday."

"I know."

"You should have called me first."

"I know. And I was going to call you once I was inside. But there was no reception."

"Iris told me." His voice was raw and open. "You nearly died."

I turned to look at him. "But part of me did die. I'm nothing without my magic," I told him, trying to fight the huge sob threatening to take over. More tears fell. I couldn't do anything about those. My body shook as emotions soared through me—fear, desperation, longing, and anger—with anger being the winning emotion. That explained the angry tears that flowed down my cheeks.

Marcus leaned closer and wrapped his big, muscular arm around my waist. "Don't say that. Being magical is just a part of you. You're more than that."

I shook my head, my body trembling. "I'm not a witch anymore. I'm a dud. Just a regular human. Ordinary."

Becoming a witch, coming into my power, had transformed me. A year ago, I was just that, ordinary. But magic had made me stronger and given me more confidence as a woman along with a belief in myself. It had given me a purpose—to help others and make our town safe.

And I had cherished it.

Now, I felt empty. I had a void inside of me, as though a physical part of me was missing, like a third limb.

"I don't care if you lost your magic," said the chief, pulling me closer. "That's not why I love you."

Well, hell. Key in the tsunami of tears followed by a very unattractive sob.

I blinked the tears from my eyes and looked at him. "Why? Why do you love me?" I asked, my voice hoarse and my heart thrashing like it wanted to burst out of my chest and tackle the wereape.

Marcus laughed. "Because you're the most stubborn person I know. You're so pigheaded that I want to smack that fine ass of yours all the time. You're strong. You never take no for an answer. You're unbelievably impulsive. You make me so angry sometimes, and you're always getting yourself into trouble."

I laughed, wiping my tears. "Yeah. That's me," I said and sniffed.

His eyes darkened with desire. "And the best part… you're sexy as hell."

He grabbed my neck and crushed his lips with mine until I was lost to the sensation. My breath came quickly as he slipped his tongue into my mouth, darting it deep, teasing. He hoisted me up onto his lap, his kiss turning urgent. My arms slid around his neck as I gave myself to his kiss. Heat shot through me, my lady regions pounding.

I shuddered under the kiss as I reached out and pulled him closer, desperate to feel something. He was so warm and solid, and I held on to him for dear life.

It felt good. More than good. It was exactly what I needed at the moment, to be swallowed by Marcus's love, his sexy hands rubbing over my body, hard, and oh so delicious.

It should have been enough, Marcus's love. But it wasn't.

I fell into his embrace, soaking him in, and made a promise to myself.

That part of me that Lucifer took—I wanted it back.

No matter what it took, I *was* going to get my magic back.

Guess it was game on, Lucifer.

Don't miss the next book in The Witches of
Hollow Cove series!

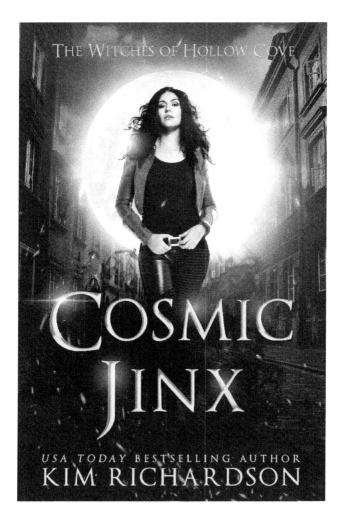

ABOUT THE AUTHOR

Kim Richardson is a USA Today bestselling and award-winning author of urban fantasy, fantasy, and young adult books. She lives in the eastern part of Canada with her husband, two dogs and a very old cat. Kim's books are available in print editions, and translations are available in over 7 languages.

To learn more about the author, please visit:

www.kimrichardsonbooks.com

Printed in Great Britain
by Amazon